Praise for Book I
Hamish X and the Cheese Pirates

Winner of the Arthur Ellis Award for
Juvenile Canadian Crime Literature

D0012311

Praise for Book II
Hamish X and the Hollow Mountain

"Hamish X, mysterious and powerful orphan with his otherworldly boots and fearless demeanour, is back for a second adventure, this time leading his cluster of friends to the remote Kingdom of Switzerland. The evil Mr. Candy and Mr. Sweet are back as well, and it's touch and go who will triumph in this fast-paced and inventive battle between good (kids) and bad (cyborgs). Seán Cullen, a Toronto comedian, has found his legs with *Hollow Mountain*.... The notion of a monarchy hidden inside the Alps, run by a boy-king served by robotic raccoons, is so pleasing that I'm happy to strap in for the ride." —*Georgia Straight*

"But the best contender for the Potter–Snicket throne may be Seán Cullen's Hamish X books. That's because they combine the best elements of both those hits—the adventure-filled plots of the Potter saga and the eccentric narrator of the Snicket tales."—*The Province*

"Cullen delivers an over-the-top action-packed adventure that is filled with buffoonery and zaniness, a compelling narrative about orphans and cyber-robots that will leave young readers laughing and craving more.... Cullen has done a masterful job of interpreting his son's imaginary land-scape with an abundance of tomfoolery."—*Hour* (Montreal)

"Weaving elements of farce, fantasy, hero tales, and science fiction of the more outrageous kind, Cullen concocts a dizzying potion about his hero Hamish X.... Sounds crazy? Well, it is, but it's the kind of craziness that kids lap up."—*The Muskokan*

PUFFIN CANADA

HAMISH X AND THE HOLLOW MOUNTAIN

Comedian SEÁN CULLEN was a member of the highly influential musical comedy troupe Corky and the Juice Pigs until 1998. His stage and screen credits include CBC's *Seán Cullen Show*, *The Tonight Show with Jay Leno*, the Showcase series *Slings and Arrows*, and the Toronto stage production of *The Producers*. He is the winner of three Gemini Awards.

Hamish X
and the Hollow mountain

SEÁN CULLEN

PUFFIN
CANADA

PUFFIN CANADA

Published by the Penguin Group

Penguin Group (Canada), 90 Eglinton Avenue East, Suite 700, Toronto, Ontario, Canada M4P 2Y3 (a division of Pearson Canada Inc.)

Penguin Group (USA) Inc., 375 Hudson Street, New York, New York 10014, U.S.A.

Penguin Books Ltd, 80 Strand, London WC2R 0RL, England

Penguin Ireland, 25 St Stephen's Green, Dublin 2, Ireland (a division of Penguin Books Ltd)

Penguin Group (Australia), 250 Camberwell Road, Camberwell, Victoria 3124, Australia (a division of Pearson Australia Group Pty Ltd)

Penguin Books India Pvt Ltd, 11 Community Centre, Panchsheel Park, New Delhi – 110 017, India

Penguin Group (NZ), 67 Apollo Drive, Rosedale, North Shore 0745, Auckland, New Zealand (a division of Pearson New Zealand Ltd)

Penguin Books (South Africa) (Pty) Ltd, 24 Sturdee Avenue, Rosebank, Johannesburg 2196, South Africa

Penguin Books Ltd, Registered Offices: 80 Strand, London WC2R 0RL, England

First published in a Puffin Canada hardcover by Penguin Group (Canada), a division of Pearson Canada Inc., 2007

Published in this edition, 2008

1 2 3 4 5 6 7 8 9 10 (WEB)

Copyright © Seán Cullen, 2007
Illustrations copyright © Johann Wessels, 2007

Manufactured in Canada.

ISBN-13: 978-0-14-305312-5
ISBN-10: 0-14-305312-4

Library and Archives Canada Cataloguing in Publication data available available upon request

Visit the Penguin Group (Canada) website at **www.penguin.ca**

Special and corporate bulk purchase rates available; please see
www.penguin.ca/corporatesales or call 1-800-810-3104, ext. 477 or 474

For Glen, my father,
who could fix anything

A Note from the Narrator

Well, hello again and welcome to the second book in the saga of Hamish X. I can only assume that you enjoyed the first book, seeing that you are reading the second. Unless, of course, you prefer to torture yourself by reading things you don't really enjoy.[1] If that is the case, you are very strange indeed and should perhaps find another hobby.

In the first book we shared a wonderful adventure complete with Cheese Pirates, daring escapes, explosions, poop-hurling monkeys, and woolly mammoths. That's not a patch on what's going to happen in the second book. Oh, lucky you.

Since I last narrated to you I have gone on a sabbatical[2]

---

[1] It sounds odd, but some people do read things they don't like. Roman schoolboys were forced to read extremely boring stories and memorize them in an effort to harden themselves against the boredom they would experience as adults. I knew a man who read nothing but phone bills. People are just odd that way.

[2] A sabbatical is a trip one takes to learn new things about one's profession. Teachers go on sabbaticals to learn better how to teach or to research things for a textbook they might be writing. The only profession that doesn't really take sabbaticals is that of travel agent, because they go on trips anyway and it would be a waste of time.

to central Tibet, where I studied with one of the finest storytellers in the world, Ta Lhasi Bo. He is a monk who is renowned for telling stories of incredible length and complexity. He once told a story so long that he died in the middle of it and his audience had to wait until he was reincarnated to finish the tale. Unfortunately, he was reincarnated as a salmon first, then a polar bear, and finally as another Tibetan monk. The process took seventeen years, and many of the original audience members died in the meantime and were reincarnated as various animals and insects. In the end, he couldn't finish the story because all the dogs, cats, mice, lemurs, donkeys, and mosquitoes were making so much noise he couldn't be heard at all.

Ta Lhasi Bo lives in a remote village reached only by catapult. I stayed there for eight months and did an incredible amount of training. He put me through gruelling exercises to improve my stamina and concentration. For example, he forced me to tell a very complicated story while being poked in the buttock with a sharpened yak bone for hours on end. Although it certainly improved my stamina, it didn't do my buttock much good. I have to wear specially designed pants now. My concentration, however, is impossible to break.

And so, fresh from the highlands of Tibet, I bring you the second tale in the series detailing Hamish X's amazing exploits: Hamish X and the Hollow Mountain. The Hollow Mountain is the home of the legendary King of Switzerland.

What's that? Switzerland has no king? It's a republic, you say? That just shows how little you know about the true state of world affairs. Trust me, everything will be explained in the pages to come. Have I ever steered you wrong? Of course I haven't.

Where did I leave you at the end of the first book? Oh, yes! A bit of a cliffhanger![3] After all, the third lesson taught at the Advanced Narrator's Certification College in Helsinki is Always Leave Them Wanting More.[4] (The first lesson is Have a Story to Tell, which may seem obvious, but I can assure you that many well-intended narrators go down in ruins because they have no idea what they want to write.)[5] The children had defeated the Cheese Pirates and were enjoying their new freedom at the cheese factory in

---

[3] The term *cliffhanger* comes from the Otaqua tribe who lived near the Grand Canyon in Arizona. The Otaquans took storytelling very seriously, and if they found a storyteller's work boring they would threaten to toss him or her off a cliff into the Canyon. This usually improved the storytellers' skills immensely and led to some of the most exciting and engaging stories. Hanging from a cliff does tend to inspire the imagination.

[4] Except when dealing with the homeless and the hungry. One should always leave them wanting less.

[5] The second lesson is Never Let Dolphins Drive. Certainly, it's irrelevant as far as narration is concerned, but prudent in everyday life. Dolphins are quite intelligent, but instead of hands they have flippers, which are prone to slip on the steering wheel, leading to many automotive accidents. Also, their skin must be kept moist, and this tends to ruin most upholstery. They have a very good sense of direction, however, so always let the dolphin hold the map.

Windcity. Mr. Kipling had proposed to Mrs. Francis. Parveen had smiled (extremely out of character for him). Then the Grey Agents of the ODA showed up in a helicopter, with a strange woman's voice luring Hamish X into their clutches. Hamish X was in a trance, unable to recognize his companions. Indeed, he even drove one of his famous boots right into Mr. Kipling's stomach. Certainly not the kind of behaviour we've come to expect from Hamish X.

Part 1

TO SWITZERLAND

Chapter 1

Mr. Sweet extended a gloved hand towards Hamish X. "Come," he said soothingly. "You are finished with them now. Time to come home."

Mimi shivered and wiped the freezing rain from her eyes. Hamish X, however, was oblivious to the cold water sifting down. He stared at Mr. Sweet and nodded.

"No!" Mimi tried to step in front of Hamish X, but he pushed her away. She fell with a splash into the mud.

Hamish X stepped over her towards Mr. Sweet.

Mimi reached up a muddy hand and clutched Hamish X's right boot. "No!" she shouted again. She spat at the agent. "He doesn't wanna go with y'all!" She pulled herself up and grabbed Hamish X's sleeve. He stared vacantly down at her tear-streaked face. "Ya belong here with us."

For an instant, confusion showed in Hamish X's eyes.

"Yer my friend, Hamish X. You saved us all."

"Little girl," Mr. Sweet laughed, "he belongs with us."

"He belongs *to* us," Mr. Candy hissed.

"No!" Mimi shook her friend. "These people don't care about ya. I don't know what they want but it cain't be good. Don't go with them. Remember who you are! You're Hamish X!" She swung around, gathered her hands into fists, and ran at the agents. Mr. Sweet stepped forward and calmly held out his arm, easily deflecting her charge and sending her off balance to fall once more in the freezing mud.

Hamish X blinked. He shook his head clumsily, as if trying to clear it. Anger showed in his eyes. "No ..." He drunkenly shambled to interpose himself between the agents and Mimi, who had fallen on her face, banging her bony nose on the ground hard enough to send blood trickling from her nostrils. "Don't touch her …"

The loudspeaker whispered again, more insistently, "Come to Mother, Hamish X. I'm waiting for you at home."

The voice had an immediate effect. "Home?" Any spark of recognition in the golden eyes was extinguished. Hamish X turned his back on Mimi and walked to the waiting agents.

Mr. Sweet reached into his coat pocket and extracted a pair of smooth white bracelets. "Excellent, Hamish X. We've wasted enough time." He guided Hamish X to the door of the helicopter. The boy didn't resist. His eyes were dull, his mouth slack.

Mimi pushed herself up on one elbow. Tears and mud plastered her face. Her hair hung in lank strips. She turned to look for Parveen but found he was gone. Had he run away and left her? She couldn't believe it. "*Hamish X!*" she wailed.

Mr. Candy stopped and turned his head towards Mimi, his goggles resembling the glittering eyes of an insect. "The boy you know as Hamish X never really existed," he shouted over the rising wind. "And soon, neither will you."

Suddenly, from the direction of the harbour, there came a crash and a rumble. The ground shook. The sky glowed red. Flames leapt into the night as several wooden buildings ignited. Over the slanted roofs of Windcity, a bizarre and terrifying shape rose.

The body was birdlike and balanced on two towering legs. A slender neck coiled with cables ended in a cluster of funnel-shaped nozzles. The overall impression was of a giant ostrich made of dark shiny metal. From the nozzles, gushing streams of flame sprayed over the tilted houses of Windcity, setting them alight, burning them despite the freezing rain that encased them. The heat baked Mimi's upturned face. As she watched in horror yet another of the strange bird machines appeared, rising above the roofs of the houses to the south. The long serpentine neck swung and the nozzle on its head began spitting flame. New fires bloomed.

"Marvellous machines, our Firebirds, don't you think?" Mr. Sweet gloated. "They'll make short work of this tinderbox town."

"You and your friends have served your purpose, little girl," Mr. Candy explained, his voice devoid of emotion. "You will be erased."

Hamish X watched the bird machines approach and something stirred in his golden eyes. "Mimi," he said groggily. "No!" He turned and looked at her. "NO!" At that moment Mr. Sweet snapped the bracelets over Hamish X's wrists. The light in his eyes dulled once more. Hamish X's head dropped forward, hanging like a lead weight.

The metal birds stomped closer, their paths converging as they moved towards the orphanage. Reaching the edge of the concrete square in front of the factory, the terrible things paused, their pointed heads swinging back and forth like snakes scenting the air.

"Destroy the town," Mr. Sweet commanded. The creatures swivelled their heads towards the sound of his voice. "Leave nothing and no one standing."

Fire spurted from the horrible heads, setting the houses next to the factory alight. Mimi scrambled backwards in terror. Mr. Neiuwendyke, still dressed as a cat, staggered out of his burning home, meowing loudly.[6] He dodged into an alleyway to escape the marching behemoths' rage.

"Hamish X! Parveen! Somebody help!" Mimi screamed.

Mr. Sweet and Mr. Candy seized Hamish X's arms and heaved him into the helicopter. They climbed into their seats and the craft began to rise above the destruction wrought by their horrible creations.

A huge metal foot crunched in the mud just in front of Mimi. She looked up into the terrible funnels and waited for the flames to engulf her.

"Hey!" Parveen's voice caused the machine's head to jerk in the direction of the ruined doors of the factory. Droplets of flaming liquid spattered and fizzed on the wet ground. Mimi spun towards the voice of her friend. In the factory doorway, Parveen, tiny but defiant, stood holding a tangle of wires and circuit boards loosely duct-taped together. "Try this." Parveen stabbed a finger into a button on the side of the bundle and hurled the object into the air.

With a loud *Crump* the device exploded, showering bits of plastic and copper wire all around. The explosion wasn't large but the effect on the mechanical creatures was

_____

6 Oh, Mr. Nieuwendyke! Still dressed as a cat. Will he ever learn?

profound. The one close to Mimi lurched back and spun in a circle. Mimi rolled out of the way to avoid being trampled by its flailing feet. Suddenly, it reeled to one side, staggered several metres, and fell headlong into a burning building with a resounding crash. It tried to rise but failed, spouting flames directly up into the night sky. Then it collapsed back into the rubble. After a single twitch of one spindly leg, it lay completely still.

The second thing fell sprawling on its front, smashing through abandoned houses as if they were all so much paper and matchsticks and skidding to a stop under a pile of burning debris.

The helicopter didn't escape unscathed. In its cockpit the two agents flailed as though an electrical current were coursing through them. The craft turned lazy circles in the sky, completely out of control. After spinning around three times and knocking down a row of abandoned shops with its tail, it dropped hard on its runners, snapping them off and slamming the craft hard onto its belly. The running lights flickered and went out. The rotors shattered against the walls of the buildings nearby. Mimi and Parveen threw themselves to the ground as a large piece of metal scythed through the air at head height, burying itself in the brick wall of the factory.

Finally, save for the crackle of the burning houses, silence fell.

As Parveen hauled Mimi to her feet she shouted, "What the heck was that?"

"EMP bomb," Parveen said matter-of-factly. "It generates an electromagnetic pulse that fries all electronic circuits. I made it from the old microwave and some other junk I scavenged. Just for fun, to see if I could do it, you know?"

"Just fer fun? Who does that fer fun? Baseball's fun! Hide and go seek. That's fun!" Mimi wiped a blob of mud from her cheek and mumbled, "Still, it did the job. Thanks for saving me. Fer a second, I thought ya'd run off and left me."

Parveen stared into her eyes. "I would never do that." Then he shrugged to dispel the serious mood. "Come on."

Mimi and Parveen ran through the freezing rain to the helicopter. Mr. Sweet and Mr. Candy lay twitching in their seats, their goggles flickering with some ghostly internal light. Mr. Sweet's fedora had fallen off, revealing a nest of circuitry that sparked and sizzled.

"They ain't people at all," Mimi breathed. "What in heck are they?"

Parveen reached down and peeled one of Mr. Sweet's grey gloves off his limp hand.

"Look," he said.

The hand was sickly pale, the veins easily seen beneath the surface. Stranger still were the fingers. They were too long. Mimi held up her own hand and compared it.

"They got one more knuckle than me! That's just weird."

"Weird, yes, but we have no time to puzzle over extra knuckles now. We've got to get Hamish X out of here before they send reinforcements." Parveen pushed Mr. Sweet aside and revealed Hamish X, lying face down behind the seats.

Mimi and Parveen dragged him out of the helicopter. He was unconscious, limp as a wet noodle. The restraining cuffs hung open on his hands. Parveen ripped them away and threw them back into the helicopter. Mimi shook Hamish X and shouted into his face. "Hamish X!

Hamish X!" There was no response. His breathing was slow and regular; he looked as if he were asleep.

"We've got to go!" Parveen insisted. They lifted Hamish X by the arms and carried him, his once-powerful boots now dull and dragging, through the mud towards the factory. Mrs. Francis met them at the door, wringing her hands in her apron.

"Oh my dears! Are you all right? I was so worried. I have all the children under the tables in the cafeteria. Mr. Kipling has broken a rib, I'm sure."

Mimi said nothing, running to the little woman and wrapping her arms around the former housekeeper's ample girth. She smeared Mrs. Francis with mud and blood in the process but the chubby woman hardly noticed, so happy was she that the children were safe. Then she saw Hamish X lying inert on the ground. "What's happened to him?" she gasped. Then, taking in the slain bird machines, the wreckage of the helicopter, and the burning town, she clutched her heart. "Oh my word."

"Load the children and all the supplies into the airship," Parveen said sharply. "Bring Viggo's strongbox and anything portable that has any value. We have to leave and we have to leave now!"

"What? We can't leave," said Mrs. Francis. "Where will we go?"

"We have no choice. The ODA will be coming back and we can't be here when they do. Also …" Parveen stopped and pointed at the advancing flames. A vast swath of Windcity's rickety wooden structures was already blazing. Hot cinders rained from above. Parveen suddenly handed Hamish X off to Mrs. Francis. "Take him!" Then he ran back to the helicopter.

"What's he doing?" Mrs. Francis asked. "Watch! Don't burn yourself!"

Parveen reached into the ruined machine and, after a moment of rummaging, pulled out the green book. Clutching it in both hands, he ran back to them. "Let's go!"

Mrs. Francis and Mimi dragged Hamish X through the ruined door. Parveen stood for a moment watching Windcity burn, the flames reflected in the thick lenses of his spectacles. Then he scuttled after them.

WHEN THE AIRSHIP ROSE into the night sky less than an hour later, the brick cheese factory, Viggo Schmatz's pride and joy, was at the centre of a sea of flames. The powerful wind that gave Windcity its name had become the instrument of its destruction. Fanning the flames to a furnace blaze, it consumed everything in its path.

Aboard the airship Parveen ran from station to station on the bridge, checking systems, inspecting upgrades to see if they functioned. Mimi, standing at the wheel, looked down on the flames engulfing the Windcity Orphanage and Cheese Factory. "Well, I never thought I'd say it, but I'll shore miss that place."

Mrs. Francis came in, supporting Mr. Kipling, whose ribs were tightly wrapped in plaster bandages. He winced in pain as he took the wheel from Mimi. "I'll carry on, dear. It'll take more than a couple of broken ribs to keep me out of action." Mimi surrendered her position to Mr. Kipling. "Heading?" he called out.

Parveen looked up from the chart table. "Due east for the moment. We just want to get as far away from here as possible."

"Aye, Captain." Mr. Kipling smiled. Parveen looked embarrassed but a little pleased, too.

IN HIS BUNK, lying under the scratchy blanket, Hamish X dreamed.

Sand and the smell of salt stung his nostrils. The sky arched overhead, a blue dome with wisps of clouds. The roar of breakers filled his ears. He stood on a beach of white sand watching the crystal blue water roll in foaming breakers towards him. He felt a strange sensation and looked down. Foamy water rolled around his feet ... Feet!

He could see his feet. The boots were gone! At first the sight of the pale flesh distressed him, but as he wriggled his toes in the wet sand, squeezing it through them, he felt a shiver of pleasure and laughed aloud. He looked out at the sea. Sunlight danced on the brilliant surface of the water. He began to run out into the waves, smiling and splashing his hands in the water.

"What is this place?" he thought. "Where am I?"

He ran until the water was up to his waist. The waves were larger and more powerful so far out. They rolled in over his head, soaking his hair and plastering it down over his eyes. Stinging salt water filled his mouth. He coughed.

Suddenly, the water seemed frightening, like a live thing pulling at him. The waves surged over his head again and the current tugged at his feet, yanking him off balance. He felt panic welling up inside him.

"Hamish!" A woman's voice cried out from somewhere behind him on the sand. "Don't go out too far!" He tried to turn and look but a wave crashed over him and he fell.

He flailed about, desperately, looking for the sandy bottom so that he could push himself upright, but his feet couldn't find it. By chance, his head broke the surface and he gasped for breath.

"Hamish! Hamish!" The woman's voice was filled with terror but he couldn't see her. Another wave crashed over him and he was pressed down into the darkness.

The darkness was full of thunder and cold. It was like a dream, but somehow Hamish X knew it wasn't really a dream. It was a memory. He wasn't going to wake up.

Chapter 2

The storm pelted the broad windows of the bridge with rain and hail. Lightning flashed, briefly illuminating the tense faces of Parveen, Mimi, and Mr. Kipling as they fought to keep the airship aloft. For several hours, relieved only by occasional cups of tea and sandwiches from Mrs. Francis, they battled the elements. The *Orphan Queen* was a noble craft and responded to the worst the storm could offer.

At long last the winds lessened, the rain slackened off, and the trio was able to relax a bit. When the clouds began to tear apart to reveal the moon, a silver crescent in the black sky, it cast a calm, glimmering light over the sea below. The waves were all crested with silver, stretching as far as the eye could see.

Parveen wearily wiped his glasses on his shirt and then pushed them back onto his nose. He bent over the radar display. "We are over Hudson's Strait. We've been blown several hundred kilometres."

Mimi's arms quivered with exhaustion as she ran her hands through her hair. "I ain't never been so tired."

Mr. Kipling stood with great care. He reached out and touched her cheek, then ruffled Parveen's hair. "No one could ask for a finer crew. We can put the ship on autopilot now. We just have to set a course."

"That in itself is a problem. Where are we going to go?" No one answered. Parveen went to the helm and locked the wheel. "For now, we'll continue to head due east. That will take us out over the North Atlantic. One good thing about the storm: it will foil any pursuit for a while."

"Let's go check on Hamish X," Mimi suggested. Mr. Kipling and the two children put aside their exhaustion for the moment, ducking through the hatchway and down the corridor through the ship to the common room. From there, they headed down the passage that held the crew's quarters.

The children from Windcity had been assigned to bunks in the crew cabins. Mimi, Mr. Kipling, and Parveen passed the darkened rooms where the orphans slept in bunks stacked against the walls like sardines in cans. Here and there, a child whimpered at a bad dream or snored in a deep sleep.

Hamish X had a cabin to himself. It had been the Captain's cabin before Cheesebeard's untimely demise. No amount of scrubbing could erase the faint stench of rancid cheese that clung to the very woodwork. Still, it had the largest, most comfortable bed, and that is where Hamish X now lay under a warm blanket attended by Mrs. Francis. A shaded light cast a soft glow over his sleeping face. His boots, once lustrous and shiny, looked inert and dull as they stuck out from under the covers. He lay there completely still, eyes closed, his breathing slow and deep. He hadn't moved or spoken since they rescued him from the helicopter. Mrs. Francis knelt beside him, lovingly pushing a strand of unruly hair from his pale brow.

"What's wrong with him?" she asked.

Parveen moved closer and looked down at Hamish. "I believe he was affected by the EMP. If he were a person like you or me, I would say he is in a coma."

"Whaddya mean, a person like you or me?" Mimi demanded.

Parveen thought for a moment, his brow furrowed. "I have a theory. I believe Hamish X is not completely human."

Mimi's mouth dropped open. "What?"

"I believe he is a machine, but an organic one."

"Orgamic?"

"Organic! Not orgamic."[7]

"Whatever. A machine? What, like them things back in the helicopter?"

"Similar but not exactly the same. The electronic pulse has, in effect, shorted him out."

Mimi looked at Hamish X lying on the bunk and shook her head. Her face darkened and her fists clenched.

"A machine? Uh-uh. No way. He's our friend, not some bag o' nuts and bolts!"

"Mimi, there's no need to shout. I'm telling you what I believe to be true. I'll have to study him more to be sure but I think I'm right. The way he behaved when he arrived: his lack of memory, his uncanny[8] abilities, the fact that according to what we know of his exploits he should

---

7   Organic and orgamic are two very different things indeed. *Organic* means living or using materials found in nature. *Orgamic* pertains to things made using the Japanese paper-folding art of origami. Orgamic machines are not very efficient because their component parts tend to unfold after repeated use. A Japanese company attempted to build robots out of folded paper, but the prototypes disintegrated in a rainstorm and the project was abandoned.

8   *Uncanny* is a word that means "too strange or unlikely to be natural or human." It comes from ancient Persia, where people who were believed to be witches were placed in a large can and dropped in a deep pool. If they escaped the can and didn't drown, they were assumed to be magical and were given a special hat made of pita bread and a beard made of leaves. The Persians were strange people.

be much older than he is. And the book ..." Parveen pointed to the green tome sitting on the small bedside table. "It all supports my theory."

Mimi crossed her arms and scowled. "Which is?"

Parveen sat on the edge of the bunk and looked at Hamish X's sleeping face. "The ODA have some sinister plot in mind of which Hamish X is an essential part. All this talk of Mother? I believe Hamish X is crucial to their plans. We can't let them have him."

"But what the heck are thur plans? How can we foil them if we ain't got an idea what they are?"

"Knowing the ODA, the plan would be evil.[9] It's enough right now for us to keep Hamish X from falling into their hands."

Mrs. Francis bit her lip. "But they are so powerful. They can find us anywhere we go."

Parveen nodded. "We need help."

"And where are we gonna git it?" Mimi waved a hand to encompass the whole ship. "We got a hundred kids, an old beat-up blimp. They got mechanical monsters and who knows what else? Who we gonna go to fer help?"

Parveen looked slightly hurt. "First of all, it's a zeppelin, not a blimp. Secondly, I have not been idle these last few weeks. I've made a number of modifications to the *Orphan Queen:* the engines are in perfect working order, the fuel

---

9 Parveen is correct. Without giving anything away, I can guar-
   antee that the plans of the ODA are evil indeed. They would
   certainly win an award for Most Evil Plan of the Century at the
   Evil Plan Awards. Of course, having such awards would be
   counterproductive for those making evil plans, as the attendant
   publicity would lead to the discovery of the evil plans in question and so lead to those plans being foiled. Still, what a red
   carpet event that would be: all the greatest evil minds together
   in one gala night of evil. But I digress.

efficiency is at optimum levels, and I've improved the stealth capabilities. We can run and we can hide."

Indeed, the zeppelin's native stealth capabilities were formidable. The secret was in the gasbag, made as it was from the skin of the endangered Chameleon whale.[10] Parveen had added a transparent sleeve of radar-repellent material that he called a "sneaky sheet" to cover the entire coiled gasbag like a sausage casing. A third precaution was the chameleon paint on the ship's hull. The pirates had devised it to imitate the effect of the Chameleon whale. The overall result was a giant airship that was incredibly difficult to pick out with human or electronic eyes.

"Run where? Hide where? We ain't got nowhere to go! They'll find us agin, just like they did b'fore!"

The little group fell silent, Mrs. Francis nervously wringing her apron and looking at the inert boy in the bed. They all felt helpless, lost in the middle of the sky with nowhere safe to go. Who could they turn to in their darkest hour? In dire times like these one would usually call upon family to help, but they had no one. Mr. Kipling's daughter was gone, drowned years before in a shipwreck that nearly took his life as well. Mrs. Francis's husband was dead from a rabid owl attack. She was alone save for her newfound love, Mr. Kipling, and the children she cared for. Mimi had

---

10 The Chameleon whale has a hide that is capable of taking on the colour of its surroundings, making it very difficult to hunt. Unfortunately, the whales are extremely friendly, loving nothing better than to frolic in the wake of ships and wave their flippers at humans, thus negating their native chameleon capability. The Chameleon whale is believed to be extinct, but every once in a while there are unsubstantiated sightings, the most recent off the beach in Santa Barbara, California, where one was reported to have been masquerading as a group of chubby German tourists.

her Aunt Jean but she would never return to that nasty, sour woman who had sold her to the ODA after the death of her father and mother. And Parveen? He had sisters and brothers somewhere but he didn't know if they were alive or dead. Truly, they had no one in the world. The cabin was a hopeless place, sad and silent.[11]

Which is a good thing, because otherwise they would never have heard the buzzing.

Parveen was the first to notice the strange sound, so subtle that the drone of the engines almost masked it. "What is that?" He cocked his head to one side and listened intently.

"I don't hear nuthin'."

"Close your mouth and open your ears, Mimi!" Parveen ignored Mimi's smouldering look and leaned closer to Hamish.

Then they all heard it: a faint buzzing, like a bumblebee trapped between panes of glass.

"It's coming from there," Parveen said, pointing at Hamish X's black boots where they stuck out from under the blanket. The buzzing emanated from inside the one on Hamish X's right foot.

The beeping and buzzing grew louder before stopping altogether. Parveen waited a few tense seconds before leaning forward, hand outstretched towards the boot.

"Be careful," Mrs. Francis fretted.

"I can see something moving … yah!" Parveen's hand jerked back in shock.

---

[11] Not so. The saddest, most hopeless place of all time was an ice cream parlour called Nahid's Num Nums. It opened in the middle of the Sahara Desert in 1754, two hundred years before reliable refrigeration was available in the region.

Over the boot top emerged a slender, silvery strand like the questing antenna of an insect. A few centimetres long and mere millimetres thick, it swung back and forth in the air, stopping to look at each of the baffled faces in turn. Finally, the antenna swung to Hamish X's sleeping face and stopped.

Out of the boot came the owner of the antenna: small and crablike, it had a shiny red body with a silver cross on its back. The thing had a number of strange legs—strange because no two legs were the same. Some were long and pointy. One was a curling spiral of metal. One actually looked like a pair of scissors, the blades splayed out like toes. The bizarre little creature skittered up to Hamish X's knee and stopped there.

"It's the knife," Parveen whispered excitedly.

"Knife?" said Mrs. Francis, bewildered.

"The King o' Switzerland's knife ..." Mimi said. "Hamish X had it hidden in his boot when he come to Windcity. He said the King o' Switzerland gave it to 'im."

"I hate to correct you, dear Mimi, but Switzerland is a republic," Mr. Kipling snorted. "It doesn't have a king."

The knife stood still for a long moment, its antenna twitching. Suddenly, the antenna went rigid, pointing directly at the sleeping face of Hamish X. The knife darted up the blanket and stopped on the sleeping boy's chest, gently rising and falling with the rhythm of his slow breathing. The antenna waved over Hamish X's face, passing back and forth repeatedly.

"Shouldn't we do something?" Mrs. Francis whispered, wringing her apron even more fiercely. "I mean, what if it tries to hurt him?"

"Wait a second." Parveen waved a hand impatiently, his attention fixed on the little mechanical creature.

A whirring sound filled the cabin. Before the spectators could move, the antenna suddenly darted up Hamish X's nose, snaking up his left nostril then farther and farther.

"Stop it! Stop it!" Mrs. Francis gasped in horror.

Mimi reached over to grab the knife but snatched her hand back. "The little critter bit me!" She held up her thumb to show a drop of blood beading on the tip. She stuffed it into her mouth as she looked around for something to smash the knife creature with.

"Wait!" Parveen urged. "Watch!"

The little cross on the knife began to glow with a pale red, softly pulsing luminescence. The antenna was now firmly inserted in Hamish X's nostril. That was strange enough, but things got even stranger when Hamish X suddenly began to speak, and what he said was very strange indeed.

"North fifty-six. East eight. North fifty-six. East eight. North fifty-six. East eight ..."

"He's talking?" gasped Mrs. Francis.

"Yeah, but what's he sayin'?" Mimi demanded.

"North fifty-six. East eight. North fifty-six. East eight. North fifty-six. East eight ..."

Hamish X's golden eyes opened. He stared at the ceiling and repeated the weird numbers again. "North fifty-six. East eight. North fifty-six. East eight. North fifty-six. East eight ..."

Hamish X's mouth moved and the words coming out sounded like him, but there was something about the cadence of his speech that was alien and machinelike.

A beam of blue light shot out of the knife, stabbing directly upwards in an inverted cone shape. Where the light hit the ceiling, a map appeared. The projection showed a map of Europe outlined in blue with a flashing blue speck in the centre of some very steep-looking mountains.

"It's showing us where we must go," Parveen said in awe.

The antenna withdrew from Hamish X's nose and back into the device. With a loud click, the knife's appendages all suddenly popped back into the knife and it fell, inert, on Hamish X's chest.

"What the heck!" Mimi shouted.

They all stood looking at the knife, waiting for it to do something else, but nothing happened. Hamish X's eyes were closed. He had returned to his sleeping state, unscathed by and apparently oblivious to the intrusion of the antenna. When Parveen was certain the knife wasn't going to do anything more, he picked it up and held it in his palm.

Parveen broke the silence. "At least we have a goal now."

Mimi locked eyes with her friend. "Whaddya mean?"

"Those numbers were map coordinates." He reached into his pocket and withdrew a dog-eared map. He opened it and flipped from section to section until he reached the one he wanted. He stabbed a finger down in the centre of the European continent. "There. We're going to Switzerland." He looked up and his usually calm eyes were glowing with excitement. "We're going to find the King of Switzerland."

"Excuse me," Mr. Kipling raised a finger in gentle protest. "I don't mean to be difficult but, as I said before, I am fairly certain the Swiss have no king. Switzerland is a republic. At least it was the last time I checked."

"That's what I thought, although I ain't had much opportunity to study gee-o-graphy!" Mimi said.

Parveen looked at the knife for a long moment. Then he spoke.

"Ever since Hamish X told me that the King of Switzerland gave him this knife, I've been doing some research. When we came back from Snow Monkey Island, I was able to rig an internet connection through the satellite television dish. This certainly facilitated my inquiries. The internet is quite a marvellous resource. I find it very useful to be able to access the great libraries of the world. Truly—"

"Parveen," Mimi interrupted, "can we get to the meat o' this particular nut, please?"

"Right, well." Parveen pulled his glasses off and polished them again with the corner of his shirt. Mrs. Francis frowned but he ignored her. "The King of Switzerland is a legend among the orphans of the world.

He is said to have a hidden kingdom called the Hollow Mountain where any orphan may seek shelter from the adults who would exploit him or her. The King is the sworn enemy of anyone who would mistreat a child. One has only to make contact with him and the orphan in question will gain his protection even against the terrifying power of the Grey Agents."

"If that's true," Mimi asked, "how can we contact this dude?"

"I believe," Parveen replaced his glasses and held up the knife. "I believe he has already contacted *us*. We must go to these coordinates and hope that he will find us."

They all looked at the knife in Parveen's hand. They had no other lead. Hamish X was in a bizarre state of shock. They were alone in the world and at the mercy of the ODA. They needed an ally.

Mimi shrugged and summed it all up. "What the heck? It can't get much worse. Switzerland it is!"

HALFWAY ACROSS THE WORLD, a boy with unruly red hair pored over his jigsaw puzzle. The puzzle, only a third of its four thousand pieces in place on the vast tabletop, depicted a field of red poppies waving in the sunshine. The pieces were very small and the difficulty very high as the flowers all looked very similar, but the boy liked it that way. He loved puzzles, the more complicated and vexing the better. He spun a piece in his pale fingers, turning it to see if it fit into a particular gap he needed to fill. Despairing, he dropped it onto the tabletop and picked up another piece.

A soft chime sounded. The boy looked up, blue eyes questioning. "Yes, George?"

"The knife, Majesty. It has been activated."

The King of Switzerland smiled. "So," he said softly. "It is finally beginning." He looked down at the puzzle and laughed. "Aha!" He placed the piece he was holding into a gap, completing a poppy's red petal. "Excellent." He reached for another piece.

Mr. Candy and Mr. Sweet

The wind pushed drifts of snow over the ruined helicopter, spilling in through the shattered windshield and pooling around the feet of the two inert agents. Already the hollows of their faces were etched in lines of white where flakes had gathered. The only sound was the high keening of the wind singing in the ruins of the town. The fires had burned themselves out, leaving a patchwork of charred foundations and blackened beams. The helicopter had crashed in the centre of the square in front of the cheese factory and so had escaped the fire. The craft sat like a black wounded beetle, lying tilted to one side.

Mr. Candy and Mr. Sweet lay strapped into their seats. Their heads were thrown back. Their mouths were open. Their sightless goggles reflected the pale dawn light. The grey pallor of their skin added to the overall impression of death. For two days and two nights they had lain, still and silent as the snow shrouded them.

At noon on the third day the sun finally broke through the heavy cloud, casting a watery white glare on the ruined town. A shaft of sunlight crawled across Mr. Sweet's face and alighted on the black surface of his goggles.

The glass of the goggles absorbed the faint trickle of solar energy. And with that, Mr. Sweet's right hand twitched.

The fingers spread and then clenched like a spider waking up from a deep sleep. Tremors passed through the agent's body. His muscles flexed and tensed painfully. Finally, he lifted his head and spat snow from his mouth in agonized, wheezing coughs. With great effort he tipped himself forward against the straps that held him upright. His right hand fumbled at the control stick of the helicopter. After two clumsy attempts, his fingers closed on a knob. With what feeble strength he had, he pulled on it, and out of the console a thin cord emerged. Drawing it towards him, he took the knob pinched in his fingers and pressed it to his head, pushing back his hat as he did so. On his forehead, in a place normally hidden by the brim of his fedora, was a black metal socket. He pressed the knob into the socket with a soft click and fell back exhausted in his chair.

Moments passed. A soft hum filled the cabin. Soon, Mr. Sweet flexed his hands, gingerly raised his arms as if testing their strength. When he was satisfied, he pulled the plug from his head and placed it into a similar socket on the forehead of Mr. Candy.

Mr. Sweet waited for a few seconds. Suddenly, Mr. Candy tilted his head forward and turned it to look at his fellow agent.

"Auxiliary battery," Mr. Sweet said simply. Mr. Candy nodded.

"Hamish X?"

Mr. Sweet scanned the horizon. He saw nothing but

lowering clouds, the precursor to a major storm. "Gone. A storm is coming. We can do nothing from here."

"Shall we begin searching for him?"

"Indeed. I'll call for transport." The agent tapped the side of his skull, tilted his head, and mumbled as if to the empty air, "HQ. Sweet. Two for extraction. Immediate. Here are our coordinates."

Chapter 3

The valley below was impossibly green and lush, like a painted rendering of an ideal spring day. Tiny star-shaped Alpine flowers, the type the Swiss call edelweiss, added a delicate sprinkling of white on the lush green turf of the meadow. On all sides the sheer mountains soared, their peaks perpetually white with snow.

A clutch of rabbits rooted in the grass, nibbling the juicy clumps of stems. Their tiny wet noses sniffed constantly for danger. For a rabbit, life is an endless round of nibbling and sniffing. Enemies are ever present.[12] Foxes prowl the Alpine meadows. Hawks circle overhead. The lynx and the wildcat stalk in a quest to feast on rabbit flesh. The rabbit must always be on the lookout for predators intent on a rabbit supper. And so the rabbits watched out for one another, shouting a warning if danger approached.[13] Theirs is a highly effective survival strategy, considering that rabbits still exist and are found throughout the world.

Unfortunately, though they were keenly aware of danger from predators, they had no way of preparing themselves for what was about to occur in the next paragraph.

---

[12] In this way rabbits are similar to the orphans of the world, but far furrier in most cases. Granted, there are bald rabbits and hairy orphans, but those cases are rare.

[13] You say you've never heard the shout of a rabbit? It is very difficult to discern in the wild, being similar to the rustling of leaves. Isolated in a laboratory, recorded and slowed down, it sounds very much like a small child licking a banana.

A huge metal spike plunged down into their midst. The force of the impact drove its point a metre into the earth. The concussion knocked the rabbits off their feet. Even the bravest of them passed out from sheer terror, after first voiding the contents of their stomachs then covering themselves with steaming, semi-digested grass.[14] These little creatures were, indeed, members of the rare species of Alpine Puking Rabbits.

Little did the panicked rabbits know they were in no danger.[15] All they managed to do in the end was to miss the arrival of the airship that had once been known as *The Vulture* but was now rechristened the *Orphan Queen*. The huge metal spike, the airship's anchor, trailed a long chain that disappeared into the vessel's undercarriage. The chain grew taut as the weight of the vessel strained against it in the stiff mountain breeze. With much ratcheting and clanking, the chain was slowly reeled in until the airship gently bumped the ground, gouging a furrow in the rich earth.

The rabbits were usually quite good at spotting danger from the skies, but they had never seen a vessel like the *Orphan Queen*. From below, the ship appeared to be the same colour as the sky: pale blue with wisps of white cloud. The section of the hull that rested on the grass had already begun to shift to lush green with flashes of colour to reflect the flowers. The chameleon paint was working

---

14 The Alpine Puking Rabbit, or *Lapina vomitus alpina*, is famous for this bizarre survival adaptation. When frightened, it vomits and falls unconscious, hoping that the predator will find its behaviour so nauseating as to refuse to eat it.

15 Rabbits rarely behave in a reasonable fashion, as jumping to conclusions is their natural inclination … jumping, I mean. They can't help it. They have thick, strong legs.

perfectly. It had even managed to mimic the splashes of lighter green that represented the vomit-covered rabbits.

A section of the airship's stern dropped slowly on hydraulic hinges to reveal the cargo hold. As soon as the ramp touched the grass several children dashed down its length, holding long ropes threaded through metal pegs. They hammered the pegs into the ground with wooden mallets.

When the ship was secure, swaying slightly in the breeze, Mr. Kipling, Mrs. Francis, Mimi, and Parveen strolled down the ramp and looked around. A little boy saluted Mr. Kipling. "The ship is secure."

"Excellent work, children." Mr. Kipling leaned on Mrs. Francis and breathed deeply. "Well, we've made it. Welcome to Switzerland."

"It's beautiful," Mrs. Francis whispered reverently. "Look at the mountains …"

"The blue sky," Parveen added.

"And get a load o' those rabbits all covered in puke," Mimi said with disgust.

"We don't have time to waste," Parveen said. "The ODA may track us at any moment."

Mimi surveyed the empty field and scowled. "Are you sure these is the coordinates? It don't seem like nuthin' is here. Either the King o' Switzerland is a barf-covered rabbit or he ain't around."

"This is the exact location stipulated by the knife." Parveen surveyed the valley, a hand shielding his eyes from the morning sun.

"But why're we out in the middle o' nowhere? Shouldn't there be a town er a farmhouse er even a barn er sumthin'?"

"I assume the King wanted us to stay away from the major centres of population to avoid being spotted by the

ODA. He seems to be cautious. Otherwise, he would have been found out long ago."

"How do we know this ain't all a trap? Maybe he's workin' fer the Grey Agents his own self."

"Why go to all this trouble?"

Mimi glowered and scuffed the grass with her toe. "I ain't figgered that out yet."

Mr. Kipling raised his ancient binoculars[16] and scanned the surrounding mountains. "No one in sight. Which is not to say that they mightn't be watching us from a hidden vantage point." He smiled and laid a hand on Mrs. Francis's shoulder. "It might be nice for the children to get out of the ship. A little sunshine, eh? Chance to play ... Blow off some steam, what? Every child needs a little playtime."

"Good idea." Mrs. Francis nodded primly and waddled back up the ramp into the ship.

AN HOUR LATER, the former inmates of Windcity Orphanage and Cheese Factory were happily playing in the shadow of the *Orphan Queen*. Certainly, they had gained their freedom from the oppressive Viggo when Hamish X had rescued them from the Cheese Pirates, but this was the first real taste of true liberty in a place where liberty might actually be quite pleasant. Being free in

---

[16] *Binoculars* is from the Latin meaning "two eyes" because of the two eyepieces the binoculars employ, one for each eye. The German company Eigenglass marketed a pair of trinoculars for a brief period after the Second World War, but the rarity of three-eyed individuals led to the item being discontinued. Trinoculars were, however, very popular among Tibetan monks, who believe they have a spiritual third eye in their foreheads. The trinoculars allowed them to see not only into the spirit world but really, really far into the spirit world.

Windcity wasn't really like being free at all. Here, under the warm sun, with beautiful mountains all around and green grass underfoot, the orphans could finally breathe easily and revel in their newfound state. Their eyes had shone as they piled out of the airship and onto the green meadow, shouting and laughing, tumbling and wrestling in the clear morning air.

The older children had begun an impromptu[17] game of soccer on the grassy meadow. The children too young to play soccer happily played tag or duck-duck-goose. The ones too small to play duck-duck-goose were very small indeed and amused themselves by gurgling and tugging on their own feet. Some of the youngest hugged soiled rabbits, much to the chagrin of Mrs. Francis, who took the rabbits from the disappointed children and rinsed the poor creatures in the galley sink.

And now Mr. Kipling sat smoking his pipe, keeping a watchful eye over the children while Mimi, Parveen, and Mrs. Francis held a meeting in the cabin occupied by Hamish X.

"SO WHAT the heck do we do? We're here in Switzerland but there ain't nobody ta meet us."

"I think we have to be cautious. We must wait. The coordinates are correct." Parveen shrugged. "We wait for this King of Switzerland to initiate contact."

"What about the ODA? Surely they are looking for us?" Mrs. Francis glanced nervously over her shoulder, as if

---

[17] *Impromptu* is a word that means unplanned or improvised. Being impromptu can be a lot of fun in the right circumstances. An impromptu birthday party is a good thing. An impromptu brain surgery, not so good.

expecting Mr. Candy and Mr. Sweet to walk in the door any moment.

"We must assume they are looking for us," Parveen agreed. "But the EMP has slowed them down and the *Orphan Queen*'s stealth capabilities make her difficult to track. Let's hope we've bought enough time for the King of Switzerland to make contact. If we haven't heard anything by dawn tomorrow, we'll have to start making a new plan. Agreed?"

Mimi nodded. Mrs. Francis wrung her apron in her pudgy fists and nodded, too. Their decision made, they looked at the object of their plans, Hamish X, lying under his blanket on the former Captain's bed.

"Looks like he could just wake up and start talkin', don't he?" Mimi said.

"Oh heavens," Mrs. Francis whispered, taking his limp hand in hers, "how I wish he would."

But he didn't. His pupils flickered under his closed eyelids. His breathing quickened but he didn't awaken.

"He must be dreaming," Parveen said softly. "What are you dreaming about, Hamish X?"

THE PAIN WOKE HIM. He arched his back until just his feet and the back of his head touched the metal table. Liquid fire coursed through him, through every fibre and nerve ending. The sensation went on and on ... and all the while he heard voices.

"Is this normal, Professor?" The voice was cold and imper-sonal with a flat, lifeless quality. The answering voice was the opposite; it had a slight quaver that betrayed tense emotion.

"Normal? Nothing about this is normal. This whole process is unethical and immoral."

"Spare us the humanity, Doctor. You have a job to do. Try to focus on the task at hand. Remember your poor mother. She needs you to do as you are told."

"Good point, Mr. Sweet." The third voice was as flat and dead as the first. "Describe to us what is happening, Professor."

The Professor swallowed audibly. After a pause, he spoke. "The augmented nerve fibres are grafting themselves onto the boy's natural nerve fibres. The process is very painful."

"Obviously," said Mr. Sweet.

"Can we not give him some form of sedative? He needn't be awake for this part of the procedure."

"He won't remember the pain, Professor. His memory will be erased."

"That's not the point!" the Professor shouted suddenly. "It's needlessly cruel!"

"Needlessly? Oh no, Professor. All cruelty is necessary. Cruelty instructs. Pain teaches lessons. Think of your mother and how she might react to such high levels of pain."

"You wouldn't dare."

"Oh but we would," Mr. Candy said softly. "But as long as you do as you're told, she will be spared."

The Professor was silent.

"Aaaaaaaaaah," Hamish X screamed unheeded, writhing in agony as a new surge of pain washed through him.

"The artificial nerve tissue is accommodating the added power flow perfectly, Mr. Candy."

"Indeed, Mr. Sweet. The genetic mapping was superb. He is ready for the memory wipe."

The pain stopped suddenly and the boy slumped onto the cold metal surface. Sweat bathed his body. He quivered with remembered agony.

"M-m-mommy," he whimpered.

The grey, goggled faces of Mr. Candy and Mr. Sweet loomed over him. The fedoras were gone, revealing the hideous nest of wiring that perched atop their skulls like bizarre multi-hued wigs. He sensed the presence of others, a silent multitude watching out in the darkness beyond the lights.

A third face leaned in. He wore a surgical mask covering his mouth and nose suspended by strings looped around his prominent ears. The eyes behind the thick glasses were watery and bloodshot.

Hamish X looked up into those eyes. "Help me," he pleaded. It came out as a croak, his voice raw from the screaming. "Where's my mother?"

The third man, the boy assumed it was the Professor, opened his mouth. "I'm sorry—"

Mr. Sweet cut him off. "He's asking for his mother, Mr. Candy."

"Fascinating. He doesn't realize what has happened to him. Should we tell him?"

"Why bother? He'll forget everything after we initiate the memory suppression therapy."

"Mommy. I want my mommy," Hamish X sobbed, a tear rolling down his cheek and into his ear.

"Your mommy doesn't want you." Mr. Sweet leaned in close, his breath faintly metallic. "You've been a bad boy and gone out too far in the ocean. You didn't stay close to the beach like she told you. You are no use to anyone but us …"

"Just do the wipe!" The Professor's voice broke into a sob. "Just do it."

Mr. Sweet and Mr. Candy exchanged a glance and nodded. Mr. Candy leaned in closer. The metallic stink of his breath washed over the boy's face. "She gave you up." Mr. Candy smiled, a hideous parody of kindness. "You have no mommy now. Except this one …"

38

A beautiful female voice filled Hamish X's head. "Hamish X. That is your name. I am Mother. Initiating memory suppression sequence."

Hamish tried to struggle but his whole body shut down. He felt a wave of nausea, and then darkness rolled over him.

Mr. Candy and Mr. Sweet

"Mister Defence Secretary," Mr. Candy said, addressing the man at the far end of the table. "Are you telling me that the most sophisticated satellite reconnaissance system in the world cannot manage to detect one slow-moving aircraft?"

The defence secretary, one of the most powerful men in the government of the most powerful country in the world, swallowed hard. He wasn't used to being called to account, especially in his own bailiwick.[18] He looked down the long table, casting his eye over the generals, admirals, and colonels who were his advisers and who studiously avoided his gaze. At last, he gulped and cleared his throat. "Of course, we have been thorough but we have not tracked an object of the configuration you described, Mr. Candy.

---

[18] *Bailiwick* is an old word that originates from Old French or Middle English. A bailiff was an official charged with keeping the public peace. His wick was his area of jurisdiction. This is the accepted definition, although I believe the word has its origin in the strange habit of a man in sixteenth-century Manchester, England, named Dan Bailey. He was very jealous of his candles and built a wicker wall around them to keep them safe against candle thieves. People passing by would ask, "What's that thing?" And they would be told, "Bailey's wicker candle castle." Over time it was shortened to Bailey's Wicker Thing and then further to Bailey's Wick. Then Bailiwick. I tend to believe the latter because it's weird enough to be true.

All our assets are being focused on the task but so far ... nothing."

The Situation Room in the basement of the White House in Washington, D.C., is usually a very busy, noisy place. Today, it was tensely quiet. The sound of computers humming and the faint purr of phones served to underline the silence as Mr. Candy and Mr. Sweet stood at the end of the long table, tall and cadaverous as they stared down the collected commanders of the United States Armed Forces. On any given day these men and women could decide the fate of the world, move nations, command vast numbers of troops and a massive arsenal. Today they fidgeted like schoolchildren under the gaze of the mysterious Grey Agents.

"Gentlemen and ladies," Mr. Sweet said, cocking his head to the side. "We have been of considerable assistance to the government of the United States over the years, providing our boundless mechanical and electronic expertise in return for your ... cooperation. Now, at last, we need you to perform one simple task using the technology we have greatly assisted in providing. And you can't seem to give us any satisfaction."

One of the younger generals, new to the job and appalled by the intrusion of these strange men into the hallowed corridors of power, decided that he'd heard quite enough. He stood up and faced Mr. Sweet. "Who the blazes do you think you are?" Everyone around the table collectively gasped.

"John!" the defence secretary snapped. "Sit down."

The young general would not be stopped. "I'm ashamed of you all." He looked around the table at the sheepish faces of the general staff. He turned back to the agents. "You can't just waltz in here and start making demands of the American military. This is a democracy! We don't answer to anyone but the American president, and he answers to the American people."

Mr. Sweet turned to face the young general. "What a quaint little speech. You, sir, do not know the truth of things. The ODA has provided many services for which the American government can never possibly repay us. In turn, we may use your resources as we see fit. Your president won his office using money from our coffers and he answers to us. These men are ours to command as we wish."

The young general's face reddened. "I won't stand for it! Do you hear me? I'm going to tell the world."

Mr. Candy stepped in close to the young military man. He said softly, "You will tell no one anything." Fast as a striking snake, he whipped off his glove and pressed his open palm to the man's face. "And you needn't stand." From the grey, clammy palm of the agent's bare hand millions of wormlike filaments sprouted and burrowed into the flesh of the general's face. The man screamed briefly and then went silent. His entire body went rigid, and as if a switch had been flipped, he slumped back into his chair. Mr. Candy removed his hand from the man's face.

Where the general's eyes had once held intelligence and

emotion, they now stared blankly at the ceiling. Drool slid from the corner of his mouth to collect on the lapel of his uniform. The faces of his colleagues around the table were frozen in shock and horror.

Mr. Candy replaced his glove. The agents looked around the table at the fear they had inspired. They nodded in unison.

"Well, then," Mr. Sweet said briskly. "We require results."

"You may contact us through the normal channels," Mr. Candy added, and the two agents strode from the room, leaving silence in their wake.

"I hate those guys," the defence secretary snarled when he was sure the agents were well out of range.

"Guh," the general barked. A rear admiral seated to his left used her handkerchief to wipe the drool from his chin.

"Get him out of here," the secretary said. "What am I going to tell the president?"

THE BLACK ODA HELICOPTER lifted off from the White House lawn and swung out over the Potomac. Mr. Candy aimed the craft north and they set off for Providence, Rhode Island, and the Orphan Disposal Agency Headquarters.

"This is a very disturbing development, Mr. Candy."

"Indeed, Mr. Sweet. Indeed." The two agents flew on in silence as the midday sun struggled unsuccessfully to force its way through the heavy clouds. The windscreen of the helicopter was streaming with rain.

Their trip back from Windcity had been arduous and humiliating. The ODA had exerted its influence over the Canadian government to divert a military jet to the remote location and extract the bedraggled agents. After a long flight, they were met at the Theodore Francis Green Airport that served Providence.

A limousine, driven by a junior agent named Miss Taffy, had met them on the runway and whisked them back to the little house on Angell Street that served as headquarters for the sinister ODA. After donning fresh clothing and undergoing a thorough diagnostic treatment, the search for Hamish X and his companions began in earnest, culminating in the fruitless trip to the White House.

The agents were quite annoyed (or at least as annoyed as they could ever be, which was only slightly by our standards). Hamish X seemed to have completely disappeared. "Shall we contact headquarters and see if any progress has been made?"

"Indeed, Mr. Sweet." Mr. Candy tapped a button on the control console. "Mother?" Mr. Candy addressed the empty air.

A faint glow flared in the space between the agents, hovering a few centimetres above the console. A cool, feminine voice filled the cockpit. "Mother is listening. What can Mother do for you?"

"Has there been any progress in determining the location of Hamish X?" Mr. Sweet demanded.

"None. I have been searching databases and coordinating

with NATO, the Russians, and the Chinese. They have been very cooperative."

"They should be," Mr. Candy said. "They know better than to cross us."

"Still, utilizing all their detection systems, I am unable to contact his locator beacon."

"It must have been disabled in the Electromagnetic Pulse blast. The one called Parveen is quite clever. I would greatly enjoy dismantling his mind," Mr. Sweet said, as if a mind were a wind-up toy or a clock radio.[19]

"Mother, give me a map of the world with Windcity as the focal point."

Instantly, the hovering glow altered itself into a globe, tiny and intricate. The globe spun until a red dot blinked to show the location of Windcity. Landmasses and oceans were illustrated in three-dimensional detail. Mountains, valleys, rivers, and oceans were startlingly clear.

"Excellent. We must assume the children are travelling by zeppelin. Given the speed of the zeppelin from existing data, represent the possible distance traversed by the fugitives up to this point." A green circle centred on Windcity appeared. The area of the circle covered roughly half the surface of the earth. "Mr. Sweet, I had no idea an airship could cover so much ground in such a short time. This

---

[19] Which it isn't. The mind is more like an electric toothbrush or one of those shoe polishers one finds in the finer hotels around the world.

doesn't really narrow down our search parameters."

"No, Mr. Candy. We must have more information." Mr. Sweet thought for a moment, his head cocked to the side. "Mother, have there been any reported sightings of unidentified craft matching the description of the pirate airship?"

"Checking ... Three hundred reports of unidentified craft. None with specific reference to airships."

"This is getting us nowhere, Mr. Candy. The number of possible locations is too great. I believe we must initiate a remote reboot."

"But, Mr. Sweet, Hamish X will be outside our control when he is restarted. His brain functions may be impaired. We don't know how he will react. He may do damage to himself. The results might be catastrophic."

"Nonetheless, the asset must be returned immediately and the only way we can retrieve it is to find it. The integration is approaching. We must restart the unit. The locator beacon will tell us where he is. It was for situations like this, when he is beyond our direct control, that we embedded the remote Mother program in his mind. The voice will prompt him to return to us. As soon as we know where he is, we will move with all speed and force to retrieve the asset. There is no other way."

The only sound was the thrupping of the rotor blades above as the Grey Agents pondered their decision. Finally, Mr. Candy ducked his head once in agreement. "Mother, initiate remote restart sequence."

Chapter 4

Mrs. Francis couldn't sleep. She lay on her bunk and stared up at the wooden planking of the ceiling. Whenever she closed her eyes, images of the attack on Windcity filled her tired mind. She imagined the bird machines approaching out of the darkness, spraying fire over the airship.

"Oh, these children. I must keep them safe somehow," she whispered to the darkness. With a heavy sigh, she gave up trying to sleep and sat up, twisting the knob on the bedside light. Blinking in the sudden glare, she swung her plump legs over the side of the bunk and slipped her feet into the fuzzy pink slippers that were her favourite. They were a little worse for wear after the stint in the pirates' custody and the escape from Windcity, but they were still serviceable. Wrapping her pink dressing gown around her chubby body, she stepped out the door.

The corridor was deserted. All the children were sleeping in their bunks, snug and warm. Mrs. Francis had made sure of that, soothing and whispering reassurances to frightened toddlers. She loved them all as if they were her own children. She dreaded the thought of anything happening to any one of them. Taking special care to make no noise, she crept down the corridor, pausing at each open hatch to look in and make sure each child was asleep.

After the last cabin was checked, she stepped into the

galley[20] to find Mr. Kipling slumped at the table, a cold cup of tea at his elbow and his chin resting on his fist. He snored softly. Mrs. Francis went to him and kissed him gently on the forehead. He opened his eyes and smiled at her.

"Just resting my eyes."

"Of course, dear." She wrapped her little arms around his bony shoulders and squeezed.

He winced. "Ribs are still a little tender, dear."

"Sorry." She released him.

"Not at all." He looked at his watch. "Why are you prowling about at this hour? Are the children all right?"

"There's nothing wrong. The children are fine. I just couldn't sleep. My mind won't stop. I'm so worried about Hamish X. And the children. And … Oh I'm just worried about everything!" She raised her hands to her face and began to sob.

Mr. Kipling took her hand and squeezed it in his own. "You mustn't cry, dear. It makes me extremely anxious. We all need you to be strong." He offered her a handkerchief. She took it and blew her nose loudly.

"I know. I just get so worried sometimes."

"I understand. I do too. But things will be all right. You'll see."

"Where are Parveen and Mimi?"

"Outside keeping a watch."

"I'll make some fresh tea."

"Lovely, dear." Kipling smiled a rare smile. "Excellent idea."

---

[20] *Galley* is the word for "kitchen" on a sailing ship. Strangely, many things have different names when they're on a ship as opposed to on land. The bathroom is called the "head." A wall is called a "bulkhead" and shoes are called "David." Sailors are odd people.

MIMI AND PARVEEN sat on the ramp in the cool evening air. The moon was a sliver in the sky, casting only a faint light. Mimi stared up into the sky while Parveen read the airship's engine manual with the aid of a small flashlight, making notes in the margin with his pencil.

"Never seen so many stars."

Parveen glanced up for a second. "Less smog. Higher altitude. Lack of light pollution."

"Whatever. It's just nice is all." Mimi was quiet for a moment. "What if nobody comes?"

Parveen didn't look up from his reading. "They'll come."

"Yeah, but what if they doesn't? What'll we do then? We ain't got nowhere to go."

Parveen lowered his book and turned the flashlight on Mimi's face. She blinked and blocked the beam with her outstretched hand.

"Mimi, we'll deal with that when the time comes. The world is extremely large. We will find somewhere to hide. Why don't you find something to do and let me read this manual?"

He turned the beam back onto his book, put the pencil back behind his ear, and continued to read. Mimi frowned. "That ain't what you do with a flashlight on a dark night when yer campin'." She suddenly reached out and grabbed the flashlight and held it below her chin. Her face was outlined eerily. "It's time for a ghost story."

"Give me back my flashlight, please."

"C'mon, Mr. Bookworm. Just one scary story."

Parveen sighed and crossed his arms. "Fine. Although I must tell you, I do not believe in ghosts or the supernatural. I believe all phenomena will one day be explained by science."

"Wow, that sounds like a lot o' fun. In the meantime, I'll tell ya a great story about the man with a hook fer a head …"

Parveen sighed again. "This seems already implausible to me."

Mimi ignored him and began her story.

"It were a dark night, sumthin' similar to tonight, in fact. There weren't no moon and two young kids, we'll call 'em Parveen and Mimi just fer simplicity's sake. Anyway, they was out walkin' in the woods and they was lost …"

"Did they have a flashlight?"

"No, they got caught unawares and din't know they would need one," Mimi said.

"Why would we go out walking in the woods on a moonless night with no light source?"

"It's just a story."

"I find it unlikely that I would venture out on such a trek without even pausing to make sure I would be able to see adequately."

"All right! All right!" Mimi rolled her eyes. "Fine. We got a flashlight. Happy?"

"Not happy; it merely seems more likely."

"Whatever. Mimi and Parveen out in the woods. They're walkin' along and they're lost. They can't see a thing—"

"I thought we had a—"

"The batteries wore out! We're walkin' along and we hear a sound like somebody is followin' us, but every time we stop … it stops."

Mimi took on a serious expression and pushed up imaginary glasses. "'Maybe it's an echo of some description. Or perhaps these woods are haunted.'" It was a quite passable impersonation of Parveen.

"That doesn't really sound like me."

"I think it does."

"Well, I would never say that."

"Quiet," Mimi snapped. "And Mimi says, 'Yeah, they're haunted all right: by the ghost o' that guy who killed people with a big hook. He eventually got his head chopped off by an angry lumberjack but now he wanders these woods lookin' fer his lost head. He's got a hook on his shoulders where his head used ta be.'"

"That is ridiculous."

"Quiet. My story! Get it? Okay, anyway ... Parveen says, 'Oh Mimi, I am experiencing such fear. Please protect me.'"

"Oh, this is completely unendurable ..."

"'Don't worry, Parveen. I'll pretect ya.' Just then, they heard a twig snap ..."

"Ridiculous."

Out in the night an owl hooted, causing them both to jump.

Mimi crowed and pointed at Parveen. "See! Ya are scared! Ha!"

"Not in the least."

HAMISH X DREAMED.

Bright lights shone down, burning through his closed eyelids. He moaned. Voices spoke nearby.

"He's stirring," Mr. Candy's voice announced. "Increase the dose of sedative."

"It's already dangerously high." The Professor sounded worried. "We don't want to lose another one."

"There are more boys where this one came from," said Mr. Sweet. "Increase the dosage, Professor."

A shuddering sigh. "As you wish."

Hamish felt the pain lessen slightly, fading to a throbbing ache that emanated from his legs.

"Excellent. Now apply the interface units, Professor. Then the process is complete."

"As you wish," the Professor said again, sounding resigned. "Applying now."

There was a pause, then a strange sensation: a cool, slick substance surrounded Hamish's feet. He murmured softly.

"The interface units are in place."

"Excellent. Activate."

"Mr. Sweet, shouldn't we wait until I've run more tests—" the Professor began.

"Do as you're told, Professor. Consider this the only test you will have the opportunity to run."

"But—"

"Remember your dear mother, Professor."

"Activating."

The cool sensation surrounding his feet and shins suddenly bloomed into white-hot pain. The sensation was bizarre and horrible—as if hundreds, thousands of tiny worms with heads as sharp as pins were burrowing into his flesh. He screamed and opened his eyes, staring down at his feet. They were encased in huge black boots, slick and shiny in the white light beaming down over the operating table where he lay. Two men in grey surgical gowns stood on either side of the table. In place of eyes, black goggles glittered in the harsh light. Between them stood the Professor, his eyes watery, swimming behind thick glasses. The Professor held a small black box in his hands.

"Why are you doing this to me?" Hamish whimpered. "Why?"

"Why?" Mr. Sweet tilted his head and looked at the boy on the table. "Why? The world is going to change and you are the instrument, the conduit, and the key! As to why you? Just unlucky I guess."

"Dear God," the Professor whispered.

The grey men looked at each other. "Hamish X," one of them said. The other nodded. "The tenth time's the charm." The man reached out, extending a disturbingly long finger, and pressed a button on the Professor's black box. The pain in Hamish's legs increased.

"Mother!" Hamish X called, terrified. "Mother?" He screamed and screamed.

"what the heck was that?"

Parveen sat up. "It sounded like Hamish X."

In the galley, Mrs. Francis and Mr. Kipling dropped their teacups when the first howl ripped through the airship.

"Hamish X!" Mrs. Francis gasped. In an instant, the two adults were hurrying down the corridor to the boy's cabin. Frightened children, startled from deep sleep, stuck their heads into the corridor. "Stay in your bunks," Mrs. Francis instructed breathlessly.

When they reached the cabin they found the room in a shambles. Hamish X was up on the big Captain's bed. All the other furniture was overturned or smashed to kindling. The bedclothes were torn to tatters. He was turned away from them, facing the wall and kicking it furiously. With every strike of boot against the wooden wall, a crackle of sparks splashed across the tortured planking. Flares of light shot off the footwear, casting a weird blue glow over the room and making Hamish X appear almost demonic. In his hands he clutched the green leather book *Great Plumbers and Their Exploits*. He turned and glared at the two adults when they rushed into the room, stopping them short with the fevered intensity of his gaze.

"I have to find my MOTHER!"

"Yes, Hamish X," the soothing voice in his head said. *"Don't let anyone stop you. Come to me now."*

He nodded and gritted his teeth. Summoning up a surge of energy, he drove a boot into the wall. The surface cracked under the furious kick. Boards shattered into slivers. The concussion was deafening in the enclosed space of the cabin. Hamish X looked like a creature possessed. His golden eyes were wild and staring. He pointed at the boots.

"These! I don't want them! TAKE THEM OFF!"

"No, Hamish X," the Voice said calmly. *"You need the boots. They are good."*

"I don't LIKE THEM. I DON'T LIKE THE MEN!"

He seemed to be trying to smash the boots as much as smash his way through the wall in the process.

"Hamish X!" Mrs. Francis cried. "Stop!"

His golden eyes blazed with terror and rage. Teeth exposed in a snarl, he shouted, "Where is my mother! WHEEERRRRRRRE?" The howl raised hairs on the back of Mrs. Francis's neck. There was no recognition in the boy's eyes, only fear. The gentle if mischievous boy who had first come to Windcity was nowhere to be seen.

"Hamish X, please! Calm down. It's me … Mrs. Francis." She held out her hands to him. "It's all right. You're safe."

"Don't listen to her. She means you harm. Come to me. Now!"

"MOTHERRRRRRRRRRRR!" The howl ripped from his lungs again. He looked at her, his eyes like slits. The fear had been replaced by rage. "Did you do this to me?" He pointed at the boots. "DID YOU?"

"Settle down, dear Hamish X," Mrs. Francis soothed, a tremor of fear in her voice. "We're your friends …"

He seemed to hesitate, confusion twisting his face. "I HAVE NO FRIENDS!" He hooked his fingers around the leather binding of the book. Squatting down on his haunches, he glared at Mrs. Francis. "I want my mother!"

"Come then, Hamish X. I'm waiting."

Mr. Kipling interposed himself between Mrs. Francis and Hamish X. His hand strayed to the sword hilt at his hip. "Son. Settle down now. There's a good lad. We'll find her."

"They mean you harm. COME!"

Hamish X barked a savage laugh and snarled again. "You can't hurt me any more! NO MORE!" He gathered himself and sprang like a cat, hands extended like claws.

Mr. Kipling dove to the side, hauling Mrs. Francis along with him. Hamish X missed him by a hair, but the momentum carried him on to the bulkhead. He swung his boots towards the wooden barrier and it exploded outwards in a rain of sparks and singed splinters. He landed in a crouch and then hurled himself down the corridor towards the cargo ramp, howling at the top of his lungs. Mrs. Francis helped Mr. Kipling to his feet. Hamish X's boots trailed wisps of blue fire.

Inside Hamish X's head, the woman's voice was speaking. Her tone was calm but insistent. "These people mean you harm, Hamish X. You must escape. You must come to me. I am in Providence, Rhode Island. Come to me now."

Hamish X shouted, "Yes, Mother! I'm coming!" and ran as fast as he could down the corridor.

Outside on the cargo ramp, Mimi and Parveen stood transfixed. "I think it was Hamish X," Mimi said. "I think he's coming this way!"

Hamish X burst into the cargo hold and skidded to a stop on the steel plating of the floor. A shower of sparks sprayed where the soles of his boots struck the metal. He clutched the book tight as if it were the only thing of importance in the world. Casting his gaze wildly back and forth, he saw the cargo ramp with Mimi and Parveen standing gaping in surprise.

Mimi's surprise turned to delight as she saw her friend up and on his feet. "Hamish X!" She smiled and held out her arms. Then she saw there was something wrong. He was sweating profusely. His eyes darted from side to side. He stood at the top of the ramp, his chest heaving and his eyes filled with panic. When she said his name, he stared at her as if she were some sort of monster.

"YOU! WHO ARE YOU? WHERE'S MY MOTHER?" His eyes narrowed. "Are you one of them?"

"She is an enemy, Hamish X," the voice said.

"Yes!" Hamish X hissed. He lunged at her, swiping the heavy book like a club.

Mimi reacted instinctively, diving to one side while grabbing Parveen's shirttail and yanking him along with her. They fell off the ramp onto the wet grass. Parveen grunted as the air left his lungs.

Hamish X leapt down the ramp and landed in the grass. His boots sizzled and steamed. "I WANT my MOTHER!" he roared and the boots flared, casting a blue light in a circle several metres across.

The light revealed the meadow around the airship, the looming gasbag above, and a few terrified, vomiting rabbits. All to be expected. What wasn't to be expected was a group of six figures dressed in dark, tight-fitting bodysuits, black goggles, and balaclavas.[21] They stood

---

21 A *balaclava* is a sort of woollen cap named for the place in the Crimean Peninsula where it originated. It can be rolled down to cover the face to protect it from the cold or to hide one's identity. Not to be confused with baklava, which is a Middle

frozen in the glare, caught in stealthy poses that would certainly have been effective in the darkness but in the bright blue light seemed superfluous, if not completely ridiculous.

"Who are they?" Mimi whispered, huddled beside Parveen in the grass.

"If I'm not mistaken ..." Parveen began.

"We come from the King of Switzerland!" the black figure in front called out. He, for indeed he was a boy, reached up and pulled off his balaclava, revealing a pale face and straight blond hair. "We've come for Hamish X!"

Eastern dessert made from pistachios, honey, and many layers of delicate, flaky pastry. It would hardly be effective as a ski mask, I think you'd agree. Although, if someone came at me wearing a load of flaky pastry on their face, I doubt I could identify them to the authorities. It might keep their face warm, too.

Chapter 5

The strange figures faced Hamish X in a loose semicircle. They were all dressed in the same black uniform. On the right breast of their bodysuits was a silver cross embroidered into the fabric. Each wore a heavy belt with small pouches on it, a coil of rope, and a bulky black holster holding a bulky black pistol. Their leader, the blond boy, took a step towards Hamish X, his hands held out before him, palms upward.

"I have come from the King, We mean you no harm."

"The King?" Mimi stood. "He sent you?"

"Yes," the boy said, "I am Aidan, Lieutenant to His Majesty and Commander of the Royal Swiss Guards. We've come to escort you to his presence."

For a moment, nobody moved. Even Hamish X, rampaging seconds before, stood frozen and dumb, staring at the strange boy and his masked cohorts. The only sound was a rabbit vomiting softly in the still night. Hamish X's boots dimmed slightly, the blue light casting an eerie glow over the newcomers.

The blond boy took a step closer to Hamish X, his hand extended. "Let's just settle down here," he said soothingly. I promise we are here to help."

Hamish X said nothing, his eyes flicking back and forth between the boy and the black figures ranged behind him. "Who are you?"

"As I said, I'm Aidan. This is my Guard Squadron." He indicated the silent group behind him. "We've come to take you to the King."

Hamish X frowned. "The King?"

Suddenly, in his head, the Voice was there, urgent and insistent. *"NO! HE IS THE ENEMY. HE WANTS TO HURT YOU!"*

The Voice was like a shout in his mind. He jerked his head in reaction to the ferocity of its tone. "What? Why?" He staggered a step forward.

"Hamish X?" Mimi breathed. "What's the matter?"

"CRUSH HIM! CRUSH THEM ALL!"

Hamish X's face darkened. He glared at Aidan and snarled like a wild animal. "You want to hurt me!"

"No, I want to …" Aidan didn't have time to finish. Hamish X sprang at him, catching the boy off guard and driving his boot into his chest. Aidan flew across the meadow, sliding on the slick grass and bouncing like a

stone skipping on a pond. When he stopped sliding, he lay on his back, groaning.

"Hamish X!" Mimi shouted. "Stop!"

One of the strangers pulled off her balaclava to reveal dark, shoulder-length hair. She hauled her pistol out of her holster. "Nobody kicks my brother." She thumbed a switch and the pistol hummed to life. She pointed the pistol at Hamish X. It had a wide barrel like the mouth of a small cannon. "Stun him!" The others drew their pistols even as she fired.

"No!" Parveen cried as he flung himself in the path of the green bolt of energy erupting from the pistol. The bolt struck him squarely in the chest. He fell in a boneless heap on the ground.

Mimi rushed over and dropped to her knees at her stricken friend's side. "Parveen? Are you all right?" She turned her friend's face up. His glasses hung from one ear. His eyes were closed and he was breathing.

Hamish X stood looking down at Mimi and Parveen. His chest heaved. His eyes were wide. "He … He tried to save me."

Mimi looked up at him, tears streaking her face. "Of course he did. He's your friend."

"Friend …" Hamish X's face was a picture of confusion. "He's my friend?"

The girl and the other Guards held their pistols ready, aimed at Hamish X.

"He tried to save me …"

"No. He isn't your friend." The Voice was so sure of itself. *"He's trying to trick you. It's all a trap."*

"No …"

"Yes. They are out to get you. They have pistols. They want to shoot you. Crush them."

Hamish X shook his head. He looked at Mimi, cradling Parveen's head in her lap. "No. They're my friends …"

"*NO! CRUSH THEM ALL!*"

Mimi was beginning to think Hamish X was going to be okay. Then his eyes clouded and his mouth drew back into a snarl. Teeth bared, he raised his boot. It flared with blue energy as he prepared to bring it down on her. He didn't get a chance.

"Fire!" the girl from the Swiss Guards ordered. All the Guards discharged their pistols. The green bolts struck Hamish X in the chest, the legs, and the right arm. He roared in pain and staggered backwards, dropping the book on the ground and falling heavily onto his backside. The air burst out of his lungs with a loud *Whuff!* He sat blinking like an owl.

"Mother?" he mumbled thickly and tried to rise again, crawling on his hands and knees towards the book lying in the grass. "Mother?"

"Fire!" the girl shouted again. Once more, green bolts splashed into Hamish X. He groaned loudly and made one more effort to push himself upright on shaking arms, but failed, slumping to the wet grass and, finally, lying still.

"Oh dear!" Mrs. Francis and Mr. Kipling rushed down the ramp, having arrived just in time to see Hamish X being stunned for the second time. Mrs. Francis gathered the inert boy into her arms, rocking him gently. Mr. Kipling came to where Mimi held Parveen and scooped up the little boy easily. Mimi went to look down at Hamish X. Aidan, walking carefully beside the other girl, came to join her.

"That could have gone better," Aidan said. He held out a hand to Mimi. "Now that the excitement's over, I'll introduce myself once again. Lieutenant Aidan of the Royal Swiss Guards."

Mimi ignored him and stepped up to face the dark-haired girl. "Who're you?"

The dark-haired girl curled her lip. "I'm Cara Doorfer. Aidan's sister."

"Well, Cara Doo-Whatever, Aidan's sister," Mimi said, "I'm Mimi Catastrophe Jones, Hamish X's friend, and I don't take kindly to people shootin' my friends, git it?"

The two girls stood toe to toe, staring into each other's eyes. For a long span of seconds, neither blinked. Finally, Cara sniffed and flicked her hair back over her shoulder. "Whatever." She turned away and went to join the other Guards, who had removed their masks and stood in a loose knot a few metres away.

Aidan shook his head. "This isn't the way the King would have wanted it. I'm sorry. We didn't expect this reaction from Hamish X."

Mimi nodded, sizing the boy up. "Yeah. He ain't been himself lately. It don't help, you folks sneakin' up like that."

"Sorry. We can't take any chances. We had to make sure you were really bringing Hamish X, and not just part of a trap set by the ODA."

"Are ya satisfied that we ain't?"

"Yes. But we're wasting time. We have to get out of here."

"And go where?"

"To the Hollow Mountain, of course."

Mrs. Francis let out a gasp as Hamish X's eyes suddenly flew open. He leapt to his feet and stared wildly around.

"I'm not going anywhere! I've got to find my Mother! MOTHER!"

Cara and the Guards reached for their pistols, but Hamish X was too quick. He lunged at Aidan and grabbed the front of his black bodysuit, lifting him into the air. "You can't stop me!"

Mimi battered Hamish X's arm with both her fists but couldn't break his grip. "Hamish X! Stop it!"

"Mother. I … You …" Hamish X's eyes suddenly rolled back into his head. He dropped Aidan, who fell to his knees.

"Mother?" Hamish X whimpered, then fell face first onto the grass. Mimi and Parveen rushed to his side, followed closely by Mr. Kipling and Mrs. Francis, with Aidan and the girl bringing up the rear.

"What happened?" Mimi asked.

Mrs. Francis pointed at Hamish X's neck. "Look."

Two small silver filaments had penetrated the skin of the stricken boy's neck just above the collar of his flannel shirt. As they watched, the filaments withdrew. With a soft rustling sound, the Swiss Army knife crawled out of Hamish X's shirt, its many blades functioning again as legs. It climbed down onto the grass, and with a click, all its blades withdrew into its body and it lay still.

"The King." Aidan smiled, rubbing his bruised chest. "He thinks of everything."

Mr. Candy and Mr. Sweet

Mr. Sweet and Mr. Candy sat at the kitchen table in the little house on Angell Street in Providence, Rhode Island. Mr. Candy's hat lay on the table while Mr. Sweet fiddled with the wires at the top of Mr. Candy's head. Mr. Sweet prodded the nest of colourful wires with a long steel pin. Every now and then the rod crackled at the end and smoke curled up in thin tendrils. The reek of burning plastic filled the small kitchen.

Mr. Sweet probed one area of Mr. Candy's cortex and Mr. Candy's right hand splayed out involuntarily. The fingers wiggled.

"That's better," Mr. Candy said, flexing his long fingers. "I was experiencing some difficulty manipulating my digits after the refit."

"I'm glad to accommodate you, Mr. Candy." Mr. Sweet laid down his instrument on a cloth beside a number of other bizarre implements whose purposes one could only guess at. As he did so a chime rang out, soft and sweet, seeming to throb in the air and coming from no particular source.

"The unit has been located." Mother's voice filled the kitchen.

Over the centre of the table an image of a spinning globe flickered into existence. The globe stopped spinning and a blue dot blinked in a mountainous region in Central Europe.

"There!" Mr. Sweet's overlong finger stabbed out at the glowing map.

"Switzerland?" Mr. Candy said, baffled. "How could they have travelled so far without being seen?"

"It doesn't matter. We have them now. Mother?"

The calm female voice filled the air. "Listening."

"Prepare an assault team. We leave within the hour."

The dot winked out. "It's gone," Mr. Sweet said.

"It doesn't matter. We have a lead now. We go to Switzerland. We know where he is. Now we retrieve Hamish X."

"We must be quick."

"Prepare the SST."[22]

---

[22] An SST is an airplane that goes extremely fast. SST stands for Super Sonic Transport. Super Sonic means the plane travels faster than the speed of sound, so don't bother to yell out the window at your friends, "I'll be there in a second!," because you'll arrive before they hear you and it will be a total waste of time.

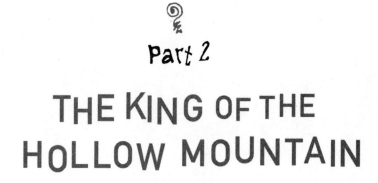

Part 2

THE KING OF THE HOLLOW MOUNTAIN

Another Note from the Narrator

Enjoying yourselves? I'm sure you are. How can I be sure? Obviously, I am an excellent narrator and any narrator worth his salt[23] knows his audience, what they like and don't like, and delivers the story accordingly. For example, if this story were aimed at a group of whales, I would dwell more heavily on aspects of the tale that might interest them, like the flight over the ocean in the early chapters. As it stands, this book is for human children, so I glossed over that part and spent more time talking about Mimi, Parveen, and Hamish X. In fact, if the book were addressed to whales, I would probably not have called it **Hamish X and the Hollow Mountain** at all. The book would likely have been called **A Whale Sees an Airship Flying Over the Ocean and**

---

[23] "Worth his salt" is an expression dating from ancient times when salt was the most important commodity in the world; being worth one's salt, then, was a sign of being valuable. Since there were no refrigerators, salt was very important as a way to preserve food. Cheese, for example, is just a way of preserving the goodness of milk for a long period of time by using salt to cure it. Not that milk is sick and needs to be cured. Curing is a process by which materials are preserved, such as leather or food. If your food is leathery, it has probably been cured improperly … unless you prefer to eat leathery things, in which case you might be a bit weird.

Then Eats Some Plankton,[24, 25] which would hold no interest for you, a human audience. That is, I assume you are human. If you aren't, please put down this book and back away slowly.

So, Hamish X is in his strange comatose state once more. Mimi and Parveen have decided to follow the Royal Swiss Guards to the Hollow Mountain. The ODA are in hot pursuit. Everything is in place for a great second section. Let's get right to it, shall we?

---

[24] Plankton is a micro-organism that grows in the sea and is a preferred food of whales.

[25] I have commenced writing this book and it should hit the shelves of major bookstores in the new year. My editor is skeptical about its possible sales, pointing out that whales rarely come out of the ocean to purchase books, as their skin must be kept moist at all times. And even if they did, most bookshops would bar them from entering because they would splash the books and ruin the merchandise. Further, a whale taking the book back to the ocean to read it quickly finds that the book becomes waterlogged and falls apart. Topping off everything, whales can't read because they are not permitted entry into most schools. So there is very little financial gain to be had in writing books for whales. Still, I do it because I am an artist and I follow my muse wherever it may lead me, regardless of monetary gain.

Chapter 6

The airship *Orphan Queen* wove its way at low altitude through the dark mountains. On either side shadowy masses of rock soared into the starry sky. The front window of the craft was etched with frost, but the heater kept the cold at bay. Here and there, a scattering of lights in the blackness below indicated the presence of a town or village. Mr. Kipling was careful to avoid the inhabited areas, clinging to the edge of the mountainsides and flying as low as he dared. The treacherous crosswinds in the mountain valleys made the flying a challenge, but Mr. Kipling didn't complain, even though his ribs were obviously sore. He bore his pain stoically.[26]

Mrs. Francis had taken the now inert Hamish X to his cabin and was watching over him, wringing her apron in her typical expression of worry. The boy was in a profound sleep, induced somehow by the knife. He hadn't so much as stirred since falling unconscious in the meadow. He lay

---

[26] *Stoically* means without complaint, and comes from the ancient Greek philosophy of Stoicism, which was practised by the Stoics. The Stoics believed in bearing all trials and tribulations of life with a stiff upper lip, i.e., without complaining. They did, in fact, have extremely stiff upper lips. So stiff were their upper lips that they were often driven head first into the gates of besieged cities and used as battering rams with great effectiveness. In a curious side note, the group actually called themselves the Storks due to their propensity for standing on one leg all day and eating exclusively fish, but they were sued by the Athenian Stork Appreciation Society for misrepresentation and copyright infringement and so had to change their name.

on his back, eyes flickering under the lids, breathing deeply. As a precaution, they had secured him to the Captain's bed using cargo straps that Parveen had managed to rummage up in the hold.

Parveen had recovered very quickly from the blast of the stun gun. He assured a fretful Mrs. Francis that, apart from a slight tingling in his fingers and toes, he was perfectly all right.

Aidan and his sister Cara stood on the bridge with Mimi and Parveen, gazing out into the night through the forward window that wrapped around the ship's wheel. Mountains loomed large as they powered through the snowy peaks. The other Guards were currently in the galley eating sandwiches thrown together by Mrs. Francis.

"Once again," Aidan said, "I'm sorry our first meeting wasn't a little smoother, but everything seems to have worked out okay."

Mimi sniffed. "Sure. Hamish X is out cold. I guess it coulda been worse."

Cara rolled her eyes. Mimi glared at her. The two girls hadn't exactly hit it off. Mimi shook her head. "So. Where the heck are we goin'?" Aidan didn't answer and Cara merely tossed her hair impatiently.

It was the fifth time Mimi had asked and she still didn't have an answer. Mimi was at the end of her patience. She was worried about Hamish X, and these strangers hadn't volunteered much beyond their names. The girl in particular rubbed her the wrong way. She was too pretty by far. Pretty girls made Mimi uncomfortable. She stole a look at her reflection in the frost-streaked window and scowled. Compared to Cara, she wasn't pretty at all. Her nose looked like a hatchet blade and her unruly hair made her feel so … well, not beautiful, that was for sure.

"Alter course, three points to starboard," Aidan said suddenly. Mr. Kipling frowned. "Are you sure?"

"Quite sure," Aidan said.

Parveen looked up from the radar screen, his face outlined in the faint green glow of the console. "But that will take us directly into the north face of Mount Nutterhorn."

"Just do it," Aidan said.

Mr. Kipling shook his head. "We'll be killed."

"Trust me," Aidan said.

"Why should we?" Mimi's temper broke. She shouted at the strange boy, venting her frustration, "Ya show up in the middle o' the night, creepin' up on us in the dark. Ya won't tell us where we're goin'. Why should we trust ya? Gimme one good reason."

Cara snorted. "Because you have no choice, that's why. So just button your lip. 'Kay?"

Mimi's face went bright red. Her fist clenched and she was about to blacken one of Cara's pretty little eyes when Parveen interjected.

"Fine," he said. "She's right, Mimi. We have no choice. We have to trust them. Why would they want to steer us into a mountain face? They'd only be killing themselves."

Mimi relaxed her fingers and with great effort let her anger drain away. What Parveen said was true. They had to help Hamish X, and at the moment the strangers were their only hope.

"Altering course," Mr. Kipling called as he turned the wheel. The ship slowly swung to the right, creaking as the wind shifted.

In the forward window loomed the bulk of a huge mountain. Outlined in the faint moonlight, it resembled a giant pyramid carved of black rock. The mountain face they approached was flat and sheer. Cloud wreathed the summit. Snow covered the peak, trailing away in a white plume blown by the wind. All in all, as mountains go, it was big, rocky, and looked very hard. Not the kind of mountain you'd really like to slam into. Come to think of it, most mountains are of that variety.[27]

Mimi watched the mountain get bigger in the window with growing unease. The wall of rock was now less than five hundred metres away. The wind was behind them, driving them quickly forward. She stole a look at Aidan and Cara. They seemed completely unfazed by the approaching impact.

"Four hundred metres," Mr. Kipling said flatly. His fingers tightened on the wheel.

Seconds ticked by and the rock face loomed larger.

"Three hundred metres."

Mimi involuntarily took a half step backwards as the black stone wall filled the window.

"Two hundred metres …" Mr. Kipling's voice crept into a slightly higher register, but he kept his hands firmly on the wheel.

"How strange," Parveen said suddenly.

"What?" Mimi stepped behind him, looking at the screen over his shoulder.

"The mountain face." Parveen had his face buried in the radar screen. "There's something weird about it. There is an area of lesser density. Roughly thirty-metre square."

---

[27] The exception to the rule is the Fluffy Mountains of Central Peru. Formed completely of naturally occurring marshmallow, they are not only safe to crash into but also extremely delicious. Recently, the UN was forced to declare the Fluffy Mountains a World Heritage Site to stop hikers from devouring them.

Mimi glared out into the night at the approaching mountain. The rock face looked like a rock face, deadly and massive. "What? What?"

Parveen suddenly lifted his eyes to the window. He didn't look alarmed. Rather, he raised an eyebrow and nodded. "A gate!"

Aidan smiled. "I love this part."

The black wall of rock was only metres away. Parveen didn't look worried in the slightest, so Mimi forced herself to take a deep breath and relax. As they approached the rock face a rumbling began, audible even inside the sealed bridge. The rock wall ahead of them shifted, swinging like a massive door on a hinge.

"That is amazing," Mr. Kipling said, awestruck.

The airship swept past the doorway into a tunnel.

They were enveloped in warm, golden light. The tunnel, carved out of the solid rock, was easily wide and high enough to accommodate the *Orphan Queen*. Banks of lights shone down from its walls. Far below, a pair of metal rails ran along the ground.

"That gate must have weighed tons," Parveen said, impressed. There was a rumble as the door swung shut behind them. "The engineering involved boggles the imagination."

"Completed during the reign of King Leopold in the late nineteenth century. It always blows my mind, no matter how many times I see it," Aidan laughed.

"It's easy to blow such a small mind," Cara cracked. Aidan ignored her.

"Ya coulda told the rest of us it was gonna open," Mimi snarled. "I darn near wet my pants."

"Are you sure you didn't?" Cara asked sweetly. Mimi glared at her.

"Cara! Zip it!" Aidan snapped. He fixed his sister with a stare.

Cara rolled her eyes, looked out the window, and mumbled, "I'm older than you, you know."

"Keep it steady, Mr. Kipling, but drop our speed to slow ahead."

"Steady as she goes," Mr. Kipling answered. "Slow ahead."

They sailed along the tunnel for several hundred metres. Ahead, a circle of bright light grew larger. The ship flew steadily towards the golden opening, emerging at last into a vast chamber. The chamber was a cavern carved out of the Nutterhorn's natural rock, easily four kilometres across and at least one kilometre high.

The *Orphan Queen* powered out into the chamber. As they passed through the gateway they saw below that the rails ended in a stone pier. The entire floor of the chamber was a vast lake, steaming gently in the golden light from some source up above. On the surface of the lake little boats floated, pushed along by small motors. Some drifted easily on the placid surface. Others made their way towards the stone pier where several boats were already moored. Children transferred boxes from the boats onto the pier and others loaded the boxes into small rail cars resting on the rails that led into the tunnel. When the children saw the *Orphan Queen* pass above, they stopped working to wave at her. Aidan and Cara waved back.

"This is an artificial lake fed by underground springs," Aidan explained. "We farm fish here and it also supplies our water needs."

"Artificial? You built this?" Parveen was amazed, pressing his face to the windscreen to look down at the expanse of water.

"Not me. King Frits. The Eleventh King of Switzerland designed and built it during his reign."

As they moved out into the chamber they saw that the walls were covered with glittering mineral deposits. Scaffolds were built into the rock to allow groups of children access to the cavern wall. The children were busy with drills and picks, prying chunks of rock away and throwing them into chutes that led down to bins at the foot of the wall. Conveyor belts whisked the rock pieces away to small stone buildings located around the base of the wall.

"We mine most of the raw materials we need to live here inside the rock."

Mimi peered closely at the scaffolds. They were far away, but she thought she could see small furry shapes moving among the children. "I must be tired." She rubbed her eyes and looked out in the direction they were headed. A pillar came into view. It was incredibly tall and thin but the mist from the water made it hard to see.

"What the heck is that?" Mimi pointed ahead of the ship where the tower rose out of the water.

"The elevator," Cara said. "And the Stair, of course."

They drew closer and saw that the tower sprouted from a wide stone base that was circular and carved from the native stone. Little boats bobbed all around it. The cylinder disappeared into the ceiling. A staircase twined around the cylinder. Here and there, a child walked up or down. On the outer edge of the staircase was a bright blue tube.

"The staircase is there in case the elevator breaks down or has to be serviced," Aidan explained.

"Yeah, but what's the blue thing?"

"A water slide."

Parveen and Mimi looked at each other. "Awesome."

"How high is that thing?" Parveen asked when he could

speak again. They were cruising straight for the structure. Droplets of what looked like rain beaded on the windscreen and the upper end of the elevator was lost in cloud.

"It runs through the entire mountain."

Parveen was about to ask another question, but Aidan held up a hand. "You'll see the whole thing soon. Don't worry. Let's bring this ship in to dock. Head for the base of the elevator, Mr. Kipling."

Mr. Kipling hesitated, looking to Parveen. The little boy nodded. "Do as he says."

"Aye, Captain." Mr. Kipling swung the wheel. Mimi flipped the trim levers and the ship began to lose altitude.

Soon a circular platform emerged from the mist. A crowd of children, all wearing loose, brightly coloured jumpsuits, stood waiting there. As the ship came closer they waved their arms and hopped up and down excitedly. When they were close enough to make out individual faces, Parveen and Mimi saw that the children represented a cross-section of every race and culture on earth. Some had brown skin, some yellow, and some pink. They were tall and short, male and female, toddlers to early teens. Such a wide range of differences, and yet they had one thing in common: they were all smiling.

"Stop her here, Mr. Kipling," Aidan said. Mr. Kipling flipped the levers that cut the power to the main engines. He manoeuvred the ship with smaller shunting engines, guiding the *Orphan Queen* expertly to the edge of the platform. The children on the platform leapt up and took hold of the mooring ropes that dangled from the nose of the airship and pulled her down. In minutes, the ship was tied to metal rings on the edge of the platform.

"Come with us." Aidan and Cara led them down to the cargo hold. Parveen pressed the red button by the cargo door and it lowered itself to the stone floor with a scrape and a clunk.

"Welcome to the Hollow Mountain," Aidan said. He marched down the ramp to the platform. Parveen, Mimi, Mr. Kipling, and Mrs. Francis hesitated. Aidan saw their worried expressions. He stood at the bottom of the ramp and beckoned, a smile on his face. "No need to fear. You're safe now under the protection of the King of Switzerland." Cautiously, the Windcity refugees walked down the ramp into a strange new land.

The locals gathered around them, their fresh, clean faces staring openly at these new arrivals. They whispered behind their hands to each other, discussing the strange new children from Windcity.[28] Oddly, when Mr. Kipling and Mrs. Francis emerged from the *Orphan Queen* the children shrank back from the adults, eyes wide with fear.

"What's wrong with them?" Mrs. Francis said. "They act as though they've never seen a grownup before."

"Most of them haven't. No adults allowed in the Hollow Mountain," Aidan explained.

Mrs. Francis gaped. "What? No adults? Who takes care of them?"

Cara squared her shoulders and answered. "We take care of ourselves."

Aidan addressed the waiting crowd. "Don't worry," he said. "I can assure everybody that Mr. Kipling and Mrs. Francis are friends to orphans of the world and companions of Hamish X." The children seemed soothed by this news and began to creep closer again. "You see,"

---

[28] Whispering about people is quite rude, but one must forgive the children in this case. Mimi and Parveen were well known in orphan circles and their arrival was highly anticipated.

Aidan explained to Mrs. Francis, "they aren't used to trusting grownups."

"Poor dears." Mrs. Francis gazed around at the children with such open affection that one of them, a small girl in a green jumpsuit, crept forward and wrapped her arms around the chubby woman's leg. Mrs. Francis stroked the top of the girl's head and smiled. The dam broke and more children clustered around her, hungry for the affection of lost mommies and daddies, half remembered but always missed.

Mimi and Parveen found themselves staring, but not at the children. Rather, they were staring at the creatures that gathered around the feet of the children. Standing up on hind legs, tiny forepaws tucked into their chests, was a pack of raccoons. They were of uniform size and identical colour, their glossy black eyes blinking in the black masks of their faces.

Parveen pointed at the animals. "I'm sorry, but are those …"

"Raccoons," all the raccoons said in unison. It was hard to decide which was more disturbing: the fact that they were speaking or that they were speaking in a synchronized way. "We are not exactly raccoons. Our outward appearance is that of a raccoon. We are actually automatons, designed to be the conduit of the central artificial intelligence that is George. We are George. George welcomes you to the Hollow Mountain."

"Wait a moment," Parveen said. "You are robots?"

"Very sophisticated robots, yes." The raccoons spoke together. They all pursed their lips in a strangely human expression. "We prefer the term Automated Mammal, but robot is accurate." Having made this distinction, they all waved a hand towards the metal cylinder. "The King is eager to meet you. Your escort is arriving."

An opening appeared in the cylinder. With a soft whoosh, two panels slid apart to reveal an elevator car. A pair of older children stood in the elevator. They wore black uniforms with the now-familiar silver cross on the right breast, a more formal version of Aidan's and Cara's bodysuits.

A frail boy with tousled red hair and pale skin appeared between them, looking small and bent in contrast to the alert bearing of his attendants. Hunched over a pair of crutches, smiling, he eased himself out onto the platform.

The effect on the crowd of children was immediate. They all bowed their heads. Aidan and Cara went down on one knee with a hand pressed over the crosses on their tunics.

"Majesty," Aidan said.

The King made his way out of the elevator car. Though he moved on crutches he was surprisingly agile, weaving his way through the children, patting each on the shoulder and greeting them as he came.

"Stand up straight, Simon. No need to bow ... Sarah! You've grown an inch or two ... Akelia, so nice to see you again!" Each child brightened as he made his little comments, glowing with delight that he remembered each of their names. Mimi and Parveen were impressed with his memory skills.

"So young to be a king," Mrs. Francis whispered. "Just a boy ..."

As they drew nearer they were able to study him in detail. He was a boy, a little older than Mimi, but he appeared frail and unhealthy. His eyes were bright blue, but dark circles beneath them spoke of sleepless nights. His skin was pale as if he rarely saw the sun. He was thin and his hands shook slightly. A shock of straight, carrot-orange hair fell over his right eye and his mouth turned up at the corner in a sad half smile.

His forehead was beaded with sweat after his walk through the crowd, and presently he pulled a white silk handkerchief from his pocket. Embroidered in one corner was the silver cross. The handkerchief, like all his clothing, looked rich and soft. He was dressed in a simple tunic and trousers cut from deep green velvet. The tunic was fastened up the front with shiny silver buttons. One of the buttons midway up was open, as though he had dressed in a hurry. Embroidered over his right breast was the silver cross.

At last he arrived in front of the little group of newcomers. He was flushed and breathing hard. "Whew, hello there. I am Liam, the Seventy-Sixth King of Switzerland. A moment, please." He held up the handkerchief and grinned. "I should get more exercise." After wiping the sweat from his forehead, he raised his eyes to take in Mimi and Parveen. "It's nice to finally meet you. When we heard you were coming, I did my best to collect as much information about you as possible." He smiled at Mimi. "Mimi Catastrophe Jones, born in Cross Plains, Texas, to William and Marguerita Jones. Mother a schoolteacher. Father played for several minor league baseball teams. In his best year, he hit forty homeruns for the Sweetwater Mudsquirrels[29] of the West Texas baseball league. Mother and father sadly deceased."

---

[29] The Mudsquirrels take their name from a local Texas rodent that prefers mud puddles to trees as a place to nest. They are a menace when threatened. A child kicking through a mud puddle might mistake a mudsquirrel for a lump of mud and kick it. The enraged mudsquirrel will use its powerful back legs to fling mud at the face of the offending child. Not fun, especially when the odd nut gets mixed in with the mud.

Mimi stood open-mouthed as the King turned to Parveen. "Parveen Paravati, youngest of thirteen children to Raj and Maraha Paravati. Father a labourer in a ballpoint pen factory. Mother a singer in Bollywood films. I hear you have a knack with machines. I think you will enjoy our technical labs. I also have a surprise for you, but it can wait until later."

King Liam winked at Parveen and turned his attention to Mr. Kipling and Mrs. Francis. "Welcome, Mrs. Francis. Your kindness and generosity are legendary among orphans. We thank you for the good works you attempted under Viggo Schmatz's difficult tenure in Windcity." Mrs. Francis couldn't restrain herself any longer. She reached out for the King. His Guards leaned in to protect him, but Liam raised a restraining hand. Mrs. Francis deftly fastened the loose button and tugged the King's tunic down gently, smoothing out the fabric with her rough, red hands.

"Forgive me." Mrs. Francis blushed as she stepped back. "I couldn't help it."

The King merely smiled. "There's nothing to forgive. And Mr. Kipling, you have helped bring Hamish X and all these children here to the Hollow Mountain. For that, you have our eternal gratitude." He leaned in conspiratorially. "I have to say, adults are forbidden in my realm, but for you two I will make an exception. These are special times. We must be flexible."

The King clapped his hands. "Let's get the other children assigned to quarters and find a place to stow this ship. Hamish X must be taken to the medical lab immediately. There's no time to waste."

The raccoons moved forward to enter the ship.

Mimi blocked the way. Hands on her hips, she scowled. "Just hold yer ... raccoons, mister. We ain't gonna jest hand ar friend over jest like that. Hamish X and the kids and nobody else ain't goin' anywhere until you tell us what's goin' on and why. We've come all the way from Windcity Orphanage and Cheese Factory 'cause our friend needs some help."

"Mimi!" Mrs. Francis was about to scold her, but the King held up a pale hand.

"Of course, you are correct, Mimi. You are being asked to trust me and take everything on faith. I know that's hard because your life up to this point has been filled with mistrust, disappointment, and heartbreak. What can I tell you that will soothe your fears?"

"Where exactly are we at?" Mimi said. "If it ain't too much trouble."

"Ah," King Liam smiled. "Let me explain. You are in my kingdom: the Hollow Mountain. The Hollow City. You are safe here for as long as you wish to stay. Come with me, please. I have food and drink and a place for you to rest. You've come a long way."

Mimi and Parveen wanted nothing more than to eat and rest. They hadn't been able to let down their guard since Mr. Candy and Mr. Sweet had come to take Hamish X away. Still though, Mimi crossed her arms over her chest and defiantly set her jaw.

"You listen here, yer worship, highness or whatever," she said sternly. "We've been brought all the way here and we ain't goin' a step further until we gets some kinda explanation. Yer Guards here"—she jabbed a thumb at Aidan and Cara—"they wouldn't tell us nuthin'. What is this place? Who are you? Why did you give Hamish X that knife and what's goin' on with ar friend? He ain't been the sanest fellar I ever met from day one but things just took a turn fer the worse and I want to make shore he's gonna be all right."

Liam looked at her for a moment and he smiled. He winked at her and chuckled softly. "You were right in your report, Aidan. She is a force to be reckoned with. Mimi and Parveen, I understand your reluctance and your fears. I'm pleased Hamish X fell in with such good souls. He has such a weight on his shoulders and he couldn't have better people to share his load. All will be explained, I promise you." He gestured towards the crutches in his hands. "I am not in the best of health, as I'm sure you've noticed. Standing for a long time can be a chore. There is another reason we've got to hurry. Hamish X is in a perilous state. Each hour that passes is dangerous for him. I wish to restore him to his proper self. My technicians and I have developed a process that may be able to waken him and heal him. I ask only that you give me the benefit of the doubt."

Mimi frowned. She looked to Parveen, who shrugged. "I don't know what else to do," he said. "I suppose we have to trust someone."

"In your shoes I'd be suspicious, too," the King said.

"Can we compromise? Hamish X must be prepared for the process. While my people are doing that, we'll eat and I'll tell you what I know. If you still feel the same fears, you can take Hamish X and go on your way. Deal?" The King held out his hand.

Mimi narrowed her eyes and hesitated. Finally, she said, "Here's the conditions: Mr. Kipling and Mrs. Francis go with Hamish X and he don't leave their sight fer even a second. We hear yer tale and if we think yer on the up-and-up, we'll let ya do yer process er whatever." Mimi held out her hand.

The King beamed and shook Mimi's hand. "Follow me."

He carefully wheeled around and started back across the stone platform, his crutches scraping on the rough surface. Aidan and Cara fell in beside him, each hovering protectively at an elbow should their King slip and fall.

Behind them Mimi and Parveen passed through the gaping crowd of children and entered the elevator. The doors whisked shut and they rose up into the Hollow City.

Mr. Candy and Mr. Sweet

The Concorde Super Sonic Transport was the ultimate in passenger transport for more than two decades. The distinctive, needle-nosed aircraft flew faster than sound between New York and London, breaking every speed record on the books. Unfortunately, the fleet was expensive to maintain and produced a great deal of noise pollution. When the planes were mothballed at the turn of the millennium, the ODA were quick to purchase them at a discount. On one of these recycled planes, zooming at twice the speed of sound across the dark expanse of the North Atlantic, Messrs. Candy and Sweet were employing the well-cushioned seats previously enjoyed by first-class passengers.

"An hour and a half until touchdown," Mr. Sweet said.

"Then three hours to the last known location of Hamish X," Mr. Candy added. "Once we've met our local operatives on the ground in Switzerland."

"We will find him."

"Yes. We will. And erase any who stand in our way."

Mr. Sweet swivelled his head, surveying the rest of the passenger seats. They were filled with other agents, clad in the grey uniform of the ODA, waiting patiently for the trip to be over.

"We shall track the asset down. He is surely in the custody of the King. When we find Hamish X, we find the King's hidden lair and we strike."

"Two birds with one stone, Mr. Sweet?"

"Indeed, Mr. Candy, two birds with one stone. The Kings of Switzerland have been a thorn in our side since we arrived in this miserable world. It will be very satisfying to destroy the line once and for all."

The plane sailed over the black surface of the ocean, its red running lights winking malevolently in the night sky.

Chapter 7

As soon as they were inside the elevator car, the doors slid shut with a thud. The King stood between Mimi and Parveen, and the Guards took up stations at the corners of the car. Mimi and Parveen discovered that, miraculously, they could see through the walls, affording them a view of the surrounding cavern.

"You're going to enjoy this," the King said. "It's quite an amazing tour for those who haven't seen it before. George?"

"Majesty?" The voice came from no single direction but seemed to be everywhere at once.

"Would you be so kind as to narrate the tour? I'm a little bit tired, I'm afraid."

"Majesty, your heart rate is elevated and your temperature is a degree above normal. You should use your motorized wheelchair."

The King waved a hand irritably at nothing. "I feel so helpless in that thing, like an invalid."

"Nonetheless," the voice said.

"The tour, please, George."

"Who the heck is that?" Mimi demanded. She found the disembodied voice disturbing.

"Hello, Mimi. It's George again. As I said, I am George. I am an artificial intelligence. I am the nervous system of the Hollow Mountain. I monitor threats to our colony, environmental systems, and all tasks too onerous for the children to do on a daily basis."

"George, as in raccoon George?" Parveen asked.

"Exactly, Parveen. I am the raccoons. They are my eyes and ears and hands when need be. They are me and I am them. We are connected."

"Impressive," Parveen said in awe.

"King Liam built me. He is very intelligent."

The King shrugged. "I have a knack for puzzles. When he starts nagging me, I sometimes regret it."

"That is very hurtful, Majesty."

"Forgive me, George, but you haven't any feelings to hurt."

"But I still understand the concept of insult and I am able to compute your disdain."

"I apologize. The tour, please, George, the tour."

"Why?" Mimi said suddenly.

"Why what?" the King asked.

"Why raccoons?"

"They aren't native to Switzerland," Parveen pointed out.

"Ah, good question. I just like them. They're cute with their little stripy tails and their black masks."

"And they have excellent manual dexterity," Parveen interjected. "Their paws are almost as nimble as human hands."

"True," the King agreed. "But they're cute, too."

They had risen high up the elevator shaft and they could see the cavern spread out below. The water glittered all around them. Small boats skimmed across the surface, leaving white wakes on the black water.

"The cave system has undergone extensive expansion during the tenure of the Kings and Queens of Switzerland. The mineral deposits in the rock are mined for processing and used here in the Hollow Mountain. The cargo platform you see below is the central hub where our most important commodity is distributed to our clients in the world outside. We float it across and then run it out of the tunnel in small rail cars."

"Commodity?" Parveen asked. "What is it?"

The King raised a hand in protest. "All in good time. Tell them about the geothermal system, George."

"Do you see the pipes running up the walls?" George began. Mimi and Parveen looked out and indeed saw sets of metallic pipes traversing the walls of the cavern. "Those pipes carry natural spring water from deep inside the rock. Some are diverted from natural hot springs and provide us with natural heating and steam power for most of our electrical energy. The cold water is used for drinking and manufacturing purposes. The water is siphoned off after use and returned below to a filtration system. We like to recycle."

As they rose, the light became stronger. The mist gathered, thickening into proper clouds as they rose in elevation.

"Heinrich's Cavern is so large that it has its own weather system. When the condensation becomes too great, there are actual rainstorms in here."

Mimi tried to imagine a rainstorm occurring indoors and found it just beyond her. This place was truly unbelievable. Presently, they rose above the cloud layer and the light increased in intensity.

They approached the ceiling of the cavern and saw that glowing panels attached to the rock gave off a golden glow remarkably like sunlight.

The elevator suddenly stopped, making everyone hop involuntarily. They had a view of the entire cavern from the very topmost point.

"The Hollow Mountain was first discovered by Heinrich the Great, first King of Switzerland. He came upon a series of natural caves in the centre of the mountain and decided it would be a perfect place to start a refuge for displaced children. The year was 1578. He began with the cavern you see below. For that reason, we named it Heinrich's Cavern."

"Makes sense," Mimi muttered.

"In the intervening years the cavern was widened and refined until it reached the proportions you see today." George's voice was quite bland even though he was relating such amazing information. "Our light source is truly remarkable." The walls of the elevator darkened, blocking out some of the glare so that the occupants could stare directly at long rectangular banks of panels embedded in the rock ceiling of the cavern. "The banks of lights you see are called Daniel's Panels. Designed and installed by King Daniel in 1972, they are capable of providing light and heat for each chamber in the facility. The Daniel's Panels cycle through a light and dark period, simulating a surface day each twenty-four hours. The panels replicate natural sunlight exactly, allowing the residents of the Hollow Mountain to enjoy all the benefits of sunlight without exposing them to the risk of discovery."

"Simulated daylight," Parveen said softly. "Much better than the fluorescent lights at the cheese factory."

"Too right," Mimi snorted. "Gave me wicked headaches."

"Hold tight, please."

The car began to rise again. They passed above the Daniel's Panels and entered the rock of the ceiling. For a few seconds, they were plunged into darkness.

"We are about to enter Frieda's Cavern. The greenhouse level."

No sooner had George made this announcement than they emerged into bright sunlight. Everywhere there was greenery and the glitter of sunlight on water. As they rose they saw they were in a cavern slightly smaller than the first, but whereas Heinrich's Cavern was rocky and barren, Frieda's Cavern was a profusion of lush plant life. Directly below them was a garden of the most brilliant flowers they had ever seen. There were fountains everywhere, sparkling as they threw up jets of water. The elevator shaft itself rose through the middle of a huge fountain that sprayed water many metres into the air. The water was lit from within and changed colours, cycling through the entire spectrum.

They stopped suddenly a hundred metres above the ground. "The Royal Park and Hakon's Fountain. The fountain was designed and built during the reign of King Hakon, fourteenth King of Switzerland. It runs completely on hydraulic pressure generated by runoff from the glaciers and the natural springs deep inside the mountain."

"I suppose it serves as a natural filter for the drinking water in the … uh, settlement," Parveen said.

"Exactly," George said in his pleasant voice. "He's very clever, this one. Very clever."

There were children everywhere in Frieda's Cavern. Some were wandering about, enjoying the flowers. Some were splashing in the fountains. Some were seated in groups around raccoons who seemed to be holding classes of some sort. The scene was one of peace and contentment, made only slightly weird by the presence of so many raccoons.

The elevator rose slowly, exposing a panoramic view of the cavern floor. "Frieda's Cavern was excavated in the eighteenth century by …"

"Let me guess," Mimi said sarcastically. "Queen Frieda?"

"The Third. Also called Frieda the Excavator. She loved to excavate, that one," George continued.

Above them, another bank of Daniel's Panels drew nearer. "The farms are located on the fringe of Frieda's Cavern. We grow most of our own food here inside the Hollow Mountain. Soybeans, corn, and wheat are our main crops, along with fruit orchards," George said. The children shielded their eyes and peered towards the outer edge of the cavern. In between the rows of crops, driving small tractors, digging, weeding, and watering, were hundreds of raccoons.

"Look at all them raccoons!" Mimi exclaimed. "It's amazing."

"Each one controlled by my central processing unit. Watch!" All the raccoons down below suddenly stopped whatever they were doing and raised first their right paws then their left paws in unison with eerie exactitude. "You see? They aren't really individuals. We're like a hive of bees, all controlled by the queen bee that is the central computer called George. In other words, me."

"So you can divide your attention up and do many different tasks at the same time?" Parveen asked.

All the raccoons suddenly pointed up at the elevator and clapped their hands. It was very disconcerting. "Absolutely," said George. "My processing power is truly incredible, if I do say so myself. I control the climate, security, food production … everything." As one, the raccoons counted on their fingers as George listed things off. George suddenly became aware that he was controlling all the raccoons. "Sorry about that." The raccoons went back to their farming tasks as if nothing had happened. The elevator entered the ceiling of the cavern.

After a few seconds of darkness, they rose into the next level.

"The workshops are all located on this third level," George announced. The cavern was smaller than the one below. They were looking out onto a circular courtyard paved with slabs of grey stone. The walls of the cavern were only fifty metres away and pierced with doorways. In the courtyard, groups of Guards practised marching in formation. Children dressed in pale green or white coats hurried in and out of doorways looking very busy. "The medical and technical laboratories are located on the third level along with the workshops that manufacture clothing and all other goods the Hollow Mountain residents require. Here, children learn trades that will help them in their lives after they leave."

"Children leave? Why would they?" Mimi asked. "This place is purdy fine."

King Liam suddenly spoke. "It's the rule. When a child turns sixteen, he or she must go out into the world. They are trained in a trade and given enough money to start them off on their own. We create a detailed history for them that we insert into the records of the world outside to hide where they have been throughout their childhood years."

"But how do ya know they ain't gonna tell anybody where ya are?" Mimi asked.

"No one has yet." The King smiled and shared a look with Aidan and Cara. "We have methods that have been foolproof up to now."

"Foolproof? But what—"

"All in good time, Mimi. George? Continue the tour if you will, George."

George jumped back in. "The Royal Swiss Guards have their barracks on this third tier. The barracks have state-of-the-art training facilities."

Mimi's interest was immediately piqued. She peered down at the Guards performing their manoeuvres. "They shore do look smart in their uniforms."

"Maybe you could join the Guards, Mimi," Aidan suggested. Cara looked mortified at the thought. Mimi scowled, trying not to look interested, but Parveen could tell that she was.

They passed through the ceiling into the next chamber.

"Welcome to the Nurtury!" The cavern was smaller again than the ones below, though still larger than the entire Windcity Orphanage and Cheese Factory. They ascended halfway up through the cavern and stopped. Terraced balconies rose all the way up the sides, turning it into a sort of ribbed bowl. Everywhere, children were sitting in groups of different ages, writing, reading, or watching a raccoon who seemed to be teaching.

"Under King Tse Shiao, the Nurtury was designed as a teaching centre for the children in the Hollow Mountain. They go to school each day." The car rose gently, passing tier after tier of classrooms. As the levels got higher the children got older. Raccoons and sometimes the older children were teaching all sorts of different classes. "The children leave here with the finest education we can provide … which is extremely good, given that I designed the curriculum."

"George," the King scolded gently. "Humility is attractive, especially in super-intelligent artificial minds."

"Of course, your Majesty."

"Thank you for the tour, George," the King said suddenly. "Take us to the Royal Chambers now, please."

"But there are still King Franklin's Hanging Gardens … and the Bubble Works. Oh, and the Raccoon Works, where I repair my raccoon units. It's very interesting."

"All in good time. I'm sure Mimi and Parveen are weary after their trip and would like some refreshment." Looking at the King's drawn face and the dark circles under his eyes, Mimi understood that he could use a little rest himself. His hands quivered where they held the crutches, and Cara's hand gripped his elbow tightly.

"Of course," said George. "Royal Chambers, next stop!" The elevator zoomed aloft. Parveen and Mimi both thought the same thing as they looked out at the disappearing terraces with their classrooms filled with happy children. *This place is heaven. I wish we could stay here and never have to worry about the ODA again.*

The elevator slid to a stop. The doors hissed open to reveal an airy, open platform finished in beautiful silver and black tiles, all bearing the silver cross of the King of Switzerland. Standing on the platform were two identical raccoons. The Royal Chambers was apparently the elevator's last stop. The shaft ended in an elaborate stone cabin.

"Majesty." The two raccoons ducked their little heads in unison.

"Some food for our guests. In the sitting room, I think."

"All prepared, Majesty." They scurried away through a stone archway. The King and his guests followed. Mimi turned to say goodbye to George but found that it was a little awkward saying goodbye to an empty car. Besides, if what the AI said was true, he hadn't left. He was there in the form of the two raccoon robot things. She shrugged. "This is gonna take some gettin' used to." The others had already headed off after their furry little guides, and Mimi hastened to catch up.

Mr. Candy and Mr. Sweet

"You are not permitted to trespass on Swiss territory. Reverse your vehicles and report to the nearest authorities immediately."

The face of the Swiss Minister of Defence was furious; the throbbing vein in the centre of his forehead looked dangerously close to bursting.

Mr. Candy and Mr. Sweet gazed up at the plasma screen emotionlessly. They were strapped into the transport truck's two swivel seats, with the screen before them serving as a map. The screen also showed little grey icons that represented agents in the other trucks in the convoy. The defence minister was relegated to a small square in the upper right corner of the screen.

"The ODA will not be interfered with, Minister. I suggest you let us go about our business before we leave your silly little country. Otherwise, we take no responsibility for the ensuing unpleasantness." Mr. Sweet sounded polite but bored.

The minister of defence went a deeper shade of purple. He leaned in close so that his face filled the screen. "Switzerland is a sovereign nation! We will not be bullied. We will react with the strongest possible measures."

"Minister, do what you must. You have harboured our

enemy in your midst for centuries." Mr. Candy was completely devoid of emotion. (No surprise, really.) "He has taken a valuable asset of ours. We will take it back. Try to stop us and you will be destroyed."

The Defence Minister bugged out his eyes in fury. Before he could retort, Mr. Sweet cut the feed.

"They can't stop us now," Mr. Sweet said with confidence. "We are about to arrive at the location where the beacon fired."

The convoy of tracked vehicles churned the green turf of the meadow where the Orphan Queen had rested only hours before. Rabbits, so recently recovered from the shock of the airship's arrival, once again voided their stomachs in a graphic display of fear.

Mr. Candy stopped the vehicle and pulled the periscope down, peering through the eyepiece. He was disappointed to find only grass, mountains, and the still forms of vomit-covered rabbits littering the ground. Gouges in the turf showed that an airship had not long ago dropped anchor here.

"We're too late."

"Indeed, Mr. Candy. Indeed."

Chapter 8

They passed through a huge stone chamber as big as a church, with an ornately carved throne inlaid with gold positioned at one end. The whole effect was very imposing.

The King waved a hand towards the throne and sniffed. "Showy and uncomfortable. I use it only when important dignitaries come to visit ..." He stopped and thought for a moment. "Which is never, actually. It's a terrible waste of space. I should convert it to a squash court or something useful like that. George, remind me later, will you?"

"Yes, Majesty. Duly noted." The two raccoons moved and walked in unison. Parveen watched them waddle ahead with fascination. He knew they were artificial, but they were so cleverly constructed that they looked absolutely real. He longed to take one of them apart and examine its inner workings. He also wanted to see the place George talked about where the little devices were repaired. Parveen hoped there would be time. He fingered the pencil behind his ear in anticipation.

They meandered through a maze of winding stone corridors lit with flickering gas lamps. "The torches run on natural gas tapped from deposits deep under the earth," the George raccoons explained as they ushered the newcomers into a comfortable little room. Broad, low tables were situated all around. On each was a complicated jigsaw puzzle in varying states of completion.

"I love puzzles," King Liam announced. "They keep my mind nimble. George devises them to be the most difficult imaginable. He's quite good."

"A pleasure, Majesty. You solve them all. He's quite clever."

"Oh, George. You're embarrassing me!" He looked around at the puzzles. "Yes. Puzzles are good exercise for the brain. And they make you see the big picture. It's helpful …" He drifted into silence as he gazed at a half-completed puzzle of a sandy beach. "Aha!" He stretched out a trembling hand and tried to pick up a piece of puzzle, but his fingers were shaking badly. Parveen reached in and scooped up the piece, slotting it home in the centre of the puzzle.

"Thanks. I guess I've had a lot of excitement today." King Liam rubbed one hand in the other. "It's gets worse when I'm tired." The rest of the room was cluttered but cozy. Piles of books leaned against the walls. A desk stood in the corner with a bright light shining overhead, illuminating an assortment of tiny tools and bits of metal and wire. The King led them past it and they saw that one entire wall was made of black tinted glass. As they were sitting down the King tapped the surface of the glass and it lightened to reveal the mountainside. The sun was up and the snow glistened in its rays.

The King smiled. "An addition by Queen Carletta. It's nice to have a view. That's one thing that's bad about living inside the mountain: it's too dangerous to have many windows onto the outside world for fear they may be discovered." He turned away from the view and spread his hands. "Sit! Please, make yourselves comfortable."

The King of Switzerland sank gratefully into an armchair, hanging his crutches on a hook installed for the purpose on the wall within arm's reach. He indicated with a sweep of his hand two similar chairs resting before him. Mimi and Parveen sat down and looked around. The walls were decorated with a series of realistic portraits. The faces, of every race and colour, looked out from the canvases with piercing, lifelike gazes. They were young faces, but they seemed to convey a wealth of experience, a weight of responsibility that was humbling.

Aidan and Cara stood by the door, casual but alert.

"I wish you would relax, you two," the King said, gesturing towards two empty chairs. "You should rest. Nothing can get us in here."

"We are resting, Majesty. Don't worry." Aidan smiled and nodded at Cara, who also nodded.

"Suit yourselves." The King shook his head. Then he turned his gaze on Parveen and Mimi. His eyes were kind. "Now, tell me your story, every bit of it. How did you come to be here? Leave nothing out."

So Mimi and Parveen told the whole sad and sorry tale of how they ended up at Windcity Orphanage and Cheese Factory. They told of Viggo and of Mrs. Francis and her kindness. They told of cheese making, misery and woe, and the arrival of Hamish X. They told of their escape plans and the coming of the Cheese Pirates led by the horrible Cheesebeard. They told of their journey north and of Snow Monkey Island. They told of the death of Cheesebeard and the defection of Mr. Kipling and his betrothal to the sweet Mrs. Francis. Finally, they related the story of the destruction of Windcity, the thwarting of Mr. Candy and Mr. Sweet, and of the knife's activation, triggering their trip to Switzerland in search of a King they weren't even sure existed.

They switched back and forth in the telling as the raccoons brought tea and cake, cheese and crackers, chocolate and more cheese. The King listened eagerly. He laughed and clapped his hands when he heard about the snow monkeys and the woolly mammoth and all the little details. When they at last reached the part about the Grey Agents and the knife and their trip across the ocean, he nodded and became thoughtful. It was completely dark outside the window when they finished their story. The King sat back as George (in the form of the two raccoons) cleared away the dishes and poured them glasses of cold glacier water, straight from the fountain.

"What an amazing tale," the King said after a moment's silent reflection. "You've already overcome so many obstacles, and then to take such a long journey on such scanty evidence." He shook his head and clucked his tongue softly. "You are very brave indeed. Hamish X was lucky to find such friends."

Mimi plunked down her glass and levelled a green-eyed stare at the King. "I think we've waited long enough. Ya heard our story. What's yers?"

"Mimi," Parveen said sharply. To Liam he said, "She's a bit rude, but she means well."

"And she's right!" The King pushed himself to his feet. Deftly plucking one of his crutches from the hook, he pivoted away to look out over the mountainside. Blue gas lamps flickered softly in an almost imperceptible breeze. He leaned his bottom on the window frame and smiled at them. "What do you want to know?"

Mr. Candy and Mr. Sweet

The valley was swarming with agents, combing the area for any sign of Hamish X's passing. The agents wore grey field uniforms, covered in pockets. They had thick belts hung with pouches and grey helmets covered their heads, leaving only their begoggled faces exposed.

Mr. Candy and Mr. Sweet sat in the cab of a truck with the engine idling. They surveyed the data coming in from the satellite cameras high above in orbit. The satellites were owned by the many governments the ODA had business with, commandeered despite vigorous protests from said governments. Nothing could be allowed to interfere with the search. Nothing.

A female agent came to the door of the truck and rapped on the window. Mr. Candy pressed a button and the window descended.

"No sign of the fugitives, Agent Candy. They seem to have vanished."

"They can't have vanished, Agent Fudge," Mr. Candy snapped. "Keep searching."

Agent Fudge nodded and turned away. Mr. Candy raised the window. Mr. Sweet was studying a small screen, his face outlined in the blue glow. He tapped a button and pictures flashed by.

"Nothing on the satellite photos. Neither in infrared nor ultraviolet spectrum."

"We must find them. They can't have just disappeared." Mr. Candy leaned in to scan the pictures.

"We must assume the King of Switzerland is involved. We find the King and his infamous Hollow Mountain, and we find Hamish X."

"Then it's the same old problem. How do we find the King of Switzerland?"

Mr. Sweet had no answer to that question. He focused his attention on the latest satellite photos instead.

Chapter 9

The two children had so many questions that it was hard to choose just one. Parveen asked, "How did all this start?"

"And while yer at it … why?"

"How and why: the simple questions are always the most profound.[30] All right, where to start? The beginning is a fine place," the King laughed. "In the beginning, Switzerland was nothing more than a handful of little provinces always at war with one another and their neighbours. The constant fighting was draining on the economy and costly in human suffering. In particular, many children were left without anyone to care for them, mothers and fathers having been lost in the wars.

"At last, the parties involved were too weary to continue. One prince, Heinrich of Bern, was determined to make a lasting peace. He was a clever young boy of twelve, wise beyond his years. He stood to become the first King of Switzerland if all the warring factions could put aside their differences and agree to unite. His heart ached for the children who had been orphaned in the fighting and left to fend for themselves. He wanted to find a way to

---

[30] I would beg to differ. The simple questions are often the simplest. For example: Do you want ice cream? Are you going to eat that last sandwich? Is the bear eating my cake? Simple questions. Simple answers. Only some simple questions are profound, like … Why do we live on this earth? Why is there war? Or, Do I look fat in these pants? Philosophers have struggled with these questions through the course of human history. I haven't. Personally, I have better ways to spend my time.

stop the fighting and take care of the lost children because he, like them, had lost his parents in the conflict.

"One of the major stumbling blocks was that the different parties couldn't agree to any one person having absolute power. So Heinrich called all the leaders to a secret conference and negotiated a compromise. He would become King but only in name. Outwardly, Switzerland would be a republic run by a democratically elected parliament. He would serve as a mediator only if disputes arose. He would live in a secret location. He would retire from public life and public knowledge but, most importantly, he would dedicate his life to the care and protection of orphans.

"It was agreed. Heinrich became the first King of Switzerland. He searched high and low to find a place where he could make his dream a reality: a safe haven for foundlings and orphans. For over a year he searched through the mountains, but he couldn't find anything that was suitable. Finally, after he had all but given up, he went on a mountain-climbing expedition. An avalanche swept down the mountain face. Everyone in his climbing party was killed and he narrowly escaped. To avoid being crushed, he ducked into a fissure[31] in the cliff face only to find the cavern we occupy today."

The King spread his hands to encompass the scene before them. "Of course, it was a good deal smaller and less comfortable then, but it was well hidden and had fresh water. It was a place to start. And so King Heinrich took possession of the Hollow Mountain and moved in the first

---

[31] A fissure is a crack or crevice. It has nothing to do with fishing. Although some say that fishing in fissures can be very rewarding. Fissure fishing is one of the fastest-growing sports in the world.

orphans. Using his own money, he outfitted the cavern with all they needed to grow and prosper.

"And so it began. When Heinrich the Great grew old enough, he chose a successor from among the children under his protection and then went out into the world a free man. Thus began the tradition of Succession. The King picks his successor when he turns sixteen. Then he goes out to live as a normal citizen, free of the burden of kingship, usually with a set of skills that will help him along the way."

King Liam smiled. "I am due to move on soon. I have yet to pick my successor, but there are many who are truly worthy. Aidan or Cara, for example."

Aidan held up a hand. "Sire, I told you before, all that responsibility doesn't interest me."

Cara shook her head. "Me neither. All that worry would give me wrinkles." She tossed her head coquettishly.

"Oh brother," Mimi muttered, earning a sneer from Cara.

"Over four hundred years have passed since Heinrich stumbled upon this refuge. Each King or Queen adds some new refinement. I've made a few improvements during my time, but perhaps my greatest contribution is yet to come …" Liam gazed off into the distance.

"Surely an operation like the Hollow Mountain must be very expensive to maintain," Parveen said. "How do you manage?"

"We're mostly self-sufficient. We grow our own food; we fish from the lake. We manufacture whatever we need here. The children and George manage very well. But besides that, we have a monopoly on a very important commodity, haven't we, George?"

The two raccoons came into the room bearing a silver

tray. On it was a wedge of yellow Swiss cheese, pocked with its famous holes. The nutty aroma of the cheese filled the room. Mimi groaned. "Don't tell me ya make cheese here, too! I thought I'd slunk free o' that when we left Windcity."

King Liam laughed. "No, not cheese. But the holes in the cheese."

"Whut?"

"The holes." Liam pointed a long thin finger at one of the hollow bubbles in the expanse of cheese. "The characteristic holes in Swiss cheese are caused by an enzyme introduced during the cheese-making process. King Ludovig discovered the process and registered the patent. Swiss cheese just isn't Swiss cheese without the holes. We collect a royalty every time the enzyme is used. The royalties add up very quickly. We have more than enough money to handle any expenses, with a sizable amount left over for investments. Through a number of false fronts and shell corporations,[32] we have invested heavily worldwide. If, heaven forbid, the Hollow Mountain is ever compromised and we are forced to flee, the money will help us relocate."

Parveen piped up. "Who would want to hurt you? All you do is take in orphans."

"Ah, Parveen, the sad reality is that there are lots of people in the world who prey upon children because they

---

[32] Shell corporations have nothing to do with shells. They are companies that exist only on paper to hide their true owners and make it too confusing for anyone to investigate their true natures. The name *shell corporation* originates from Central America, where a group of Guatemalan businessmen dressed as crabs and tried to get a bank loan. The bank was so confused and disturbed by the arrival of human-sized crabs at its door that it granted the loan without question to avoid a confrontation with the giant crustaceans.

are helpless. Children have no voice in the adult world, and so they fall victim to those who would abuse or mistreat them. By taking these poor young ones in, we deprive the predators of their livelihood.

"When the Hollow Mountain was first established, the goal of the Kings and Queens of Switzerland was to fight these terrible people and protect the children. It was bad enough when all we fought were ruthless businessmen and cruel, indifferent governments. In the last century, these more mundane threats have been eclipsed by the arrival of the ODA.

"The ODA hates us the most. If they found their way in here … well, I hate to imagine the ruin they would wreak upon our happy little enclave."

"But why do they hate you so much?" Parveen asked.

"One can only guess at the ultimate goals of the Orphan Disposal Agency. The name suggests they have little respect for orphans, and their actions prove it. Naturally, since we try to help children in need, the ODA views us as a threat. Up to now they haven't managed to find us. We hide our tracks pretty well. I hope they never do—the consequences would be disastrous. We do our best to be secretive. All our business dealings are handled through the Super Secret Swiss Bank. The SSSB[33] is so secretive that it makes the other Swiss banks seem positively forthright."

---

[33] Swiss banks are renowned for their policies of absolute confidentiality where their clients are concerned. The Super Secret Swiss Bank takes secrecy to a ridiculous level. Most of the employees don't even know they work at a bank. Most don't know what a bank is. The president of the bank thinks he's a chair. This leads to a lot of misunderstandings, but in the end, the system is very effective.

"But how kin ya be shore that no one's gonna squeal on ya?"

"In over four centuries, no one has done it yet. The gift we give our children is precious: a new start, a place to grow up in safety, a family. You wouldn't squeal on a brother or a sister, would you, Mimi?"

"Nope, I wouldn't but I cain't speak for nobody else."

"You can barely speak," Cara muttered just loud enough for Mimi to hear. Mimi gritted her teeth and her eyes smouldered, but she held her tongue.

The King went on. "We have another way of ensuring our secrecy, which we will show you later if you decide to stay." He winked at Mimi. "The years passed. The Kings and Queens of Switzerland prospered. The Hollow Mountain became more refined and safer. Now we take in a few hundred orphans every year. Our agents, children trained as Guards and sent out into the world, find the vulnerable, exploited children and bring them here. At any given time we have up to three thousand children living in the Mountain, ranging from newborns to sixteen years of age. We put them through school, train them, and then send them out with enough money to get started and with connections to the field they would most like to pursue."

"Three thousand?" Mimi shook her head. "I don't mean to spit inta the wind here but that don't seem like much in the grand scheme o' things. I mean ther's thousands o' poor orphans out there in the world … millions!"

Before Parveen could scold Mimi for rudeness, the King raised a weary hand. "I agree, Mimi. I wish we could bring them all here, but there just isn't enough room. I like to think, however, that each one of these children we save and send out into the world makes the world a little better.

They make the people around them care a little more and so, slowly, the world changes."

Mimi thought about this for a moment. "That sounds like it'd take a heck of a long time."

The King laughed. "Good! Where was I? Ah yes. So these children we save are sent out into the world at the age of sixteen. The time is fast approaching when I myself must choose my successor and head out into the world." Liam raised a crutch and shook his head ruefully. He looked out into the darkness of the cavern, the lamps glinting blue under a simulated moon. "I can't say I'm looking forward to it. I've enjoyed my time here and the world can be … difficult for someone like me. More than that, I have yet to complete my legacy." He turned and looked at Mimi and Parveen. His eyes were shining. "Your coming has made it possible, now. You have brought Hamish X and that makes all the difference."

Parveen and Mimi looked at each other. Mimi nodded at Parveen and he spoke for them both. "We are here because we had no other place to go. The knife was our only clue. We don't know what you want from us and we don't know what you want from our friend Hamish X."

"I understand. You have questions." The King hobbled back to his chair and sank down gratefully. Hanging his crutch on the hook, he took a sip of water and then settled back in his chair. "Ask what you will and I'll answer as honestly as I can. I want you to trust me."

"First off, who the heck are the ODA? I seen the Grey Agents who brought Hamish X and I seen 'em after Parveen nailed 'em with his PME."

"EMP," Parveen interjected.

"Whatever. They ain't quite human."

"No. They are not. We don't know exactly what they are but we believe they are not wholly of this earth."

"What?" Even Parveen couldn't keep the surprise from his voice.

"It'll be easier if I just show you. George? The screen, please." The King pointed at one of the George raccoons and the tiny creature waved a paw. The light dimmed. With the wave of another paw, a painting—a portrait of a chubby girl in pigtails—slid up to reveal a large white projection screen.

Chapter 10

A beam of light emanated from a small window set high in the wall. Through the window a raccoon could be seen operating a projector. The beam shone down, illuminating the screen. King Liam narrated the images.

"The Orphan Disposal Agency." A stylized logo of the ODA hung in the middle of the screen, three letters inter-woven like snakes. The letters were a sickly yellow colour that was somehow unsettling, as if the vile hue had been chosen from an alien pallet.

"That logo is horrible. The colours ..." Parveen stopped to rub his eyes.

"Indeed," Liam nodded. "Where most companies want a logo that attracts attention, the ODA wishes to drive the observer away. They love to work in secret, away from prying eyes.

"For almost a century, the ODA has taken unwanted, unloved children—of which there are far too many, I'm sorry to say—and distributed them among clients world-wide." A series of photos flashed by showing children working in mines, workhouses, factories—miserable children all over the globe, dirty and fearful. Mimi and Parveen recognized only too well the look in their eyes. They'd seen it in the mirror every morning when they lived under Viggo in Windcity.

King Liam continued. "As I said, until the ODA arrived on the scene, the King of Switzerland had only to worry about saving children orphaned in war or forced to slave for heartless industrialists and the like.

The ODA are something altogether more sinister.[34]

"No one knows exactly when the ODA came to be, but our researchers believe that their appearance coincided with the Eastern Russian meteor strike called the Tunguska Event."[35]

The screen flickered, then filled with a grainy photograph of a blasted forest landscape. In the foreground, men in old-fashioned army uniforms pointed at flattened trees and a giant gouge in the earth. They wore extremely odd, old-fashioned hats.[36]

The picture changed to show a man with pale, staring eyes wearing a monk's robe. His hair was lank and his

---

[34] *Sinister* is a word that has come to mean "evil," but it literally means "left." The inference is that all people who are left-handed are evil and all people who are right-handed are good. Of course, anyone can see that this assumption is simple-minded. The only truly evil people in the world use both hands with equal agility and so are called ambidextrous. (Just kidding … sort of.)

[35] The Tunguska Event was an enormous explosion in Siberia that devastated forests and left massive craters all through the Tunguska region. The nature of the event is still much debated. Some say it was a meteor strike, others an anti-matter explosion. Still others claim it was children playing with matches, but adults are always trying to blame children for things they don't understand. One very silly scientist from Portugal asserts that the event was caused by an angry duck with gastro-intestinitis.

[36] In the nineteenth and early twentieth centuries putting on pointy hats and pointing at things while posing for photographs was a time-honoured tradition, especially in Russia where awards were given for Most Rigid Finger and Most Interesting Facial Expression While Pointing at an Object. Sadly, this practice of pointing at things has gone out of fashion because people became very competitive, developing elaborate false fingers to extend the range of their pointing. The practice was banned after, inevitably, someone lost an eye. Mothers around the world were smug.

beard tangled and wild. He stood beside a man in an elaborate white uniform encrusted with gold braid and medals on ribbons. Behind them a line of men in various uniforms stood looking on.

"Who's the creep in the dress?" Mimi said.

"Rasputin.[37] And that man beside him is Tsar Nicholas the Second of Russia."

"Rasputin? That sounds like a dessert," Mimi snorted.

"Believe me," Liam shook his head, "he was not sweet at all.[38] He was cruel and mad, eventually driving the people of Russia to rise up and overthrow the Tsar." Liam raised a crutch and used it as a pointer. "I am certain that Rasputin was really just a puppet for ... *them*." The tip of the pointer rested on a pair of figures tucked away in the back of the group. The two men were swathed in grey monks' robes, but the strange black goggles and pale faces were unmistakable.

"Grey Agents," Parveen gasped.

"Exactly. The Grey Agents first enter history in the early twentieth century in the court of the Tsar Nicholas the Second. They are referred to in court records in Saint Petersburg in 1911. The official records called them Grey Monks and suggest they had some connection with Rasputin. George?"

---

[37] Rasputin was a Russian monk who is blamed for the downfall of the Romanoff dynasty of Russia. They said he could control people with his mind. Whatever powers he may have had, grooming was not his strong point.

[38] King Liam is obviously not aware that there was a dessert named after the mad monk Rasputin. It was a giant pastry covered in chocolate and filled with intensely sweet custard. So sweet in fact that it would cause anyone who ate it to go mad. Certainly an apt tribute to Rasputin, but not a quality that would make it a popular dessert.

The King waved his crutch. The raccoon in the projection booth changed the picture. In the new photo, a man with a thick moustache and long heavy coat stood on a stone balcony looking down over a military parade. Tanks rolled by. Soldiers marched in formation down the street. Missiles on trailers were pulled along by trucks. Behind the moustached man, in a group of other officers, the ODA agents huddled again. This time they wore military uniforms and peaked caps.

"When the Tsar was killed by the new regime, the ODA didn't miss a beat. They became close advisers to the new government in the Soviet Union. They traded technical expertise for the right to conduct their business without interference. Soon they were insinuating themselves into the lives of the wealthy and gaining influence with many other governments."

A series of photos showed Grey Agents dressed in many different national costumes, always in the background, almost hidden in the crowd of anonymous advisers to famous people. They stood in the shadows behind prime ministers, kings, presidents, and potentates, always close enough to have the ear of important people but far enough away so as not to attract attention. Black goggles masked their eyes. Their faces were as grey as their clothing. The agents blended into the background.

"Through the years, they slowly went about their business. They gathered unwanted children for reasonable fees. Their contacts in government protected them. They distributed children and took back the orphans as they turned fourteen ..."

The pictures became more and more recent, until they were in the modern era. The ODA were shown dropping off loads of miserable children at clothing factories and fish canning operations. There was even a picture of Mr. Candy and Mr. Sweet looking on with a vilely grinning Viggo as the first lot of orphans was delivered to the cheese factory in Windcity. In the background of the photo, Mrs. Francis looked very nervous and sad, her apron much newer and less wrinkly than it currently was. Another series showed the Grey Agents herding adolescent[39] boys and girls onto trucks, boats, and cargo planes.

"No one is sure what happens to these returnees, but we do know where they are taken ..."

The picture changed. Now there was a pretty little house on a lovely, tree-lined street.

"The ODA headquarters in Providence, Rhode Island. The children go in but they don't come out. We've never been able to get an operative into the HQ. Anyone who tries isn't heard from again."

"I know the ODA is bad news," Mimi's voice interrupted the King. "That ain't nuthin' new. But what's the connection with Hamish X? And how did Hamish X end up with yer knife in his boot?"

"Excellent questions. I'll do my best to answer you, dear Mimi." The picture changed. An image of Hamish X filled the screen.

"Hamish X. Hero to orphans everywhere. His exploits are the stuff of legend."

The picture was poorly centred and out of focus, as though the photographer had been hurried or was just

---

[39] *Adolescent* is a word that means "early teen." Adolescence brings with it pimples, irritability, and the uncanny ability to believe oneself right even when one is obviously wrong. Fortunately, adolescence doesn't last long and is replaced eventually with adulthood, which is the state of knowing less and less as time goes on but letting on it doesn't bother you much.

plain bad. It was clearly of Hamish X, however. He stood on top of a building, balancing on one boot at the peak of a steep roof. He was smiling and waving to a crowd of people in a public square below.

"This is the first public appearance of Hamish X. He has just defeated the Moscow Seven, a notorious gang of cutthroats who kidnapped children and sold them into slavery. The photo was taken by one of the freed children. This was over eleven years ago."

"But," Mimi said, "Hamish X cain't be more than ten. I'm older than him."

"Exactly." Pictures flashed by in quick succession. Hamish X clinging to the side of a burning building. He was caught in mid-shout, his boots blazing. The Kickie Shoe Factory sign burned merrily behind him. "Hamish X destroys the Kickie Shoe Factory that employs all child labour. Who delivered him there? The ODA." A picture of Mr. Candy and Mr. Sweet delivering Hamish X to the front gate of Kickie Shoes. "This picture was taken two weeks before Hamish X led the rebellion in the shoe factory. Note the strange handcuffs." Indeed, the glowing plastic bracelets secured Hamish X's hands.

"The pattern repeats itself ten months later." The picture shifted. Now Hamish X was on the deck of a ship surrounded by cheering children.

"Hamish X defeats Soybeard the Pirate and smashes his child piracy ring. Six months later, he destroys the child slave rodeo of Spicy Tuna, the infamous Mexican Wrestler." The next picture showed Hamish X in a wrestling ring fighting a huge man in pink tights.

"Next we find Hamish X in Colombia where he smashes the Malinqué Coffee Cartel. The unscrupulous company exploited child labour to produce cheap coffee

beans." The next
picture was bizarre: Hamish X
battling a giant octopus while riding a donkey.[40]

"And of course, the now famous dance with the Yeti.
Hamish X challenged the Abominable Snow Man to a
break dance contest.[41] He won the dance marathon and
so freed hundreds of children from the Tibetan Silver

---

[40] The Malinqué Coffee Cartel was indeed a strange group. The
idea of Hamish X battling an octopus from a donkey's back may
seem crazy but the head of the cartel, Don Pinque Malinqué,
revelled in breeding sea animals that could survive on land for
extended periods of time. He had several guard octopi, a
number of attack lobsters, and a swarm of ninja shrimp.

[41] Most people are unaware that the Yeti is a devoted fan of
hip-hop. Considering that few people have ever seen the Yeti,
it is understandable that its dance preferences are not common
knowledge. In a similar shocker, Bigfoot, the Yeti's American
cousin, is an accomplished tap dancer ... but that is hardly
relevant to our story.

Mines." The photo showed Hamish X dancing with a large hairy creature. Hamish X was frozen in mid-air as he prepared to undertake a break dancing move known as the "aerial worm."

Most of the pictures were grainy and looked as if they were taken by eyewitness amateur photographers. Some were of excellent quality. Some were pulled from the newspapers and some were cut from news broadcasts. The King spoke as the pictures flipped by.

"For over a decade, Hamish X has made appearances all over the world. He comes out of nowhere, thwarts some evildoer, and then vanishes without a trace for months on end. Where does he come from? Where does he go?"

"The ODA delivered him to Windcity," Parveen said. "And then they came to take him back."

The King nodded. "Strange, isn't it? The ODA agents seem to be everywhere Hamish X is. In fact, they seem to deliver Hamish X to a location where he can damage their interests and the interests of their clients."

"It don't make no sense."

"No, Mimi, it don't. Unless Hamish X is part of some larger plan of the ODA, one in which they are willing to sacrifice a few lesser plans to achieve the greater." He pointed to the latest photo. Hamish X filled the screen, his body displayed from head to toe. The backdrop was a jungle, lush and green. In his hand he held the book *Great Plumbers and Their Exploits*. The boots shone slick and black in the sunlight. The golden eyes were wary as they looked at the camera. "Here is a truly remarkable boy," the King continued. "These boots he wears: Where did he get them? Why can't he take them off? What is their ultimate purpose? And the book: Why does he carry it everywhere? Why does the ODA allow him to keep it?"

"I have a theory about the book," Parveen offered. The King leaned forward expectantly. "I have read it very closely. On the surface, it is exactly what it appears to be: a very boring book about plumbers and plumbing. On closer inspection, I have found patterns in the text, repeated words and phrases. I believe the book has a hidden code. Hamish X is compelled to read the book and it teaches him computer code subconsciously."

The King's mouth popped open in surprise. "Of course. What a brilliant deduction, Parveen!" Liam clicked his tongue and shook his head. "All this time studying Hamish X and that never occurred to me. What a clever person you are." Parveen blushed. The King's eyes were bright with excitement. "It all fits with my own observations. But I need to prove it once and for all. That's why I need you to trust me. I know your life up to this point has left you mistrustful of anyone but each other, but I need you to believe I have Hamish X's best interests at heart." The King hobbled over to Parveen and Mimi until he could reach out and grasp their hands. "I have made Hamish X my lifelong project. I believe that if we can unlock his secret we will be able to defeat the ODA and, hopefully, free Hamish X."

"I got a question," Mimi said suddenly.

"Ask away."

"The knife," Mimi began. "How did Hamish X git it in the first place?"

"Ah," the King chuckled. "One of my operatives planted it in his boot. It was in Egypt, four years ago …"

"The Happy Smiles Incident?" Parveen asked. "I heard rumours about the uprising there."

"Correct. I learned that Hamish X had been confined at Happy Smiles, and I decided this was my chance …"

HAMISH X STOOD AT THE GATE of the Happy Smiles Orphanage and Souvenir Factory. The entire compound was a smoking ruin. Happy Smiles was a workhouse that churned out cheap plastic replicas of the Pyramids, the Sphinx, mummies, and all sorts of Egyptian memorabilia. Up until that morning it had been run with child labour provided by miserable orphans who slaved under the owner of the factory, Mahkmed Abdul Smith. Mr. Smith, the son of an evil English chiropractor and an Egyptian seamstress, had run the factory with an iron fist. The children were given a handful of rice every day and a cup of water. The poor inmates were expected to work fourteen-hour shifts turning out plastic trinkets that were then sold at the market in Mahkmed Abdul Smith's souvenir stalls.

The children had been resigned to their lives of eternal drudgery and woe until the ODA had brought Hamish X to the factory one day as a new worker. Within two weeks, rebellion was brewing.

In the dark of night, Hamish X led an assault on the guards and captured Mahkmed. The children ran riot and broke down the front gates. Unattended, the plastic pyramid machine overheated and burst into flames. Now, with the children safely fleeing into the streets of Cairo, beyond the reach of the ODA, Hamish X stood in front of the blazing factory enjoying the sight of the conflagration.

"What a magnificent spectacle, eh Mahkmed?" Hamish X sighed. "I've never seen this place look better."

Mahkmed's only answer was a miserable whimper. Certainly, the sight of his life's work going up in flames was enough of a blow, but the added humiliation of Hamish X standing on his chest made everything slightly more depressing. The soles of the fabled boots dug into Mahkmed's puffy flesh, causing him a great deal of discomfort. His hands and feet were bound tightly together behind his back.

"Well you should whimper, Mahkmed. Does it hurt to be trampled on? Imagine how the children ground under your boot heels these twenty years might feel."

Hamish X hopped down onto the ground. He picked up his backpack and took one last look at the burning factory. Turning to walk up the street, he was surprised to see a boy his own age standing in his path. The boy was dressed in rags, but Hamish X didn't recognize him from Happy Smiles. Perhaps he was one of the many children who lived rough on the streets of Cairo? He didn't look malnourished. In fact, he looked healthy and fit.

"Hamish X," the boy said. His teeth flashed white in contrast to the dark skin of his face. "I come from the King of Switzerland."

"Who?" Hamish X was confused. "There is no King in Switzerland."

The sound of a distant helicopter made the boy jump. His voice became urgent. "I haven't time. They'll be here soon. The King wants you to have this." The boy thrust out his hand. In his palm was a pocketknife, shiny and new. A silver cross was inlaid on the side. "Keep it secret. Don't show it to them." He pointed at the approaching black helicopter. Quickly, he slapped the knife into Hamish X's hand, and with a small wave he darted between two buildings and disappeared.

Puzzled, Hamish X looked at the knife. He hefted it. It felt impossibly light in his palm. The helicopter was coming closer. He looked up into the sky, shielding his eyes against the midday sun. Dust rose as the helicopter descended. Hamish X felt a growing dread as it approached. Looking down at the knife in his palm, he felt a sudden urge to hide it from view. Some instinct told him he should keep the strange object a secret from whoever was in the helicopter. He slid the knife into his left boot.

"Hamish X ..." A beautiful female voice emanated from a

speaker on the belly of the helicopter. "Stay where you are. Mother's here."

"Mother?" The helicopter bore the logo of the ODA, sickly and yellow. Hamish X knew he should run but somehow the Voice compelled him to stand still.

When the craft was on the ground, a side door opened and Mr. Sweet stepped out into the dusty street. "Hamish X. It's time to come back with us ..." Hamish X climbed into the hatchway, the knife in his boot forgotten.

THE KING COUGHED as he finished his story. A raccoon offered him a glass of water which he accepted gratefully. "Thank you, George." Liam took a sip, his hands shaking so badly that he almost spilled his drink. Refreshed, he went on speaking. "The knife is made of an alloy that is undetectable to X-ray and deep radar. It's a tracking device that has helped me keep tabs on Hamish X and his movements. We found a very interesting pattern."

The King indicated the screen. A map showed a series of red lines criss-crossing the face of the earth. Hamish X had travelled back and forth in the last four years and there was a definite pattern. All the lines radiated out from a central location on the eastern seaboard of the United States.

"They all lead back to Providence, Rhode Island."

"The HQ of them Grey Creeps."

"Every three or four months, Hamish X is released into the world. He has an adventure. The ODA then retrieve him."

"So he's workin' for the ODA?" Mimi shook her head in disbelief.

"No, dear Mimi. I don't think Hamish X has any idea that they're using him."

"Why doesn't he remember anything of this?" Parveen asked. "His recollections of his past life and adventures are vague at best. He seems to retain skills and abilities but no long-term memories."

The King nodded. "Here's where a strange story becomes even stranger. You're right. His lack of memories is very weird. What if I told you that Hamish X, the boy who is your friend, might not really be a boy at all?"

"Wuh?" Mimi crossed her arms. "Whaddya talkin' about? He's a boy all right."

"A boy in appearance and function, but he is also something more ..."

"A computer!" Parveen breathed.

"Got it in one!" Liam smiled.

"A com*pu*ter?" Mimi scoffed. "That's just stupid. Anyone can see he's a kid just like you and me."

"I don't know, Mimi ..." Parveen said. "A boy who never ages? A boy with superhuman abilities? He's like no other boy on earth."

"He's our friend," Mimi said flatly. "Shore he's weird and jest now he's more than a little wacko but ... he ain't just some ... machine." Mimi's voice cracked as she tried to hold back tears.

The King's voice was calm. "Mimi, I know you care for Hamish X. You're a good friend and that's just what he needs right now. He can't make this decision for himself." Liam squeezed her shoulder and smiled. "This may be the greatest gift you could give him. Maybe we can find some way to set him free."

Mimi looked into the King's eyes. She saw nothing but concern. "Will it hurt 'im?"

Liam frowned. "Perhaps."

Mimi sat back, a fierce scowl on her face. The thought

of people hurting Hamish X made her angry, but she could see no other way.

"Mimi," Parveen said softly. She turned and looked into his eyes, large and brown behind his thick glasses. "Hamish X is not happy as he is. You can see that. The only hope we have is to trust these people. I suggest we do so."

Mimi looked at the King. His blue eyes were filled with sympathy. "I promise, we will do everything we can to make sure he isn't harmed."

Tears welled up in her eyes. She roughly knuckled them away. "Okay. Let's do it. But if anybody hurts him, they answer to me. Understood?"

"Understood." The King pushed himself to his feet. Reaching for his crutches, he called, "George! Prepare the computer lab!"

Mr. Candy and Mr. Sweet

The rain soaked the agents to the skin as they all lined up in front of Mr. Candy and Mr. Sweet. They were spattered in mud up to their knees. The green meadow was green no more. The search had churned up the once lovely turf into a morass of black mud.

"Report," Mr. Sweet demanded.

"No sign of the fugitives, Mr. Sweet. We have searched everywhere in a two-kilometre radius and there is no clue as to their whereabouts."

Mr. Sweet stood silently for a full minute in the drizzle. The searchers waited patiently in their drenched ranks for his pronouncement. "Pack up," he said finally. "We can't stay here. We will attempt to track him by other means."

The agents broke ranks and trotted for their vehicles. Mr. Sweet and Mr. Candy walked towards a waiting helicopter.

"This is most annoying, Mr. Sweet. Most annoying."

"Patience, Mr. Candy. We have a little time yet. We will find them."

They reached the helicopter. Mr. Sweet opened the door and said, "Mother?"

"Yes?" The feminine voice filled the cockpit.

"Run another scan of all the satellite data. Concentrate on the moment the tracking device went down."

"Running."

Chapter 11

Less than an hour later, after a swift journey down the elevator to the Technical Department on the third level, they found themselves looking down through a window into a darkened operating theatre.[42] Hamish X lay on a shiny metal table. He remained in his sleeping state, oblivious to the activity around him. A team composed of children and raccoons in white surgical scrubs ranged around the sleeping boy. The team was busy attaching a bewildering array of cables to Hamish X's hands, forehead and most of all to his big shiny boots. The cables were fixed in place with a clear glue applied to round pads that were then stuck to his skin.

Hamish X's clothes were gone, replaced with a thin paper surgical gown. The boots seemed even stranger than they usually did, stuck as they were on the ends of his bare legs. Mimi's heart went out to her friend. He looked so vulnerable in the midst of all the machines, in an island of light surrounded by darkness.

"Poor boy ..." Mrs. Francis said. She and Mr. Kipling

---

[42] An operating theatre is a room where medical procedures take place. The name is a holdover from the Renaissance, when all doctors had to supplement their income through acting. They would perform plays that involved medical procedures. Needy audience members who couldn't afford surgery would come out of the crowd to receive treatment. It was highly entertaining but not very sanitary. Some of the best plays from the Surgical Drama Era were *Danny Gets a Kidney*, *The Tonsils of Julius Caesar*, *The Tragedy of Lucretia and Her Burst Appendix*, and *Hernia!*

had accompanied Hamish X from the airship and they stood in the little group clustered at the window.

"I assure you he's in good hands," King Liam said.

"Not him," Mrs. Francis said, clucking softly. "It's you I'm worried about. Don't you ever brush that hair?" She licked her palm and tried to flatten a stray lock of red hair that stood straight up from the King's scalp. He squirmed under her attentions. "And those clothes. Have they never seen an iron? Did you dress in the dark? Honestly!" She tugged at the King's tunic, trying to straighten out some wrinkles. Aidan and Cara strained to stifle their giggles at the King's discomfort. "No adults indeed. It shows. Believe me, it shows!"

"Please, Mrs. Francis!" the King begged. "I am trying to concentrate."

Mimi laughed. "Give it up, yer Majesty. You lost that battle when ya let 'er in the front door."

The King groaned and submitted to Mrs. Francis's ministrations with as much grace as he could muster. Parveen tried to distract him from his discomfort. "Tell me, what are all the machines and cables for?"

"The machines are monitoring and imaging devices. They are attached to important nerve centres in Hamish X's body, and using the data they generate ... Ow! Mrs. Francis, *please* ... we can build an internal picture of his body. We want to take a close look at him before we attempt anything drastic."

"Majesty," a raccoon voice came from behind the group. They turned to see one of the little creatures standing at the door of the little observation room. It held a small black remote control in its paw. "The imager is prepared."

Grateful for the opportunity, King Liam pulled gently but firmly away from Mrs. Francis's attentions. He went to the raccoon and took the remote. Pointing the small device at the empty space in front of him, he thumbed a button.

Everyone gasped as an image appeared, hovering in space in the centre of the room. It was Hamish X, about three times his natural size, floating a metre above the ground. Every feature was picked out in minute detail, from the dishevelled hairs on his head to the individual pores in his skin.

"Amazing," Mr. Kipling breathed.

"Truly." Liam moved forward until he was standing right beside the projection. "George and I have been working on image projection together for a long time. George really is very clever."

The George raccoon bowed. "You are too kind, Majesty."

The King beckoned to the others, who began to gather around the giant Hamish X.

"Come closer. The detail is marvellous. My technical staff is amazing. These images are miles ahead of anything you can find in the commercial holographic projection field." The King punched another button. The image spun slowly to show the sleeping boy from all angles.

"The MRI, or Magnetic Resonance Imaging, machine will allow us to look inside Hamish X and see what there is to be seen.[43] Our machine is somewhat more advanced

---

[43] Magnetic Resonance Imaging, or MRI, makes pictures of the interior of the human body using magnetic waves. Before the MRI, pictures of the interior of the human body could be achieved only with cameras attached to highly trained shrews (very tiny mammalian carnivores). Shrews are difficult to tame, and so training was extremely costly and time-consuming. Add to this the fact that many shrews refused to come out of the human body after going in, and the invention of the MRI was long overdue.

than what the average hospital provides. Using our technology, we can peel away the layers without harming the patient."

The image changed and now they looked at a Hamish X without his skin. All his muscles were exposed to view. Mimi felt slightly sick but fascinated at the same time. Ropy cables of red and purple stretched along the bones of Hamish X's skeleton. His face was a grinning, skinless skull.

"Goodness," Mrs. Francis gasped, burying her face in Mr. Kipling's chest.

"Gross," Mimi said.

"Neat," Parveen pronounced.

"Believe me, Mrs. Francis, Hamish X doesn't feel a thing."

Mrs. Francis reluctantly turned her face to look at the image.

Mimi forced herself to examine the disgusting sight. Something was strange about the picture. She thought for a moment and then realized what it was.

"The boots!"

"Yes, Mimi, the boots. They don't register at all on our scans. They are made of some material that we have never seen before."

"Weird," was all Mimi could say. Hamish X stripped of his skin looked bizarre enough, but without the boots and his skin he looked positively naked.

"It gets weirder," the King said. He reached out with one finger to touch the image. The tip of his finger passed through the muscle covering Hamish X's bicep. "The muscles are all in the right place but they are much denser than they should be in a child of Hamish X's apparent age. In fact, they are denser than the muscles of even a professional body builder."

"How is that possible?" Parveen peered closely at the projection.

"On its own, we could dismiss his strange strength as a freak of nature, a fluke that allows Hamish X to perform amazing feats of strength. But it isn't the only thing that's odd. Let's look deeper." The King toggled another button. "It gets even more interesting." The image jumped again and the muscles disappeared. A network of thin lines outlined the shape of a human body. "The nervous system. Each one of these little filaments is a nerve." The nerves looked almost like the roots of a plant. There was a thick central root that ran down the centre like a tree trunk. Branching off into finer and finer filaments was a network that formed the shape of Hamish X's skull, arms, hands, legs, and feet. The farther away from the spine, the thinner the filaments became.

Liam broke the silence. "Notice anything strange?"

Mimi shrugged. "It's all pretty screwy."

Parveen whistled. "There are too many nerves. Especially around his feet."

"What do you mean?" the King's eyes sparkled.

Parveen peered at the image for a moment longer and said, "There are roughly three times the number of nerves running through his body than are found in a normal human being. That's just a guess."

"A good guess, Parveen. Yes. His nerve structure, like his muscle system, is much denser. That gives him faster reflexes. The other advantage for him is that he can carry more information to his brain."

Mimi pointed. "That's where the boots are, ain't it."

"Yes. They are integrated into his nervous system. That's why he can't remove them. They have become part of his flesh. Someone has altered Hamish X's nervous system to accommodate huge volumes of energy, sensation, and information and grafted the boots onto his body."

"The ODA?" Mr. Kipling asked.

"Of course. They have modified Hamish X for some purpose. We need to know what that purpose is." The remote slipped from the King's fingers. Mimi reached out, quick as a cat, and caught the little device just inches from the tile floor. She handed it back to the King. "Thank you, Mimi. I'm a little overexcited." He pressed another button. "Let's look at the brain scan."

The image jumped, and there, turning slowly, was a colourful, pulsing mass of wrinkled tissue. Split down the middle, it was like two beans pressed together. The ghostly outline of Hamish X's skull was barely visible.

"Incredible," breathed the King.

"That's his brain?" Mimi gasped.

"Yes," Liam whispered. "But … it's impossible."

"What's impossible?" Mrs. Francis was finally able to speak.

"It's so … hot!" Parveen said softly. The image looked like a throbbing ball of fire, flaring in space. Its entire surface rippled with colours ranging from deep orange to bright yellow.

"A good choice of words, Parveen. Yes. Hot indeed." The King punched a button. A second blob appeared beside the first. The second blob had some orange, but most of its surface was a cool blue with some orange flashes. "Here … This is a normal human brain. We use only about ten percent of brain capacity. Hamish X's brain looks closer to eighty percent. It's amazing. The ODA have made him into a walking computer processor. His whole body is like a conduit for energy."

"Why would they do that?" Parveen rubbed his glasses with his shirttail, drawing a disapproving glare from Mrs. Francis. He dropped the shirttail and switched to a handkerchief dredged from his pants pocket.

"We can only guess. That is why I coaxed Hamish X back here."

The King turned to them and addressed them earnestly. "I believe that only Hamish X can tell us what has been done to him. First, however, we must break down some of his system software."

"You can't talk about him that way," Mrs. Francis cried, close to tears. "He's a little boy, not a machine."

King Liam took Mrs. Francis's hand. "No. He is both a little boy and a machine. What I hope to do, I do for the little boy, Mrs. Francis. He will be whole only when he is free of the Grey Agents' influence. Please, you must understand that what I must do, I do for all the children in the Hollow Mountain, all the children around the world who fall under the ODA's sway, but most of all … for him."

He pointed through the window where Hamish X lay on the silver table. The medical team was finished with their preparations. They stood waiting, looking up to the window for some signal from their King.

"It may be dangerous. Together with my technical team, I've created a program that will be uploaded into Hamish X's consciousness. Then I will attempt to enter his sleeping mind through a new experimental procedure. I won't lie to you: the procedure will be dangerous for us both. I am going to try to restore his memories and revive him. I know that you are all his friends and I won't do anything without your permission."

Mimi, Parveen, Mrs. Francis, and Mr. Kipling pressed forward, huddling together to look down at the sleeping boy. Mr. Kipling put an arm around Mrs. Francis and held her close. Mrs. Francis draped her warm bulk over the two children. For a long time, they just looked down at their friend, imagining a world where he didn't come back to them. At last, Mimi stepped forward and stood nose to nose with the King. Her green eyes stared hard into his blue ones.

"Listen and listen good," Mimi said, even and slow. "You do what you gotta do to bring 'im back. We'll be watchin'. If it looks like anythin's goin' wrong, I'm comin' down there and I'm pullin' the plug." She poked Liam's chest with a long bony finger. "Anythin' happens to my friend Hamish X and yore gonna hear from me direct. Understand?"

The King's face was serious, his blue eyes intense. "I wouldn't expect anything less from Miss Mimi Catastrophe Jones." He winked. He nodded. Pressing a button next to the window, he said, "Prepare the link. I'm coming down."

Chapter 12

The Memory Party

He didn't know where he was. He didn't know who he was. He had to call himself something. He decided to call himself The Boy.

The Boy looked around and discovered he was standing on a gravel walkway. On either side of the walkway, perfectly clipped grass stretched out as far as the eye could see. He looked up into the sky and saw a million stars in the black sky. The moon hung yellow and full above.

The walkway was made up of hundreds and thousands of tiny white stones packed together. The Boy scuffed the stones with his feet, sending a bunch of them skittering onto the manicured grass. Immediately the stones leapt off the grass and back onto the walkway, as if the grass were repelling them.

The Boy laughed. "That is certainly odd." His voice sounded loud and strange in his ears. He noticed another strange thing: he was wearing huge black boots. They glistened in the starlight. "Weird."

"Excuse me, sir." The voice made him jerk his head up in surprise from contemplation of his odd footwear. Directly in front of him there now stood a large stone house. Tall stained-glass windows shone from within. The light spilled over the grass in long coloured pools. He found himself at the bottom of a set of stone steps that led up to an arch filled with an ornately carved wooden door. The door was open.

Standing in the doorway was a boy, a little older than

himself. He was tall and well proportioned, dressed in a plain green suit with a silver cross embroidered over the right breast. The boy had red hair tangled in an unruly mop on his head and blue eyes that crinkled around the corners. "You're here for the Memory Party, aren't you?"

As soon as the stranger said these words, The Boy heard music and laughter and realized there was a party going on.

"What's a Memory Party?"

"It's like a party, only better. You like parties, don't you?"

"I guess so," The Boy said.

"Come in then, come right in." The Red-Haired Boy opened the door wider and stepped aside to allow The Boy to enter. The Boy climbed the steps and went in. "Everyone is waiting."

He found himself in a foyer.[44] *The Red-Haired Boy closed the door and stood beside him.*

"Who are you?" the Boy asked.

"We've never met." The Red-Haired Boy smiled. He held out a hand, pale and thin. "I am Liam."

The Boy shook the hand. It was soft and warm. "I'm glad to meet you. And I'm glad to know your name so I don't have to keep thinking of you as the Red-Haired Boy. Liam is shorter and easier."[45] *The Boy paused. "You wouldn't know what my name is, would you? I can't seem to recall."*

---

[44] Forgive me for interrupting this dream sequence, but *foyer* is such an odd word, I couldn't keep quiet. A foyer is the room directly inside the entrance of a building. Many people don't have foyers and so don't know this. I believe this is a great tragedy and I work with a charity organization for the foyerless called The Space Inside The Door Association, or TSITDA. We help bring foyers to those who haven't any. This is a very expensive process, as most homes that don't have foyers must be renovated drastically to accommodate a foyer and so much money has to be raised to offset the costs. Please give generously

[45] Amen to that.

Liam laughed. "You are Hamish X."

"I am?" the Boy said. He thought for a moment. "Yes, I am. I remember that now. What a relief." Hamish X looked around at the foyer. "Where are we, Liam, if you don't mind me asking?"

Liam laughed again. Hamish X decided he liked the sound of Liam's laugh. "I could give you a complicated answer that would take a long time, but I think I'll just say we're inside your head."

"How strange," Hamish X said. "I must have a huge head if I can fit both you and me inside it."

"When I say inside your head," Liam smiled, "I mean to say that we are in your mind. This whole place is constructed from your memories. I have inserted myself into your mind to be a guide."

Hamish X knitted his brow. "So this isn't real?"

"Oh it's real, in the way that dreams and memories are real, but it exists only within your consciousness." Liam held up his hands and flexed his fingers. He laughed with sudden delight. "I couldn't do this anywhere else." He did a little jig, kicking his feet. He laughed again and Hamish X laughed at his infectious good humour. "Yes, I could grow to like this." Liam stopped dancing and looked at Hamish X. "I'm being foolish. We haven't much time. They're waiting."

"Who?"

"Your memories."

"Oh."

Liam set off down a corridor. Hamish X followed.

The din of the party grew louder as they moved down the dark corridor. Voices were raised in laughter and music swelled. They turned a corner and came to a large open room. The party was in full swing.

A huge banner hung on one wall. It read WELCOME HAMISH X in big red letters. Under the banner, a small band made up of children dressed in tuxedos and evening gowns played a variety of instruments: violins, horns, saxophones, and guitars. The room was decorated in bright streamers of red and gold. The floor was made of hardwood, polished to a gleaming honey yellow. Standing around on the beautiful floor was the strangest collection of people one could imagine. They were of every size and shape, every colour and culture, male and female, young and old. They were all chatting animatedly and holding cups of sparkling red punch.

"Who are they?" Hamish X asked Liam.

"Your memories. Do you recognize any of them?"

"I can't say I do."

Suddenly, a tall bony man turned and looked directly at Hamish X. He smiled, exposing yellow teeth. "Surely you remember me?" He held out a tiny tray with a single cube of bluish-white cheese on it. Hamish X reached out, took the proffered cheese, and popped it in his mouth. Its pungent smell instantly permeated his mouth and stung his nostrils. His eyes widened as memories of Viggo and the Windcity Orphanage and Cheese Factory flooded his mind.

"Viggo," he whispered. "Viggo Schmatz."

Viggo winked and turned away. Hamish X stepped into the throng, immersing himself in the noise and heat of the crowd.

He bumped into a man wearing a pair of pink tights and a golden mask. The masked man was in the middle of a conversation with a dignified gentleman with blond hair and a gold crown perched on his head. They smiled at Hamish X.

"Bueno! The little Hombre himself." The man in tights grabbed Hamish X by the hand and squeezed it in a bone-crushing grip. In the midst of the pain, the man's identity leapt into Hamish X's brain.

"Spicy Tuna!" Hamish X cried. "The Mexican wrestler!"

"The same!"

Hamish X gritted his teeth and squeezed Spicy Tuna's hand. The eyes in the holes of the mask went wide. The huge man fell to his knees. "Oh, so strong! You defeat me once again!"

Hamish X released the wrestler's hand as the blond man touched his shoulder. With the contact, Hamish X remembered. "King Olaf of Sweden. I'm sorry I had to steal your helicopter."

"Sink noting ov it, my boy! I have many udders." The King of Sweden waved a hand in dismissal.

"'Ere's the man of the hour!" A heavy hand landed on his shoulder and spun him round. Two men with beards loomed over him. The first had a beard matted with waxy cheese, stinky and tangled. It covered his broad chest and dangled to his belly. The second had a beard more elegantly trimmed. Tied in the strands of his facial hair with red ribbons were cubes of brown-rubber soy curd.

"Cheesebeard and Soybeard!" Hamish X exclaimed. His initial delight at being able to remember who the brothers were gave way to wariness. He raised his fists to defend himself. He needn't have worried. The brothers just laughed. Soybeard pointed. "Look, Cheesebeard! He wants to fight! No! No! We're all done with that."

"Aye," Cheesebeard agreed. "We're just memories now, lad, and memories hold no grudges." He winked and the brothers strolled away arm in arm, leaving Hamish X bewildered.

"This is crazy," he muttered. Suddenly, the boy named Liam was at his elbow. "Not crazy, Hamish X. You're just getting your memories back. And there are many more to come."

Liam guided Hamish X through the crowd, stopping here and there to greet the strangest array of characters. Some were old foes and some were old friends. As he met each one, he found that the memory of their encounter came flooding back. The party became more and more raucous, with pirates and bandits, ninjas and monks, kings and queens shouting and laughing as they drank punch and ate cubes of Caribou Blue.

Hamish X began to feel claustrophobic as the room seemed more and more crowded, his memories pressing in from all sides. The strange but familiar faces became a blur to him as Liam pulled him this way and that.

Suddenly, two great brown hands lifted him up into the air.

"Hamish X!" Liam cried but his voice was lost in the din.

Hamish X was hoisted into the air and brought face to face with a strange ape face. The face was missing an eye but was joyful despite the deformity, its great yellow teeth twisted into a parody of a human smile.

"Winkie!" Hamish X laughed aloud. The huge snow monkey grinned even wider and swung Hamish X in a great arc. The crowd stepped back and began to clap in time to the music. Hamish X was at the mercy of the great ape, who flung him like a doll up into the air. He looked around at the swirl of faces and began to fill decidedly ill. Winkie was oblivious to his discomfort. The big primate hooted loudly and pranced about the room.

Hamish X saw the faces spinning around him, enemies and friends blending into one. He was whirling so fast he couldn't focus.

"Winkie! Stop! STOP!"

Winkie abruptly did as he was told. Hooting softly, he put Hamish X down on the floor, the big boots clicking on the shiny wooden surface. The boy had trouble standing up, he was so dizzy. He staggered a step and went down on one knee, staring at a single wooden tile in front of his face in an effort to get his bearings. The crowd all around was shouting and laughing, a great incoherent roar.

"Hamish." The high voice of a woman cut through the din. "My Hamish," the woman called again. The voice struck deep at Hamish X's heart. He raised his head and looked for the source of the sound. In the middle of the throng he saw the back of a woman's head. She was pushing through the crowd, moving away. Hamish X couldn't see her face, just a thick sweep of brown hair. "Mother!" he called but she didn't turn. He pulled himself to his feet and staggered into the crowd.

He tried to move in her direction but it was tough going. People clogged his path, patting him on the back and shaking his hand. "Excellent party!" "Remember me, lad?" With each contact more memories flooded in, adding to his disorientation. Hamish X pushed his way past an extremely fat man wearing a pointed helmet and a wedding dress.[46] He caught a glimpse of the brown hair at the edge of the crowd, moving away.

"Mother, wait!" He felt a growing desperation. Throwing himself against the people in his path, he called upon his boots. He reached with his mind down into their dark well and instantly felt them stir. "I'm coming, Mother! Wait for me!" The power surged up his legs. Using his newfound strength he pushed against the crowd, plowing forward like a bulldozer. His memories protested as he cast them aside.

At last, he came out into the open. The polished floor was empty in front of him. A few metres away was a simple wooden door. He caught a glimpse of brown hair as the door closed.

"Wait!" he shouted. "Mother, don't go!" Tears prickled in his eyes. He dashed across the shining floor, his boots squeaking on the slick surface. His hand reached for the door handle. He was almost there when the door burst open.

Two men in grey suits stepped into the room. They wore grey fedoras and gloves. Black goggles covered their eyes. Hamish X skidded to a stop, his boots leaving long black marks on the floor. The men stood staring at him, their heads cocked to one side.

---

[46] Probably the Crown Prince Garbonzo of Humnubble, who is known to wear a wedding dress most of the time. He is also said to wear a pointed helmet, and he encourages his subjects to toss doughnuts over the point. He is an extremely silly person.

"Hamish X," one of the men said in a flat voice. The voice was lifeless and mechanical, the kind of voice that a can opener or a toaster might have, should it be able to speak.[47] "We've come for you."

"Indeed," the other said in an equally lifeless tone.

They lunged, grabbed him by the arms, wrestled him to the floor. Memories of the metal table and the horrible lights flooded back. Hamish X screamed and screamed. "Candy and Sweet! No! No!" He remembered all the pain he had suffered at the hands of the Grey Agents.

Suddenly, a voice cried out. "Let him go! He's just a child!" Hamish X looked to the doorway and saw a skinny bald man standing there. He wore thick glasses perched on his long nose. His face was pale, almost as white as the surgical gown he wore.

The Grey Agents seemed momentarily surprised. Hamish X took the opportunity to wrench himself free.

Mr. Sweet pointed a long bony finger at the man. "Professor, do not interfere."

"He is ours. We made him," Mr. Candy added.

The agents turned to the boy lying on the floor. "He is ours ..." They moved towards him together.

Hamish X cowered away as they approached. He didn't want them to touch him again. Those horrible hands and faces filled him with dread.

"No!" the Professor cried, covering his face with his hands.

Suddenly Liam was there, kneeling by Hamish X's side. "Not

---

[47] Thank goodness they can't. Can you imagine having a talking can opener? What could it possibly have to say? "The beans are now unlidded!" or "Look at me: I've opened the soup." Or even worse: a talking toaster! "Hey, the toast is burning, you fool!" And "How dare you put a toaster pastry in me! I'm an artist!" Toasters are truly the prima donnas of the appliance world.

feeling too good are you, Hamish X. It's a lot to take in all at once."

Mr. Candy and Mr. Sweet stopped and stared at the boy. "Get away from him," they said together. "He's ours."

"Nonsense," Liam said with a chuckle. He took Hamish X's hand and pulled him to his feet. "You don't feel well, Hamish X." Hamish X nodded. "I can help." Liam went around behind Hamish X and, wrapping his arms around the boy's stomach, the red-haired boy heaved as hard as he could.

Hamish X gagged once, twice, and then out of his mouth a sickly green object popped. It fell to the floor with a wet splurt. It was a slimy little bug, a disgusting cross between a beetle and a cricket. The bug immediately began to skitter across the floor.

"After him," Mr. Candy said. The Grey Agents set off after the little creature, following it in a meandering pattern across the room, weaving here and there, wherever the bug's fancy led them.

"They won't be able to find you now," Liam said.

"That's amazing," breathed Hamish X.

"A little trick my technical people and I dreamed up."

"Technical people? Who are you?"

"All in good time. You've had a lot of excitement. It's time to leave." Liam handed Hamish X a cup brimming with rich, red liquid. "Drink this."

Hamish X took the cup. Suddenly, he remembered. "Mother!" He looked for the door but there was nothing but wall in front of him, a smooth surface covered in floral wallpaper. It was as if the door had never existed. The Professor was gone, too. Hamish X turned and saw that the room was empty. The crowd had disappeared. Only he and Liam remained.

"Drink," Liam said again. Hamish X found he couldn't resist. He tipped the cup up and drained it in one long gulp. As soon as he did so, he felt a warm heaviness come over him.

"That's it, Hamish X. Close your eyes."

He did as he was told. He felt a strange falling sensation. He wasn't afraid. In fact, the feeling was rather pleasant. He plummeted through warm darkness.

As he fell, he heard a sound. A voice called from far away. It was familiar.

"Hamish X. Wake up!"

The voice was getting closer.

"It's us! Y'all right!"

His fall was slowing.

"Mimi?" he murmured.

He was stopping now.

"HAMISH X! Wake up! Wake up now!" She was shaking him.

"Mimi! Stop shaking me! I'm awake already!"

Mimi's eyes went wide. "Hamish X? You know who I am? You remember me?"

"I remember you, Mimi. I remember Parveen." He looked at Mrs. Francis and Mr. Kipling. "I remember you, too ..."

He turned his head, cables and wires making the movement difficult. Lying on a table beside him, he saw the red-haired boy from the party. The boy's hair was plastered down with sweat and he looked pale but he smiled.

"Liam?"

"King Liam of Switzerland. Welcome, Hamish X." The King's blue eyes closed. He was exhausted.

Hamish X suddenly remembered the woman with the brown hair. He had only caught a glimpse but he knew who she was. "Mother."

Hamish X gulped against a swelling ache in his throat.

Parveen stepped close and took his friend's hand. "Are you all right, Hamish X?"

"I don't know," he said. "I remember so much …" and he began to cry.

Mimi wrapped her arms around her friend and held him close to her as he began to sob.

One of the medical team members, a tall, thin girl, stepped up in front of Parveen. Her skin was a chocolate colour where it showed between her mask and her white cotton surgical cap. Her brown eyes were wide. "Your name … is Parveen."

Parveen nodded. "Yes."

The girl pulled off her mask and cap. A glossy ponytail fell over her shoulder. Her smile was bright. "Parveen! Don't you know me?"

"I … I …"

"I'm your sister, Noor." And she crushed the little boy to her, lifting him from his feet with the ferocity of her embrace.

Mr. Candy and Mr. Sweet

Standing in the rain, Mr. Sweet and Mr. Candy looked around the ruined meadow, the brims of their sodden grey fedoras dripping.

Behind the two agents, the helicopter idled in the darkness as they surveyed the empty valley. Their goggles, misted with rain, scanned the surrounding mountains for a clue as to the whereabouts of their quarry.

The agents rarely showed irritation, but they were obviously annoyed. A rabbit hopped near Mr. Sweet's foot and he kicked it. The rabbit immediately vomited on the agent's shoe and fell comatose in the grass from terror.

"What silly creatures. When this world is ours, we shall eradicate all such useless beings, Mr. Candy."

"First things first, Mr. Sweet. We must find our asset. The tracking device flared for only three point two seconds. Somehow, they managed to switch it off. Mother was unable to pinpoint the exact location but it was somewhere in the Alps."

"They are not in Switzerland by accident, Mr. Candy."

"They must have already made contact with the King. We must finish off the King once and for all."

"We have the firepower to destroy the Hollow Mountain and the King. The only problem, Mr. Candy, is finding the

Hollow Mountain. How do you propose we do that?"

Mr. Candy tilted his head back. The moonlight glinted off the goggles covering his eyes. "We ask directions, Mr. Sweet."

They climbed into the helicopter.

"Mother?" Mr. Candy spoke as they fastened their seatbelts.

"I'm listening."

"Run a scan of all adoption data for the last fifty years. Focus on children who have inherited large sums of money upon reaching the age of majority."

"Any geographical restrictions?" Mother asked.

"Central Europe only, for now. Keep it local."

"Running."

The rotors spun up as Mr. Sweet took the controls. Mr. Candy shook his head. "We've run the same search three thousand and forty-seven times. Why waste our time again?"

"Perhaps we'll be lucky this time," Mr. Sweet said. "And the King of Switzerland won't." He pulled back on the control stick and the aircraft lifted off into the grey dawn.

Part 3

GOOD AND BAD
THINGS HAPPEN

Yet Another Note from the Narrator

Oh my! What a dramatic moment! Hamish X has returned to himself, only more so. At last he is able to remember the events of his past. Most of them anyway. Still, he is unable to remember clearly the one thing he wants to remember most: his mother.

Isn't that always the way with memory? The one thing you are racking your brain to recall is the one thing you can't quite seem to grasp. For me, it's where I put my favourite trousers. They are such beautiful trousers: thick corduroy with glittering gold piping down the outside of the leg. They are fastened by a polished, pure silver button in the front and the zipper is fashioned out of diamonds. In the sun, the zipper and button combined with the gold piping is quite a dazzling spectacle. If I am planning to wear them on a sunny day, I am required to report my intentions to the local traffic authorities as a safety precaution: the majesty of my glittering trousers has been known to cause traffic accidents and to dazzle pilots in low-flying aircraft. The pants were a gift from the Sultana of Benmurgui as a reward for a particularly well-narrated story at her thirteenth birthday party.[48]

The point is, I put them down somewhere and I can't remember where. The more I try to remember, the more I can't quite seem to recall. Highly annoying. One might wonder how such a shining pair of trousers might be overlooked. Surely they'd be difficult to miss, which leads me to believe that perhaps they have been stolen by a rival narrator, jealous of my success and my clothing. Time will tell.

I digress. Let us return to the story. Weeks have passed and the former residents of Windcity are settling in to their new home. Everyone seems happy ... everyone but Hamish X.

---

[48] The Sultana is not a raisin but rather a female Sultan (a variety of ruler of an Arab state). It would be very difficult for a raisin to give anyone a pair of trousers, as it has no hands, nor does it have a good grasp of the concept of trousers, as it has no legs either. Not that raisins aren't generous: they are among the most gentle and giving of dried fruits.

Chapter 13

He was lying on the steel table again, under the intense lights. He tried to get up but he found he couldn't move. Every muscle of his body was paralyzed. Fear twisted in his stomach, winding in his bowels like a cold snake.

Only his eyes were capable of moving. They darted back and forth, looking from one side to the other. In the darkness, outside the pool of light, he sensed that someone was watching. There was danger close by but he couldn't make himself move. He tried to scream but his throat was frozen shut.

"You are ours, Hamish X," the voice of Mr. Sweet hissed from the darkness.

"You will be the key that opens the door." Mr. Candy's flat tones echoed in the emptiness. "You will build a bridge to join the worlds."

Out of the shadows the Grey Agents came, leaning over him, staring down with their black goggles reflecting his terror-stricken face.

"You are one of us," they said together. Slowly, they reached up with their gloved hands and with a wet sucking sound, removed their goggles. Their eyes were terrible, moist and bulging. The most horrible thing was the colour of those eyes: golden, like his own.

"NOOOOOOOOOOOOOOOOOOOOO!"

Hamish X screamed, sitting up in his sweat-soaked bed to find himself in his quarters in the Hollow Mountain.

"Hamish X? Are you all right?"

A George raccoon sat on the floor next to the bed, reared up on its haunches, black eyes blinking.

"Nightmare, I guess."

"Again? Should I schedule an appointment with medical?"

"No, no. I'm fine, thank you."

Hamish X looked out the window. The artificial sunlight from the Daniel's Panels cast a glow of simulated morning over the Hollow Mountain. He heard children's voices calling to each other as they went about their business. They were making their way to the raccoon-taught schoolrooms or the workshops on the lower level, happy and content. Hamish X envied them.

"George?"

"I'm here, Hamish X."

"What time is it?"

"It is currently eight oh seven and thirty-two seconds in our local time zone."

"Seven minutes past eight would be enough."

"Do you require breakfast?"

"Can I have some toast and some orange juice?"

"We have seventeen types of bread available. Rye, sourdough, cornbread, brown, seven-grain, white—"

"White. Just plain white toast and jam, please."

"There are twenty-three types of jam. We have—"

"Strawberry."

"I will prepare the toast and jam."

The raccoon turned and waddled out the door. George the raccoon was assigned to take care of all Hamish X's personal needs. Hamish X couldn't quite get his head around the idea that all the raccoons were actually just one raccoon with an interconnected mind. Hamish X got out of bed.

Ten minutes later he was sitting at the small breakfast table in the kitchen. He had his own little apartment to live in. It wasn't very big but it was private. Mimi, Parveen, Mrs. Francis, and Mr. Kipling all had similar units along the same strip of terrace on the residential level. The breakfast room had a sliding door that was open to allow the fresh air in as Hamish X chewed on his toast.

Great Plumbers and Their Exploits sat on the table by Hamish X's elbow. He hadn't opened it in days. Before he regained his memories he'd pored over the book with rabid intensity, certain that the pages held a clue to the location of his lost mother. But since King Liam had awakened his memories he'd lost the desire to read the book. Parveen believed that *Great Plumbers* was part of the ODA's plans, and that since Hamish X was now free of their programming he was also free of his compulsion to read the boring book.

He laid a hand on the green leather cover, tracing the gold lettering with a fingertip. He felt a pang of loneliness. "How could I miss reading such a boring book?" he mumbled to himself.

"Are you addressing me?" The George raccoon roused itself from sleep mode at the sound of his voice. George had been standing silent and still against the wall as it always did, resting until required.

"Sorry, no. Just talking to myself."

"Very well." The George raccoon went back to sleep.

Hamish X looked at the name of the author of the book. *Professor Magnus Ballantyne-Stewart*. He found himself wondering who the man was, or if he even existed at all. Probably just a name the ODA agents made up to amuse themselves as an elaborate joke to play on Hamish X.

"George?"

The raccoon's eyes opened. "Yes, Hamish X, I'm listening."

"Where is everybody?"

"Shall I list them alphabetically? Anthony Aaron is working in workshop 21 at workstation 7a. Andrea Aato is in the gardens in the park by the Hakon's Fountain. Fredirick Afalati is training in the gymnasium ..."

"Not every single person in the Hollow Mountain!"

"You'll have to be more specific with your commands."

Hamish X rolled his eyes. "All right. Where *specifically* is Mimi?"

"Sarcasm is unnecessary. She is in the courtyard on the workshop level. More specifically, she is training in the Guards' facility, practising hand-to-hand combat. She has just knocked Guard Captain Aidan down for the fourth straight time in a judo demonstration."

Hamish X grinned at that. "I'll bet he isn't very happy."

"No, he is not happy."

Hamish chuckled and took a bite of his toast. The toast was perfectly golden and crisp. George was great at making toast.

In the two weeks they'd been guests at the Hollow Mountain, Mimi had taken to the idea of becoming one of the King's Guards. She was progressing quickly. Her raw strength and agility helped her excel. Her hot temper was a bit of a drawback, however. Aidan was one of the few sparring partners brave enough to trade blows with her in the practice ring. Despite her lack of formal training, she was fast becoming the best hand-to-hand fighter in the Hollow Mountain.

"Where is Parveen?"

"He is in the electronics lab with his sister, Noor."

Parveen's sister: that was a still a surprise. Parveen had thought his entire family gone forever until Noor removed her mask in the operating theatre that day. She had been scooped up by the ODA to work in a factory in Malaysia that manufactured sharp and pointy toys for third world children. She had managed to escape with the help of the King's agents and had come to live at the Hollow Mountain. Technical expertise ran in the family. She was brilliant with electronics and computers. Most of the program that had allowed Hamish X to remember his past was her work. Now Parveen and Noor were practically joined at the hip. After having thought each other lost, they didn't want to lose each other again.

"Mrs. Francis? Mr. Kipling?"

"They are the only adults in the Hollow Mountain."

"I know *that*," Hamish X said, exasperated. "Where are they right now?"

"Mrs. Francis is supervising the preparations for the wedding feast later today. Mr. Kipling is at the tailor's undergoing the final fitting of his dress uniform. He is complaining that the seat of the trousers is too snug."

Hamish X sighed. The wedding was tonight. The union of Mr. Kipling and Mrs. Francis was to be a grand affair, a highly anticipated social event officiated by the King on the lawn of the Royal Park in Frieda's Cavern. Mrs. Francis was worried that the army of George raccoons in the kitchens would not prepare food properly. She fretted day and night about the ingredients, the tablecloths, the napkins, which spoons went where, which fork was left and which right.

He smiled when he thought of the stout housekeeper he'd first met in the receiving area at the Windcity Orphanage and Cheese Factory. She had been a fretful, nervous little woman wringing her dingy brown apron, hardly a heroine. Even then, however, he had seen her goodness in the secret smile she gave him on that day. In their struggle with the Cheese Pirates she had proven her bravery and loyalty, even melting the heart of Mr. Kipling, a pirate himself until she taught him how to love again.

Everywhere Mrs. Francis went in the Hollow Mountain, she was followed by a swarm of young children, all eager for the love of a mother that no raccoon or computer could provide, however cleverly constructed or ingeniously programmed. She could be found tying shoelaces or reading stories on the lawn, mending tears in clothing or having tea parties with any number of dolls. Mrs. Francis was unofficially the mother of over three thousand orphans. Mr. Kipling bore all this with stoic patience,

knowing that he would always have to share his futur bride's love with an untold number of young children.

Hamish X was happy for Mrs. Francis and Mr. Kipling and for Parveen and Mimi. They were busy. All the chil dren who had come from Windcity in the *Orphan Quee* had been absorbed into the population of the city unde the mountain and they all had a job to carry out or a schoolroom to learn in or a duty to perform.

Everyone was taken care of. Everyone had a purpose. Everyone, that is, except ... Hamish X. He was at a loss.

He was left to wander and explore. He read in the library or watched the raccoons building in the workshop. He tagged along to watch Mimi train or Parveen tinker with some device or other he was working on. A lot of the time he just sat in his little kitchen, looking out over the busy little colony of children, each with a place and a purpose, wondering what his place and purpose might possibly be. He had tried to get an audience with King Liam to discuss his future but the George raccoons had regretfully informed him that the King was receiving no visitors and that all requests and queries should be delivered through one's raccoon and would be addressed in due time.

Hamish X was frustrated. Why had Liam gone to all the trouble of planting the knife on him, bringing him here, and reviving him if he wasn't going to tell him what he should be doing? He stuffed the last morsel of toast into his mouth and, chewing in a manner that suggested he was annoyed with the world, clomped out the front door to the elevator.

The only drawback to the Hollow Mountain that Hamish X had discovered was that one could wait forever for the elevator. There was only one car and it serviced all the caverns. He joined a group of children waiting for the

next car. One of them, a young girl of about eight, glanced over at him and immediately her eyes went wide.

"You're Hamish X, aren't you?" she said breathlessly. The other children's heads whipped around. In a second, Hamish X was surrounded by a press of children eagerly asking him questions about his adventures and about his boots. He suffered their attentions as best he could, all the while feeling uncomfortable. They even asked to touch the boots, running their fingers over the slick surface of his footwear.

Since the restart, his boots had felt strange to him. Certainly, they were strange in the first place, but now that he remembered when they were grafted onto his body against his will, they felt alien. He could still feel their power like a soft hum, waiting to be unleashed. He had experimented on his own, late at night while lying in his bed. He would look down at the boots, focusing his mind on them. They would glow with blue radiance, reacting to his attentions. He felt the incredible power, the destructive energy they could release, but he could control it. He was becoming more adept at focusing the power. At first, he could only make the boots throb with energy, scorching his bedclothes and causing George to worry as he set the fire alarm off in his apartment. After some practice, though, he was able to control their intensity, letting it trickle through the boots at whatever level he wished. He could make the boots cling to the wall by sending the right amount of power to the knobbly soles. He could regulate his leaps and monitor his speed. In short, he was learning how to master the boots rather than be mastered by them.

The elevator car arrived. The doors opened and a crowd of children, chattering happily, stepped out as Hamish X and his newfound admirers stepped in. Again, he was

subjected to stares of fascination. He moved to the back of the car and tried to concentrate on the scenery outside.

His thoughts returned to the boots. Since the King had revived him, there had been another development. The voice that had spoken to him was silent. He spent the dark hours of the night straining to hear the beautiful woman's voice, yearning for its soothing tone. The voice had always spoken when he was in need. He had identified it with his mother. Now that he knew the boots were all part of some plan of the ODA's, he understood that the voice was merely part of that plan and so couldn't be anything good. The book that he had also cherished as a link to his mother was just a mass of codes and hidden programming language.

He knew that the voice was nothing but a construct. He still missed it, though. Now he felt so alone in the world. Now that he knew there was no mother for him, he wished he still had that hope. At least he wouldn't feel so lonely and adrift. Parveen had found Noor. Mimi had the Guards. He had nothing. Again, a little bubble of resentment towards King Liam rose to the top of his mind.

The car arrived at the Workshop Cavern. He stepped out into the courtyard with a couple of other children. Immediately a barrage of shouts and cheers assaulted his ears. A crowd was gathered in front of the doors to the Guards' barracks. Hamish X couldn't see what was happening, but he heard sharp cracks as if someone was banging sticks together. Then there was a meaty *thwack!* and someone yelped in pain. Cheers went up again.

"MI-MI! MI-MI! MI-MI!" the children chanted.

"Uh-oh," Hamish X chuckled and walked towards the crowd.

Chapter 14

Hamish X joined the spectators, pushing his way through the children until he got to the front. At the centre of the throng, a large stone circle held only two people. Mimi stood gripping a wooden stick about a metre long. Aidan held a similar weapon and stood across the ring from her. Mimi was flushed in the face, her eyes alight and her teeth bared in a fierce grin.

"Best four outta seven? How 'bout it, Aidan?" Mimi brandished her stick over her head.

Aidan's blond hair was plastered down over his forehead. He was breathing hard and rubbing his right buttock. His face was grim.

Mimi looked fresh by comparison. She wore a T-shirt and black cotton trousers. She hopped easily from foot to foot.

"Beginner's luck," Aidan huffed.

"I'm shore I'll lose this time," Mimi smiled sweetly. "Do ya feel lucky?"

Children hooted with laughter, catcalling Aidan and whistling.

"She's good."

Hamish X turned to find Cara standing beside him. She was dressed in her everyday black uniform. Her arms were crossed and her hip cocked as she watched her brother glare at Mimi across the empty ring.

"Hello, Cara," Hamish X said. He felt a little uncomfortable with the pretty girl. She was slightly taller than him and it made him feel a little self-conscious. Her perfectly arranged hair hung framing her face as she watched the match. She turned and caught him studying her. Hamish X flushed and shifted uneasily from foot to foot. She merely looked at him with her serious brown eyes.

She spoke again, her tone casual and easy. "Stick fighting isn't as easy as it looks," she said. "To the layman, it's a matter of merely hitting someone with a stick. But in the hands of a master, a simple stick can become an instrument of beauty and a lethal weapon. Mimi and I don't get along too well, but I can appreciate her natural ability. I've never seen anyone beat Aidan more than once."

"All right," Aidan said through gritted teeth. "Let's do this."

He launched himself across the ring, bringing down his stick. Mimi parried the blow easily and laughed as he counterattacked with a side swing. She leaned away from the swing's arc, dancing out of reach. Aidan grimly pursued her.

"How did you end up here, Cara?"

"You really want to know?" Hamish X nodded. The girl looked at him, her brown eyes searching his golden ones. She seemed to make a decision. Shrugging a shoulder, she turned to watch the fight as she spoke. "My parents owned a big multinational gourmet dog food company. They made what they claimed was the most delicious dog food in the world. Fifteen different varieties, from Chicken Cordon Bleu to Veal Scallopini, all created by the best chefs on the planet. How a dog would tell the difference I'll never know. They hardly care what they eat—I mean, these are animals that sniff each other's bottoms." Hamish X laughed at that and she shook her head. "Anyway, they made a packet of money. We had a huge house with a swimming pool, fancy cars, a jet … everything we ever wanted. Yes, Aidan!" This in response to an excellent attack by Aidan that Mimi turned aside with some difficulty. Cara scowled and continued her story. "There was an accident. My mother and father's jet went down and they were never found."

"I'm sorry."

Cara shrugged. "I was really young, Aidan was barely walking. I can't really remember them." Her eyes were distant for a moment, then she continued. "We were supposed to inherit everything but we were too young to take possession of the estate. So the bank appointed a guardian." She sneered. "My dear Uncle Bertie.

"At first he was nice to us, but I could tell there was something wrong. His smiles and his jokes were all a little too jolly. He tried really hard to make us like him. Bit by bit, he began to change. He started spending: fancy clothes, different girlfriends every day of the week, a yacht and private jet. I tried to tell people but no one paid any attention to me. I was just a kid.

"In less than a year our inheritance was all but gone. He started to go into debt. He got phone calls from bill collectors and the banks. Soon he had no way to pay the bills. He blamed us for everything, saying that if it wasn't for us he'd be okay; that we didn't do anything but eat and take up space. He said he'd be better off without us."

Aidan rained blows down on Mimi, backing her away, forcing her to defend herself. She was panting now, her wiry hair dripping sweat.

"One day, Uncle Bertie called us into the den. He was talking to two people, a man and a woman all dressed in grey."

"Grey Agents."

"Yes. Bertie sold us to them. They took us away and we were sent to work at a seaweed farm in Russia on the freezing coast of the Baltic Sea. To Uncle Bertie's credit, he looked sad when we were led to the helicopter. As we lifted off, he came running out, shouting and waving, tears in his eyes. I like to think he'd changed his mind, but it was too late by then."

Hamish X didn't know what to say. It was such a terrible story. Sometimes he felt he'd missed out by not remembering his mother and his family. When he heard stories like Cara's, though, he figured it was a mercy to have no memory of his mother beyond a fleeting impression.

"Anyway," Cara said brightly, "I managed to steal a raft and float us to Finland, where we were contacted by the King's agents and brought here."

In the ring, Mimi ducked a wild swing by Aidan and then stepped up close to him while he was vulnerable and drove her stick into his back. Aidan fell on his face and Mimi pinned him to the ground. He struggled, but Mimi held him fast.

"Who's the best?" Mimi crowed.

"Let me up," Aidan growled.

"Who's the best?"

Aidan grimly tried to rise. Mimi refused to let him get up. "Just say it: Mimi is the best." The children were laughing and shouting. "*Mimi! Mimi! Mimi!*" The chant was taken up quickly and soon everyone was clapping.

Hamish X saw that Aidan was humiliated and he decided it was time to put a stop to it. He was about to open his mouth when Cara's voice cut through the din. "Let him up." The children stopped chanting. The girl strode into the ring, her face like thunder, and stood a few metres from Mimi. Mimi's eyes narrowed.

"Ya have ta fight yer brother's battles?"

"Let him up." Cara's voice was measured and strong. "You won. A bad winner is just as nasty as a bad loser. Let him up." The crowd was completely quiet now.

Mimi looked at Cara. At last, she lifted the stick from Aidan's back. She reached down and took his hand, pulling the boy to his feet. "I'm sorry. I git a little carried away."

Aidan shook his head and laughed. "You're amazing. You should be leading the training sessions."

"Uh-uh. I ain't no teacher. I ain't got the patience."

Cara picked up Aidan's stick casually. Then with blinding speed, she drove it between Mimi's feet and twisted. Mimi fell hard on her bottom. Everyone in the crowd crowed and hooted. Cara handed the stick to Aidan.

"Never let your guard down," Cara said.

"You sneaky …" Mimi leapt to her feet, her stick at the ready. Cara bunched her fists. Hamish X stepped into her path, grabbing the stick.

"Mimi, she's right. You let your guard down." Mimi tugged at the stick but Hamish X held it fast. The two girls glared at each other.

Aidan laid a hand on Mimi's shoulder. "Mimi, I think we've done enough demonstration for today. I admire your tenacity. You managed to beat me in judo and in stick fighting. That's never happened before." He grabbed her wrist and held her hand in the air. "Three cheers for Mimi Jones! Undisputed Champion of Hand-to-Hand Combat in All of Hollow Mountain!"

The crowd erupted. "Hip! Hip! Hooray! Hip! Hip! Hooray! Hip! Hip! Hooray!"

Mimi's shoulders dropped. She released the stick, letting Hamish X take it from her hands. Looking around at the cheering children, she allowed herself to smile. She sketched a comical bow to her admirers.

Aidan waved his hands. "All right. That's all. You have things to do, all of you. The show's over."

Chapter 15

The children groaned but started to disperse, some heading to the workshops and others for the elevator and the stairs. Soon, Mimi and Hamish X were alone with Cara and Aidan. Aidan rubbed his buttock. "Ow. That really stings. You sure pack a wallop, Mimi."

"I gotta learn to pull those a little bit. I get a little riled up."

Cara rolled her eyes. In a fair imitation of Mimi's Texan accent, she said, "Silly ol' me. I don't know ma own strength."

Mimi tensed. Aidan interceded. "Cara, I think you've done enough. Let's go get something to eat." Cara flipped her hair in Mimi's direction and the brother and sister headed off towards the barracks across the courtyard.

"Ooo. She burns ma biscuits."

"She sure knows how to push your buttons."

"What did I ever do ta her?"

"Nothing, Mimi. She's had a hard time and all she has is Aidan. She's very protective of him."

"I didn't hit 'im that hard."

Hamish X laughed, remembering his first day in the cheese factory in Windcity. "No, you've hit me harder."

Mimi sat down on the flagstones and pulled a knapsack into her lap. "I gotta say, I love the fightin' classes. I'm thinkin' I'd like to be a Guard, mebbe, if we end up stayin' here." She pulled her father's ball glove out of the knapsack, the smell of seasoned leather filling the air. She extracted a baseball from the pack and began whacking the ball into the pocket of the glove. "Mebbe I could even teach people how ta play ball. Start a team."

Hamish X scuffed at the floor with one of his black boots. "It's nice to see you're fitting in here. I wish I could say the same."

Mimi looked at Hamish X and frowned. He didn't seem to be the same boy who had led them on their trek to defeat Cheesebeard and his Cheese Pirates of Snow Monkey Island. That boy was confident and happy. He never got down even in the face of incredible odds. But ever since he'd undergone the process in the King of Switzerland's medical laboratory, he lacked the spark he once had. He hardly spoke to anyone and he kept to himself. Guiltily, Mimi realized that she hadn't been spending much time with him, absorbed as she was with the training sessions in the Guard barracks. Parveen had been preoccupied as well with his newly recovered sister. And Mr. Kipling and Mrs. Francis were spending all their time getting ready for the wedding. Anyone who had been his close friend was now too busy to spend time with Hamish X.

Mimi stuffed the ball and glove back into her pack. She slung the bag over her shoulder and picked up her fighting stick. She put an arm around Hamish X's shoulders. "Hamish X, I'm sorry I ain't been such a good friend. I know ya got a lot to sort out and we ain't really talked much."

"No, Mimi." Hamish X shook his head. "You have to live your life. I know you've got a lot to do and I want you to enjoy your new life here." Hamish X looked into her face and his golden eyes were filled with sadness. "I thought it would help me to remember, but it only makes things worse. I don't know where I fit in any more. I want to know where I come from and what I'm supposed to do."

"Have you talked to the King about it?"

"That's just it. Ever since I woke up he's been too busy to see me. Every time I try to go and see him, George tells me he isn't available or to come back later. I don't understand. I thought he'd tell me everything. It's maddening."

As they walked towards the barracks where the showers were, Mimi tried to cheer him up.

"I think you oughtta cut the King some slack. He's got a lot on his mind."

"I'm sure he does," Hamish X agreed. He tapped his own forehead sharply. "So do I. I have a mind that I don't know what to do with. You, the King, Parveen, everybody here knows who they are, at least. I need some help. I'm just feeling so … lost."

Mimi stopped outside the barracks. Guards were walking in and out of the large metal doors. She grabbed Hamish X by the shoulders and looked into the face of her friend. "You ain't lost. We're right here with ya and we know who ya are even if you don't."

"Oh yeah? Who am I?"

"You're my friend, Hamish X. Ain't nuthin' gonna change that. Not the ODA or the King of Switzerland. Nobody." She hugged him to her.

Hamish X laughed and squirmed out of her grip. "Ew. You really need a shower."

Mimi raised her stick in a mock threat. Hamish X danced away. "See you at the wedding." He set off across the courtyard in the direction of the technical laboratories. Mimi lowered the stick and watched him until he turned the corner, a line of worry creasing the bridge of her nose. "I gotta spend some more time with 'im. After the weddin'."

She pushed open the metal door and went in, whistling to herself and thinking about what she might call a baseball team.

Chapter 16

Hamish X was in a less buoyant mood. He crossed the courtyard, skirting King Stephen's Stair[49] and heading for a pair of large white doors. Written across the doors in red lettering was "Technical Department." Mimi called the place "the gadget factory." It was where all the clever inventions the King and his people used in their struggle against the ODA were manufactured. Most of the children here were older. They were chosen for their skill with machines and electronics, using special aptitude tests devised and refined by the Kings and Queens of Switzerland down through the years.

As Hamish X walked through the doors the temperature dropped by a few degrees. He'd come here often for tests since that first night when the technical team had revived him. They wanted to make sure that his condition remained stable and that he felt no ill effects. He couldn't exactly say this was his favourite place in the Hollow Mountain. He had a feeling that in his previous life, the life he couldn't remember, he hadn't liked going to the doctor.

---

[49] King Stephen, thirty-third King of Switzerland, was a fitness fanatic. Much to the chagrin of his subjects, he closed the elevator and replaced it with the staircase that wound up around the elevator shaft from the bottom to the top of the Hollow Mountain. Children were forced to run up and down the stairs as a form of exercise instead of being lazy and using the easier elevator. As soon as King Stephen left the Hollow Mountain at the age of sixteen, the elevator was immediately reopened by his successor, Gerta, the Chubby, Twenty-Fourth Queen of Switzerland.

Pushing that thought aside, he walked along the central corridor. Hallways branched off every few metres, curving away out of sight. He walked past open doors of workshops where children laboured over lathes and worktables, past knots of children conferring over blueprints tacked to walls, past a lecture hall where a child held forth to a small group of listeners about the electrical conductivity of aluminum. At last he came to the nondescript door that was the entrance to the laboratory Parveen had been assigned to work in. A red light blinked above the doorframe. Hamish X listened at the door for a moment before he opened it and went inside.

The entire room was in darkness. Hamish X could barely see his hand in front of his face. After a few seconds there was a click and a single light came on, shedding a cone of illumination in the centre of the room. Standing in the shaft of white light was a figure that struck dread into Hamish X. A man in a grey overcoat and fedora hat turned towards him. The black goggles glittered in the harsh light. A Grey Agent! How did a Grey Agent get into the Hollow Mountain?

The agent cocked his head to one side. "Hamish X? What are you doing here?"

The voice was tinny and metallic, but something about the inflection was familiar. Hamish X crouched. Calling on his boots, he leapt at the agent, propelling himself across the room in one powerful lunge. Before he reached him he slammed into an invisible barrier, falling backwards with a crash.

The lights went on. He sat up, shaking his head. The lab was cluttered with many small worktables and half-assembled machines. Parveen and Noor stood behind a console covered with knobs and buttons, looking wide-eyed at Hamish X. Parveen was wearing a strange suit over his normal overalls: it was like a web of wires with white balls at regular intervals over all his limbs and head.

"Didn't you see the red light?" Parveen demanded. "You know you aren't supposed to enter when the light is on."

Hamish X saw that he had slammed into a transparent plastic booth enclosing the Grey Agent. The agent was still looking at him but making no other threatening movement.

Noor came rushing over. "Are you all right?" She lifted his chin and looked him in the eyes. "Who am I?"

He looked up into the girl's face. He could see a clear resemblance to Parveen in the round shape of the dark eyes and the slightly pointed chin. She kept her hair in a glossy black ponytail bound with an elastic band. Her face was full of concern. "You're Noor, Parveen's sister," Hamish X mumbled. He shook his head again. "I'm fine. What is *he* doing here?" He cocked a thumb at the Grey Agent in the booth.

"It is a remotely controlled robot," said Parveen. "It is linked to my body and mimics my movements through this motion capture suit." He flicked one of the white balls with a small brown finger. Then he pushed his glasses up onto the bridge of his nose. The Grey Agent pushed a pair of imaginary glasses up onto the bridge of his nose. "I can also direct him using that remote control." He pointed to a small black object on the table. "We built him to test out some new weapons systems. I've been trying to improve my microwave oven bomb. A smaller, more refined version of the EMP bomb that knocked out Candy and Sweet in Windcity."

Noor held up a small object in her palm. The thing was

spherical and covered in downy orange fur. "We were about to try it. Want to watch?"

"Will it knock me out too, like the EMP did back in Windcity? I'd rather not go through that again if I can help it."

"That's part of the refinement," Parveen said. "We've made the pulse effect more localized and invented a more accurate delivery system. You'll be quite safe."

"We think," Noor added. The tone of her voice didn't exactly fill Hamish X with confidence, but he shrugged and walked over to Parveen at the console.

Noor joined them and tapped a button. The lights dimmed again. The Grey Agent stood patiently in the booth. Parveen waved and the Grey Agent waved back at them. Hamish X found the jaunty gesture somewhat disturbing in the sinister creature.

"All right," Parveen said. "We're set. Deliver the weapon."

Noor lowered the furry sphere to the floor. It lay there inert for a second, then quite suddenly it sprouted stubby pink feet and a head with pink ears and black beady eyes.

"A *hamster*?" Hamish X snorted. "What's it supposed to do? Cuddle the agent to death?"

Parveen ignored his tone. "Watch and learn."

The hamster raised a pink quivering nose into the air, questing from side to side until it focused on the Grey Agent in the booth. Like a shot it beelined across the floor, passing into the booth through a small opening. Parveen started stomping his feet and the Grey Agent did the same, trying to stamp on the scurrying rodent but failing to strike it. The hamster leapt in the air and landed on the agent's trouser leg, crawling up the grey fabric and under the grey coat. Parveen started slapping himself and the

Grey Agent imitated him. The hamster managed to avoid being crushed and came up out of the collar of the coat. Climbing the agent's neck, it reached the right temple of the Grey Agent robot and stopped. There was a dull pop and a flash as the hamster exploded. The robot went rigid and then fell in a heap, motionless on the floor of the booth.

Hamish X felt a slight wave of nausea. He reached out and braced himself against the edge of the worktable. The nausea passed quickly. Noor touched his shoulder. "Are you all right?"

Hamish X nodded. Parveen grasped Noor's hand excitedly. "See? It works."

Noor nodded. "By changing the wavelength of the pulse we were able to adjust it to make it less harmful to you and more harmful to the Grey Agents."

"Now we have a new weapon. The first we've developed together." Parveen's chest puffed with pride. "I did the circuitry but Noor was able to alter the pulse generator and make it more compact. She's very clever."

Hamish X smiled and gripped his shoulder. "She would have to be. She's your sister."

Parveen blushed. Noor kissed her brother's cheek. "No need for that!" Parveen wiped his cheek with his hand. Noor laughed and pinched his other cheek. "You're such a little old man."

Hamish X watched as she teased him and felt a swell of joy. How wonderful for Parveen not to be alone in the world any more. Now the little boy had someone to belong with. Hamish X had no such luck. He sensed a wave of sadness threatening to sweep over him and so changed the subject. "Hey, are you all ready for the wedding?"

"Yes," Parveen nodded. "Of course. We have made a wonderful gift for Mrs. Francis and Mr. Kipling. It's—"

Noor clamped a hand over Parveen's mouth. "It's a surprise is what it is, little brother."

Hamish X laughed. He headed for the door, calling over his shoulder, "See you in the park then. I'll take the red light more seriously next time."

He stepped through the door and left them bent over, heads together, examining the inert robot.

Chapter 17

Hamish X headed across the courtyard to the elevator. There was a crowd of children waiting for the next car. He didn't feel like being the centre of attention any more today. He decided to take the stairs.

His quarters were three levels above. For a normal child without the benefit of Hamish X's augmented footwear that would be a lot of stairs. Hamish X was bitterly aware that he was not a normal child. He wasn't really a child at all. He concentrated on his boots, feeling them respond with a trickle of power. He began to run.

He took the stairs three at a time and he still wasn't going all out. He probably could have leapt from level to level if he really wished to, but he didn't want to attract any more notice. He flashed by other children on the stairs, their astonished faces blurring by as he jumped over or sped around them. As he fell into the rhythm of the climb he felt the familiar joy that came from using the boots. The power surged through his legs, lifting him up, up, up. The wind whistling past his ears, the stunned faces of the children he passed, the pounding of the soles on the stone all served to lift his spirits.

For the first time in a long time, Hamish X laughed. He laughed because it had suddenly dawned on him that he was free. The ODA could not reach him. He laughed because he was young and powerful and alive. He laughed because he realized that even though he might never find his mother and never be a normal child like everyone else, he was alive—and when you are alive, all things are possible.

After only a minute he reached his goal, the residential level. He felt almost disappointed that the trip was over. "It doesn't have to be," he hooted to himself and turned back down the stairs. He ran all the way to the bottom and back again, his boots leaving a trail of blue fire. He arrived at the residential level again, having hardly broken a sweat. He was tempted to run back down to the bottom and up once more, just for fun, but he stopped himself. The wedding would be starting soon and he had to get ready. He let the power flow away, feeling the sense of loss he always felt at the end of a boot-driven episode. He allowed himself to feel a little sad at the absence of the Voice before heading to his quarters.

When he pushed open the door and entered the kitchen, the George raccoon was standing in the middle of the floor, waiting for him.

"Hamish X," George said, "the King wishes to see you."

His happiness drained away. "Now? I've been waiting to see him for weeks. Tell him I'm getting ready for the wedding and I'll see him afterwards."

"He has attached an urgent tag to this communication. That means immediately."

Hamish X snorted. "Weeks of ignoring me and now it's 'urgent.'"

"No need to be peevish." The George raccoon sounded wounded.

"Don't pretend I hurt your feelings. You're a computer."

"Now, that *did* hurt my feelings." The creature stuck its nose in the air and waddled off.

Hamish X shrugged. He went into his bedroom. He decided to get dressed for the wedding and then go to see the King. *Let him wait for a while. See how he likes it.*

The George raccoon had put out his wedding suit. The tailors had decided to give him something in keeping with his name. On the bed was a formal Highland Scottish outfit. There was a beautiful kilt in red tartan shot through with yellow and green. A white shirt with a ruffled front lay beside the kilt. Draped over the back of a chair at the foot of the bed was a black velvet jacket. The jacket was edged at the waist and adorned with polished, diamond-shaped silver buttons.

At first Hamish X had turned up his nose at the outfit, but when he'd tried it on he grudgingly changed his mind. The kilt was the ideal garment for wearing with the strange boots. When he wore trousers he was forced to slit the pant legs and install zippers to facilitate the bulky footwear. The kilt was easy to put on over the boots, and as an added bonus, movement was easy, not to mention the fact that a kilt was naturally ventilated.

Hamish X donned his wedding outfit and appraised himself in the mirror. He looked himself up and down and smiled. Somehow, he felt at home in this outfit, as if he had worn it before. Maybe, he thought, I *have* worn a kilt before. Hamish is a Scottish name … Maybe that's where I came from originally. Maybe my family is still there. Maybe the seashore from my memories is there and my mother too …

He looked at the clock and realized he'd spent too long getting dressed. He grabbed the pocketknife from his dresser and tucked it into the top of his boot. Prepared, he dashed out of the room on his way to the Royal Terrace.

He got into the elevator, which was mercifully empty for once. As the doors closed he said, "Take me to the Royal Terrace, George."

"Right away, Hamish X." The doors closed and the elevator rose sharply. It passed through the ceiling of the residential level and stopped at the Royal Level.

Hamish X was expecting to be taken to the King's study, but the George raccoon that greeted him led him down a corridor into a brightly lit room lined with grey metal lockers. One stood open. In it hung some gym shorts and a T-shirt.

"Put them on, please, and then go through that door," the George raccoon instructed. "The King is waiting for you."

The creature waddled out through the swinging door he had indicated.

Hamish X grumbled at having to take off his good suit and kilt, but he did as he was told. He stepped through the door and found himself in a brightly lit gymnasium. The hardwood floor gleamed golden in the warm light. At either end of the rectangular room was a basketball hoop and backboard.

"What are we doing here, George?" Hamish X looked about, bewildered.

"The King instructed me to bring you here. So I have." The raccoon stepped back against the wall and went into sleep mode.

On the far side of the gymnasium a door opened. Into the room stepped a bizarre figure. It was shaped like a human being, with arms and legs, feet and hands, and a bulbous head, but its silver metallic skin gleamed in the light. Though it looked very heavy, it strode across the wooden floor with incredible grace and left no mark on the polished surface. Where its face should have been there was instead a mirrored visor that reflected the entire room in a stretched parody of itself. The hands and feet were sheathed in a black, rubbery coating. In its right hand it held a brown sphere about the size of a small pumpkin.

Hamish X crouched, prepared to defend himself. "Who are you? What do you want?"

A strange sound emanated from the thing. It reached up with its left hand and jabbed a small button on the side of its head. The visor whisked open to reveal the pale, smiling face of King Liam. "It's me, of course! My, you look a little tense. Haven't you ever seen a basketball before?"

Chapter 18

The King winked and spun the basketball, for indeed that was what the brown sphere was, holding it on the tip of one rubber-coated finger and watching it revolve like a leathery planet.[50] He tossed the ball into the air, caught it, and then launched it towards the basket at the far end of the gym. The ball sailed unerringly in a perfect arc. It fell into the hoop with a whiffing sound as it passed through the twine netting.

"Amazing," Hamish X said, reaching out to touch the polished silver surface of the suit.

"Yes!" The King laughed, pumping his fist. "Three points. Oh, you mean the suit. Nice, isn't it?' He spun slowly, allowing Hamish X to see the suit in its entirety. "George and I built it a little while ago. I am not well, as you know. The disease is slowly eroding my physical strength and coordination. I have always been weaker than all the other children. It's all because I was ..." His face darkened, as if he remembered something bad. "Regardless, it has forced me to develop in other ways ..." He tapped the side of the helmet with a rubber finger. "But I always wanted to know what it would be like to run

---

50 The thought of a leathery planet is very odd, but a group of cattle farmers from Wyoming became obsessed with the idea of covering Venus in a vast leather coat in an attempt to promote the wearing of leather. They ran into a few difficulties: inability to find a cow large enough to provide sufficient leather for a coat that size, NASA's refusal to lend them a spacecraft, and opposition from animal rights activists.

and jump and play like a normal child. So …" He held out his arms and sprang into the air, did a back flip, and landed lightly on his feet.

Hamish X's mouth fell open in awe. "That's incredible."

"Now that you've come along, I finally have a worthy opponent. Shall we play a little one-on-one? To twenty? You and your boots versus me and my suit."

Hamish X smiled and shrugged. "I'll try to take it easy on you."

"Oh, please don't."

King Liam smiled behind the visor and bounded out to the centre of the court. Hamish X took up position opposite. A George raccoon took the ball in its palms and, checking that the opponents were ready, threw it straight up into the air. Hamish X and the King sprang up, striving for the ball. Hamish X brushed it with his fingers but the King clamped his hands onto it and hauled it down.

Hamish X spread his arms wide to block the King's path but Liam laughed and jumped right over him, bounding once, twice, and then slamming the ball through the hoop.

"Two for me!" The King clapped his hands together and trotted back to his own side of centre.

Hamish X gaped in amazement. No one had ever beaten him so handily in a physical contest. He went and picked up the ball. The King crouched and waited.

"I'll try to take it easy on *you*," Liam said sweetly.

Hamish X scowled. Gritting his teeth, he called up the power of his boots. He felt a surge of energy. As he bounced the ball he blurred straight at the King, stopping and spinning around him. Before Liam could even move, Hamish X had darted straight in at the opposite basket and launched himself into the air, spinning like a helicopter and delicately rolling the ball off his fingers and into the basket. He landed in a crouch and smiled at his opponent.

King Liam smiled back. "This is going to be fun."

For the next hour they played, the score crawling slowly upward. The speed of the game was incredible, and had anyone been there to see, they would have called it the greatest one-one-one battle in the history of basketball. Unfortunately, the only spectator was George the raccoon. Being an artificial intelligence, he wasn't a huge fan of sport and so remained unmoved by all the amazing dribbling, slamming, and blocking.

At first the two players traded baskets back and forth until the score stood at twelve–ten for the King. Hamish X had the speed and agility, but the King's suit gave him superior strength and stamina. As a result, they were evenly matched. The game settled into a defensive battle. They ground each other down basket by basket.

They laughed and shouted at each other, enjoying the game and each other's company. For a while, they weren't Hamish X, the strange boy with the odd boots, lost and lonely in the world, and King Liam, weighed down with responsibility, sickly, careworn, and sad. They were just two boys playing a game.

Now they were deadlocked at eighteen apiece and neither could get the final basket. Hamish X sent a long skyhook arcing for the hoop but the King leapt up and slapped it away at the last possible second. He caught the ball in his hands and grinned at Hamish X through the faceplate of his helmet. Sweat dripped from his nose. His red hair was plastered to his forehead.

"Are you getting tired, Hamish X? Shall we call it a draw?"

Hamish X bent over with his hands on his knees. He was breathing heavily and his body was covered in sweat. He hated to admit it, but he'd never felt so hard-pressed to beat any opponent. He'd been pushed to his limits, but he also felt so alive and happy, all things but the game forgotten. "I think we should see who wins. Unless you need to rest."

The King grinned again. "Not today!"

Liam pounded down the court, bouncing the ball as he came. Hamish X stood, watching him approach. He waited until the King was about to run him over then reached out and slapped the ball out of his hands, sending it bouncing towards the King's basket. Laughing, Hamish X immediately sped after the ball.

He grabbed the ball and dribbled it twice. He heard the King's footsteps thudding behind him. Revelling in his speed and strength, he called up a burst of power from his boots and leapt for the basket, holding the ball over his head. He felt pure exhilaration as he hammered it into the metal hoop with a tremendous force that drove the ball down to the ground and shattered the floorboards under the basket. Landing easily, he roared his triumph. He turned, arms raised, to celebrate his victory.

The King was lying face down on the floor. His limbs thrashed weakly. Hamish X rushed to his side and turned him over. Liam's face in the frame of his helmet was flushed and sweaty.

"Are you all right?" Hamish X asked, levering the prone boy into a seated position.

"Oh, I'm fine," he said weakly. "Just ran out of battery power, that's all. This thing becomes a dead weight if it has no power."

The George raccoon scurried over and pushed a button on the side of the suit. With a hiss, the entire device cracked open down the front, unfolding like a flower. The King, his green tunic and trousers soaked to the skin, pushed himself up out of the suit and took a deep breath. Hamish X grasped him by the arm and supported him as they walked carefully to a bench at the side of the gymnasium. Liam eased himself down and Hamish X sat beside him.

"So, you won the game. Well done."

"It was hardly fair. I mean … you're …"

"Sickly? Feeble? Oh, don't look so uncomfortable. I'm used to it," the King laughed. "Just don't feel sorry for me. It's the worst feeling when you see that look in someone's eyes. 'Poor little Liam.' That makes me feel truly sick."

"Sorry," Hamish X said. "I don't mean … Did you really bring me up here just to play a game of basketball?"

"I understand your impatience, Hamish X. I just want you to answer me one question." The King picked up a chilled bottle of water, popped the cap, and drank a long swallow while Hamish X waited in frustration. Finally, Liam lowered the bottle and wiped his mouth. "Nothing tastes sweeter than water. Now, my question: Did you enjoy our game?"

Hamish X snorted. "What's that got to do with anything?"

"It has everything to do with everything. Did you enjoy it?"

"Yes. It was fun."

"Good. You looked like you were having a very good time out there. I want you to realize how wonderful that is. These boots of yours have been a curse to you. They've ruled your life in a way, and while you were wearing them you were a pawn in whatever plan the ODA might have for you. But now you are free. You can do anything you want. And you still have these amazing boots. I envy you."

Hamish X sat for a moment thinking about what the King had said. He realized it was true. He looked down at the boots. With a flicker of a thought, he caused them to burn bright blue. With another flicker of a thought, he extinguished them again. He scanned his newly recovered memories, looking back on all the amazing things the boots had done. Now he truly controlled them. He looked at the King and smiled. "It *is* kind of cool, isn't it?"

"Cool. Yes, very cool. You are free to come and go as you please. The Grey Agents can't track you any more. Remember the bug you coughed up in that crazy dream?" Hamish X nodded. "That was our software turning off the tracking device."

"That dream …"

"It wasn't a dream, really. It was a virtual world created by a program we shunted into your brain. Fun, wasn't it? I was able to walk and run, released from this afflicted body." He looked wistfully at the inert suit of armour. "I would give anything to be free of this slow, wasting sickness. I devise any number of ways to circumvent it, the armour being only the latest. Alas, it's all a waste of time. It will destroy me in the not so distant future."

The King looked Hamish X in the eye, suddenly serious. "I have to admit something to you, Hamish X. I didn't bring you here just to set you free and thwart the ODA. I confess that I was hoping I might glean something in the analysis of your amazing physiology that would give me a clue as to how to save myself from the disease. After all, it was the ODA who made me this way."

Hamish X was aghast. "What are you talking about?"

Liam held up a shaking hand. "I was once a prisoner of the ODA. They did experiments on me, trying to alter the functions of my body, my muscles and nervous system. I was a guinea pig in the project that eventually produced you."

"You were their prisoner?"

"Yes. Fortunately, I was rescued in a raid by King Juan's Guards. He was my predecessor. I was rescued and brought here. My body was damaged beyond repair. As a result, I was forced to develop my mind. When Juan left, he made me King." Liam smiled. "I've enjoyed my reign. I've tried to do good, but I must admit, I'd hoped we could find out some way of fixing the damage wrought by the ODA through careful study of you. Selfish, wasn't it?"

"That's not selfish," Hamish X said. "It's human."

King Liam smiled. "The ODA have altered you in many ways, but they neglected to tamper with the one thing that will bring them the most grief: you have a kind heart, Hamish X."

The King clapped his hands. The George raccoon scurried over with a manila envelope. It handed the envelope to Liam.

"Thank you, George," the King said, holding the envelope against his chest. He turned back to Hamish X. "I haven't spoken to you sooner for two reasons. I wanted you to have some time to adjust to the boots and grow to understand that you are free. The second reason is that I have been sending my agents out searching for information on you. I wanted to help you figure out who you really are. I have compiled everything we could find that is pertinent to your identity. Here it is."

He handed over the envelope. Hamish X took it and tore open the top with greedy fingers. He tipped the envelope over and his heart sank when all that came out was a single black and white photograph, a scrap of paper, and a small key.

Hamish X couldn't help but feel a little disappointed. An exhaustive search and this was the result? He held up the picture. Staring back at him was the face of the Professor, bringing back the terrible memories of the Grey Agents and the procedure that had grafted his boots onto him. The eyes were fearful and the man seemed older, his face drawn and haggard. He was photographed from a distance and was obviously unaware of being observed. In his hand he carried a small suitcase and he was stepping down from a small plane onto the tarmac of an airport. The photographer had caught him in the act of looking over his shoulder. The eyes were watery and wide behind thick bifocals.

"It's the man from my memories! He was there in the operating room when the Grey Agents put the boots on me."

"His name is Professor Magnus Ballantyne-Stewart."

Hamish X's eyes went wide. "The man who wrote my book!"

"Exactly. He was a brilliant genetic engineer and neurologist before he was contracted by the Grey Agents. Supposedly he died in a car crash, but we believe he staged his death to escape the ODA. He is now in Central Africa under an assumed name, providing medical care for remote villages."

"I have to find him. He might know something about who I am."

"I agree."

Hamish X fell silent. He held up his hand, turning it back and forth, examining it.

"What's the matter?" King Liam asked.

"It's funny. I don't know how to feel about all this. At first, the only question I had was 'Who am I?' Now, it's 'What am I?' Am I even human?"

"Hamish X, have you ever heard the story of Pinocchio?"

"No."

"Pinocchio is a wooden boy who wants to be a real boy. He goes into the world and has many adventures, but in the end he returns home and discovers that it's love that has transformed him into a real child. You are going through something similar, I think, but in reverse. You thought you were a real boy but you've discovered that you are not. I think the lesson you have to learn is that it isn't the parts and pieces, the muscle and tissue, the blood and bone that makes you human. No," the King smiled. "It's what's in the heart that makes us real people. And you, my friend, are as real as can be."

They sat in silence for a minute or two. At last, Hamish X held up the slip of paper. There was a four-digit number written on it. "What's this?"

"It is the number for a locker in the Athens train station. The key opens the locker. There you will find some money and the documentation you need to make your way to Central Africa and seek him out."

Hamish X looked up from the photograph into Liam's eyes. "I don't know how to thank you."

The King shook his head. "You don't need to thank me. Just find out what you need to know. Hopefully, with that knowledge, you can stand against the ODA and bring us one step closer to defeating them."

"When should I go?" Hamish X asked.

"I wouldn't waste any time. Whatever the ODA have planned it must be happening soon or they wouldn't be so desperate to get you back. I think you should go tonight after the wedding."

"But the others ... Mimi and Parveen ... If I tell them

I'm going, they'll want to come along. I won't be able to stop them." Hamish X frowned. "They seem so happy here. They've found a home. I wouldn't want them to give that up."

"Slip out secretly during the reception. George will show you the way. I'll explain everything to Mimi and Parveen once you are well gone. Now hurry! Shower and get ready for the wedding. You don't have much time."

Hamish X stood up and slid the picture carefully into the envelope. He began to walk away but stopped, turning slowly to face the King. "Why do you trust me not to tell anyone where you are? The ODA could capture me and find out the location of the Hollow Mountain."

"If they capture you, Hamish X," King Liam smiled sadly, "it won't matter any more."

Hamish X thought about that for a moment, then turned and went through the door to the locker room.

"Well, George," the King said softly to the raccoon standing quietly to one side. "I've done what I can. It's up to him now."

"Indeed, Majesty. Shall I ready your dress tunic?"

"Yes, please, George."

Mr. Candy and Mr. Sweet

Mr. Candy and Mr. Sweet stood in the rain, water dripping from their grey fedoras. They had been very busy in the two weeks since they lost Hamish X's trail in the Swiss Alps. After exhausting every search method they could muster, from satellite photography to deep sonar to orbital heat scans, they had concluded that the King of Switzerland's hidden refuge could not be located by any practical means at their disposal. They had decided to attack the problem in a different way. When confronted with a puzzle, they always looked for the weakest link in the chain. And to the ODA, it was the human element that invariably represented the weakest link in any chain.

The problem they faced was that the Kings and Queens of Switzerland commanded incredible loyalty from their subjects. No former resident of the Hollow Mountain would willingly betray the haven's secret location. All the orphans helped by the King earned his undying gratitude. They were trained and educated, and given a nest egg that could start them in their new life. A history was fabricated for them that covered their tracks and kept the King's involvement in their lives hidden.

Loyalty alone was a strong motivator, but the Kings and Queens of Switzerland had learned that loyalty was no match for a determined interrogator. Besides, even the most loyal person can let a stray fact slip by accident, and with disastrous consequences. To defend against these dangers, the Kings and Queens had engaged in extensive experiments involving memory suppression through hypnosis and subconscious sleep teaching. When orphans left the Hollow Mountain they underwent a week of deep hypnosis to suppress their memories of their time there and to implant their false history. Over the centuries the process had become quite effective. No one had ever betrayed the location of the Hollow Mountain.

The Grey Agents knew that the refuge was called the Hollow Mountain by listening to the whispering of the orphans they had traded in down through the years. They had never managed to glean its precise location. Mr. Candy and Mr. Sweet knew they had to find and break one of the King's former subjects, and so they had instructed Mother to search all the online databases it could hack into and find an orphan whose background might not add up. The resulting candidates were compiled into a long list and weeded out, until at last the Grey Agents focused on one person in particular. The search had eaten up quite a chunk of their precious time, but finally they were ready. They had their weak link.

That is why they stood on a cobbled[51] street in the Swiss city of Bern. The sky was heavy, with roiling black clouds

---

[51] Cobbled roads are made up of many small stones laid together to form a bumpy surface. Not to be confused with cobblers, who make and repair shoes, although one Moghul Emperor

spilling their contents on the city with a vengeance. The shop fronts were time-worn and respectable. They were in the oldest part of the city, near the cathedral, or Munster,[52] as the locals called it. Its steeple rose over the red-tiled roofs of the ancient buildings, silent and tall like a stone finger.

In the daytime the old quarter was host to an open-air market of crafts and farmers' wares, but at that late hour there was no one about. The empty stalls stood silent and dripping with rain and the arcades[53] were deserted. The pedestrians[54] had long since gone home

---

ruling in India in the twelfth century cobbled an entire road with cobblers. He was a rather nasty man, though, with a cruel sense of humour.

[52] Munster is a small town in Germany. It is also a kind of German cheese and the German word for cathedral. This all points to a time in the dim past when Germans worshipped cheese.

[53] Not pinball or video arcades. An arcade in this sense means "a covered passage with shops on both sides." Of course, the Swiss do love pinball and video games. The first pinball machine was invented in Zurich in 1762. It involved a silver ball being manipulated through the holes of a Swiss cheese using wooden paddles driven by metal springs. On hot days the cheese would melt, and so all pinball parlours were located in cool underground chambers. As a result, to this day all video and pinball games in Switzerland are played underground.

[54] *Pedestrian* is a word meaning "travelling by foot." The word originates from the city-state of Pedestria in ancient Greece. The Pedestrians worshipped a giant stone foot that they insisted was the foot of the god Zeus. They also dressed themselves as giant feet, wore shoes on their heads, fished out of boats shaped like feet, and travelled around in chariots shaped like giant sandals. The entire city was wiped out during a particularly nasty Athlete's Foot epidemic.

with their purchases, leaving the streets to less savoury types.

Mr. Sweet and Mr. Candy were definitely of the less savoury variety.[55]

The two Grey Agents stood dripping before a shop with the gilded sign REICHARD FULCHER'S CONFECTIONS AND CHOCOLATES. The large front window was covered with a metal shutter. The awning that usually shaded the window was wound back into the wall. The door was shut and a sign saying "closed" hung in plain view. Light seeped out from under the door, though, denoting that someone was inside.[56]

Mr. Sweet turned to watch the street as Mr. Candy glided forward. He took hold of the doorknob. His overlong fingers clamped tight on the cold brass. The agent squeezed and twisted hard. A squeak of tortured metal was muffled by the drumming rain. With a soft snap, the lock shattered. Mr. Candy nodded to Mr. Sweet and opened the door. They quickly ducked inside and closed the door behind them.

Inside, the shop was a wonderland of chocolate. Shelves covered every wall and every shelf was itself covered with

---

[55] The practice of calling bad persons "unsavoury" dates back to London of the Middle Ages, when convicted criminals were forced to walk around the streets dressed as not very delicious foods. Thieves dressed as Brussels sprouts, dishonest business-men dressed as cabbage sandwiches, and murderers were attired as very unappetizing meat pies.

[56] Wow, what a lot of footnotes on these two pages! Crazy!

some form of delicious chocolate confection. Wrapped in beautifully coloured foil were bars of chocolate in multiple flavours: butter cream, caramel-filled, nougat, cherry, peanut butter. A long glass counter ran across the entire shop. Inside, trays and trays of individual chocolates lay arranged in perfect rows. The person who had created these displays was obviously someone who loved chocolate, and who had raised the craft of chocolate-making to an art form.

The artistry was most brilliantly displayed in the window. When the shutters were raised people outside could see the most incredible sight: dioramas made entirely out of sweets. There was a chocolate castle built of tiny chocolate bricks with candy soldiers defending its ramparts against a vast dragon of spun sugar breathing clouds of candy floss. A chocolate waterfall fed the moat, a rippling stream of pure dark chocolate in which marzipan crocodiles floated, their candy eyes glaring. A village of gingerbread houses nestled at the foot of the chocolate hill below the castle, roofs constructed of hundreds and thousands of tiny chocolate tiles. Cotton-candy sheep grazed, herded by tiny chocolate shepherds. It was truly a candy masterpiece. Any human being with a soul would have been moved by the attention to detail and the palpable love poured into the display.

Of course, Mr. Candy and Mr. Sweet had no souls to speak of. Ironically, though they were named Sweet and Candy,

they were unmoved in the presence of their namesakes.[57]
They stalked through the darkened shop in their agile yet
awkward way, all pointy limbs and darting heads. They went
around the glass counter towards a doorway hung with a
red velvet curtain. At the curtain they stopped, cocking
their heads to the side to listen. A golden light emanated
beneath the curtain and they heard a man humming softly.
They nodded to each other and ducked inside.

They found themselves in a workshop.

A long table sat in a pool of bright golden light. Over
the table was a metal grid suspended by chains at its four
corners. Dangling from the grid and within easy reach
were tools of every description: drills, sanders, chisels,
hammers of various sizes, pliers, and electric saws with
strangely shaped blades.

The tools were amazing enough, but what was on the
table itself was truly awe-inspiring. Hundreds of chocolate
carvings in various states of completion stood silent in the
golden light.

The surface of the table was taken up by an oval structure composed of a series of chocolate arches. The detail

---

57 Irony is a difficult concept. Irony occurs when something
appears as if it should be one way but is actually the opposite.
Candy and Sweet don't like candy and sweets. Ironic. Other
examples: a bald man winning a year's supply of hair cream. Or
a man with no head winning a free hat. (Although, a man with
no head has bigger problems to worry about than having a free
hat and nowhere to put it. Life without a head is a challenge at
the best of times.)

was breathtaking. Each brick was individually cut and fit into place. Tiny flags of spun sugar stood on tiny candystick poles all around the top of the walls. Contained within the walls, terraced seats contained hundreds and hundreds of tiny candy Roman citizens, each in a tiny toga made of white frosting.

Sitting with his back to the door was an old man. His white hair was neatly trimmed around the shiny bald spot on the top of his head. His shoulders were hunched. He wore a white linen jacket of the sort that a doctor might wear.

The agents glided across the floor until they stood at the old man's elbows. So silent were they in their approach that the old man didn't even notice they were there until they grabbed him by the elbows and lifted him from his stool. The old man dropped the chariot he had been working on. It shattered on the floor, sending a spray of chocolate fragments shooting across the room.

"Ach! What do you want? The shop is closed."

Mr. Candy and Mr. Sweet held the man off the floor, his little legs kicking as he scrambled for purchase in the air. Finally, he ceased struggling and hung limp in the agents' grip. He was terrified of the strange grey-coated men with their dripping hats and cold black eyes.

"You are Reichard Fulcher?" Mr. Sweet said.

The old man blinked, his eyes watery behind thick spectacles. Attached to one lens was a magnifying device, called an ocular, of the type that jewellers use for fine work. It had the effect of magnifying one of Reichard's eyes grotesquely.

That didn't bother the agents. They fixed their goggled eyes on the old man in a predatory fashion. He felt a desperate urge to run, but while his feet were out of contact with the earth, running was not an option.

"What is the meaning of this intrusion? I am a simple chocolate maker. Take what you want and get out. There is some money in the cashbox at the front counter."

"We don't want money. You know who we are, don't you?"

Reichard was about to splutter a denial, when Mr. Candy slapped him across the face with the back of his hand. Reichard's glasses were knocked askew to dangle by one arm from his left ear. The jeweller's ocular fell to the floor and shattered. The agents threw him roughly to the ground. Mr. Sweet stood over the cowering old man while Mr. Candy perused the detailed sculpture work on the tabletop. Reichard, shaken and stunned, sat on the floor adjusting his glasses.

Mr. Candy leaned low to look at a tiny statue of a gladiator in full armour with a trident raised in one hand.

"Detail," said the agent. "So important in every true work of art." Mr. Candy picked up a small paintbrush with only a single bristle in its head. He dipped it in some red candy paint and drew a frown on the gladiator's chocolate face. "And you, Herr Fulcher, are an artist. So are the people who designed your history to disguise your past."

Reichard's stomach dropped. He had no idea what these strangers were talking about, but just seeing them made him feel deeply uneasy. He decided to be blunt. "I don't know what you're talking about."

"I think you do." Mr. Candy picked up a lion from the coliseum floor. The animal fit into the palm of the agent's gloved hand. "We looked into your background and found something very interesting. You were an orphan, weren't you?"

Reichard nodded.

"According to the official files, you were brought up in a state-run orphanage in Basel. On the day you turned sixteen, you discovered that you had a long-lost uncle who died and left you a healthy amount of money. Enough to buy this shop and start you off in the chocolate business. What a stroke of luck."

"I was very lucky, yes. What does it matter to you?"

Mr. Candy held the lion up and admired it under the light. "It matters a great deal to me. Because it is all a pack of lies." He crushed the lion, sugary crumbs tumbling through his spidery fingers as he ground the creature to dust. "We've checked into the orphanage. We were very thorough, interviewing all the people who were there at the same time you were supposed to have been there. No one remembers you. Do you know why?"

"I kept to myself." Reichard began to feel peculiar. The stranger's words seemed to jog something deep in his memory, but it remained just beyond his mind's grasp. He also felt that if he did remember, he mustn't tell the sinister men in grey.

"You were never there, that's why no one knows you. I have a theory. Do you want to hear it?"

"Not particularly," Reichard said with a defiance he didn't truly feel.

Mr. Candy picked a hammer from the rack overhead. He tossed it in the air and caught it, the metal head spinning end over end above the elaborate model of the ancient Roman Coliseum rendered in such scrupulous detail. The model represented hundreds of hours of devoted craftsmanship. "I believe you are one of the orphans from the mythical Hollow Mountain, a ward of the King of Switzerland, our mortal enemy. I believe he provided you the cover story, planted those lies in the public records, and gave you the money to start this enterprise." Mr. Candy stopped flipping the hammer and stared at Reichard. "What do you think? Is that a good theory?"

The old man looked completely confused. He laughed in disbelief. "I ... I really don't know what you are talking about. Truly, you are quite mad. A hollow mountain? There is no King of Switzerland. Switzerland is a republic. Everybody knows that!"

Reichard felt the viselike grip of Mr. Sweet as the agent pressed down on him, grinding the bones of his shoulders in a long-fingered grasp.

"I don't believe you are lying. I think you really do believe you don't know what we're talking about." Mr. Sweet let go of one of Reichard's shoulders and tapped his gloved finger on Reichard's forehead. "You have the knowledge but you don't even know it's there."

The chocolatier squirmed, trying to escape the prodding finger. "How is that possible? How can I know something and not know it at the same time?"

"You have been made to forget it," Mr. Candy said, smiling. "But don't worry. I will help you remember ..."

Mr. Sweet held his victim in place as Mr. Candy removed the glove from his right hand. He held the hand up. Reichard found the pallid flesh of the agent deeply disturbing. Waxy, greasy, plastic ... the flesh looked almost artificial. The old man's skin crawled at the thought of the agent touching him. As he watched, his eyes went wide. From Mr. Candy's fingertips, tiny wriggling threads appeared like the heads of tiny worms. They strained blindly in the light. Mr. Candy lowered his hand towards Reichard's face.

"No! No!" The old man desperately tried to turn his face away, but Mr. Sweet grabbed his head and held Reichard fast. Paralyzed by terror, he watched the wriggling worms descend. The tiny filaments wriggled sickeningly against the surface of his skin as if thousands of little tongues were tasting him. With a sensation like needles piercing his flesh, the tendrils burrowed into his face. For a sickening moment he felt them squirming like maggots, writhing up through his sinus cavities and through his skull. After that he remembered nothing more.

REICHARD WAS ON HIS KNEES in front of his burning shop when the firefighters arrived on the scene an hour later. A firefighter knelt beside the old man, wrapping a blanket around him. The flames crackled and blazed despite the drizzling cold rain. The firefighter tried to shake Reichard, but he just stared into his hands.

"Sir. Sir? What happened here?"

Reichard suddenly turned and stared into the face of the firefighter. His eyes were wild.

"It's too late."

"No," she said. "We may save some of it yet."

"No," Reichard cried. "No. It's too late for the King of Switzerland. The Hollow Mountain will be destroyed. The end is coming. The King of Switzerland will fall." Having uttered these strange words, the old man fell in a heap on the wet pavement.

The firefighter called for the paramedics. While she waited she held the man's head in her lap. His breathing was ragged and his skin grey.

"Poor old fellow," she murmured. "Obviously, he's delirious. Everyone knows that Switzerland is a republic."

Chapter 19

The King of Switzerland had decreed that the wedding of Mr. Kipling and Mrs. Francis was to be the most lavish and wonderful the Hollow Mountain had ever seen. George had been very busy making preparations for the happy event. Through his raccoon surrogates he had spent the better part of a week transforming the Royal Park in Frieda's Cavern into a wonderland.

Every tree and bush had been meticulously groomed. Every blade of grass was trimmed, all the weeds pulled, every flowerbed manicured and pruned. The result was stunning. The colourful flowers, already beautiful, had been coaxed forth until they were breathtaking to behold. Their sweet scents wafted gently over the park, adding an air of magic to the day.

Every branch of every tree had a bright silver streamer woven through it, the effect magnified when the Daniel's Panels shone down from above, striking the streamers' reflective surfaces and casting spots of light over the entire cavern. It seemed to be filled with water, rippling and shining.

White and silver balloons bobbed on threads all around Hakon's Fountain. The younger children batted at the ones they could reach, laughing and calling to each other. Their laughter mingled with the sound of the orchestra that was set up on a temporary stage on the lawn. The orchestra comprised the most gifted musicians among the children of the Hollow Mountain. Dressed in beautifully tailored, identical white tuxedos sewn by the students in the clothing and fashion department, they played their instruments with studied precision. This was the first time many of them had played in public and they wanted it to be absolutely perfect. Their faces as they followed their music and their conductor, an older girl with a severe, scowling expression, were serious and concentrated. No one wanted to make a mistake.

The children were all dressed in their finest tunics, cleaned and pressed. The George raccoons had made them wash behind their ears[58] and scrub their hands and scour their fingernails before they were allowed to come down for the ceremony. George was very strict about personal hygiene.[59]

Every child of the Hollow Mountain had been relieved of his or her normal duties to attend the celebration. As a result, the mood in the Royal Park was exuberantly festive. Children were streaming down the stairs from the residential level, all cleaned and pressed in their immaculate tunics. Even the Royal Swiss Guards, who were normally quite stern-looking, managed to smile once in a while. They looked spiffy in their dress grey uniforms, with their silver buttons and black boots polished to a high gloss.

---

[58] The expression "wash behind your ears" comes from the steppes of Russia, where peasants were forced to scrape soil out from behind their ears. The peasants were so poor that they would try to steal dirt, one earload at a time, from the farms they worked on in hopes of one day accumulating enough soil to start a farm of their own.

[59] Maybe this was a holdover from the raccoon mind that the George/Raccoon bots were based on. Raccoons are very careful to clean their food before eating it. Some have even been rumoured to brush their teeth between meals, but this has never been documented.

A canopy had been erected beside Hakon's Fountain. Beneath its shade stood the wedding party. Mimi looked uncomfortable in a pretty pink dress specially made for the occasion. A lacy belt cinched the dress tightly around her waist and the sleeves were puffy, edged with frilly cuffs. She fidgeted and plucked at the satin as if contact with it burned her skin. Her long face was wrinkled in a scowl. Mrs. Francis had attempted to put her hair up in a bow but Mimi flatly refused to be subjected to such indignities.

Hamish X stood beside her, barely able to stifle his laughter. She saw him snickering and drilled him hard in the shoulder with her fist.

"What?" he said, all innocence.

Mimi glowered. "I seen ya laughin'. I'm only wearin' this get-up 'cause Mrs. Francis asked me to." She pinched a piece of pink lace as if it were something she'd found under a rock. "I mean, pink? Are ya kiddin' me?"

The look on her face was so pained that Hamish X was about to laugh again, but he stopped. Looking at that hawkish, hatchet nose and those green eyes, he was struck suddenly by how close they had become and how much he would miss her. He felt a weight settle around his heart.

Mimi sensed his change of mood. "What's the matter with ya? Ya look like ya just lost yer best friend."

The words struck so close to home that Hamish X almost broke down and told her about his plans to leave later that day. Just then Mr. Kipling stepped into the tent, ducking under the edge of the canopy. He was freshly shaven, his moustache waxed and stiff, and he wore a beautiful white dress uniform complete with gold braid at the shoulders, white gloves, and a white peaked cap tucked under his arm. He beamed at Mimi and Hamish X. "What wonderful dresses you both have on." Hamish X was about to protest but Mr. Kipling laughed and held up a hand. "Just teasing you, Hamish X. The kilt is a noble garment." He bent over and kissed Mimi on the top of the head. "You are a vision, my dearest Mimi. An absolute princess."

Mimi blushed a bright pink, only a shade lighter than her dress. "Ain't no princesses come outta Texas."

Mr. Kipling laughed again and looked Hamish X up and down. "What a fine Highlander you would make, Hamish X. That is the Royal Stewart tartan[60] if I'm not mistaken." Something caught his eye. "Ah, and speaking of royalty, here comes his Majesty now."

All eyes were focused on the broad doors of the elevator. A long red carpet had been laid out between the doors and the canopy. The doors whooshed open to reveal the King.

King Liam stepped out of the elevator and the crowd cheered. He was dressed in a simple green doublet of silk, trimmed with white fur. Long suede boots came up to his knees and a simple circlet of pale metal rested on his unruly red hair. He was flanked on either side by George raccoons, each carrying a corner of his long grey velvet cloak in their mouths. Aidan and Cara led the way in their dress uniforms. Cara's hair was piled on top of her head in an elaborate network of knots and braids. A detail of Guards formed a line on either side along the carpet stretching from the elevator doors to the canopy.

---

60 Highland society is divided into "clans," or extended family groups. Each clan has a tartan pattern so that people can recognize other family members in the middle of a battle. As more and more clans developed tartans the process of identification became increasingly difficult, until entire battles had to be halted while people sorted out who they were supposed to be chopping. This led to war being abandoned in Scotland. Instead, people discuss their tartans. Much less dangerous and far more interesting.

The Royal Party stepped out to the increasing cheers of the gathered throng. The King smiled and waved to his subjects as the orchestra let loose with a stirring fanfare. The children threw handfuls of confetti, turning the afternoon into a colourful snowstorm of paper. King Liam smiled brightly. Then he turned and held out a hand towards the open doors of the elevator. The cheering died to a murmur as the crowd waited with bated breath.

Mrs. Francis had never been what fashion magazines would call beautiful. She had always been a little on the short side and a little bit on the chubby side. Her complexion had never been peaches and cream. Her hair was mousy and brown, shot through with grey. Her hands weren't soft after years of drudgery and toil in the kitchen at Windcity. And yet when she stepped out of the elevator, her hand resting on Parveen's elbow for her walk down the aisle, she was beautiful. All the eyes that looked upon her that day knew. She was beautiful because love had made her so.

Her hair was done up in ringlets interlaced with tiny white flowers. Her dress was the colour of ivory, made from the softest silk. She held a bouquet of delicate blossoms clutched in her chubby little hands.

The King led Parveen and Mrs. Francis down the red carpet towards the canopy where Mr. Kipling waited. Mrs. Francis beamed, her cheeks dimpling and her eyes shining as she gazed at her betrothed. Hamish X glanced up at Mr. Kipling's face and saw the same glow in his eyes. The smile on the man's face was warm and sure. He looked younger and stronger than he had ever seemed before. All the time the children had known him there had been a trace of sadness about the old sailor. The loss of his daughter years ago had left a hole in his heart. Now, watching his bride approach, it was as if that hole might finally be filled with a new love and a new purpose in life.

Mrs. Francis arrived under the canopy and the King turned to face the crowd. Parveen offered Mrs. Francis's hand to Mr. Kipling. The man took it in his own and bowed. "Thank you, Parveen." Parveen smiled one of his rare smiles and went to stand at Hamish X's side. He had dressed in a simple black tunic for the ceremony, but the stub of pencil remained behind his ear.

Mrs. Francis and Mr. Kipling stood before the King. Suddenly, Mrs. Francis handed her bouquet to Mimi. Her hands thus freed, she reached out and straightened Liam's tunic and rearranged a stray lock of his red hair that had fallen over his forehead. King Liam rolled his eyes and smiled. "Thanks, Mrs. Francis."

Mrs. Francis blushed and curtseyed. "I can't help myself, your Majesty."

The gathered children laughed and the King laughed with them. He then placed his hands over theirs.

"Dear friends. You were strangers only a few weeks ago, but since you arrived to live among us all have come to know your sweetness of spirit, kindness, selflessness, and sacrifice.

"Mrs. Francis … You were the one bright light in a dark place for so many children. Without you, Hamish X, Parveen, and Mimi would have been lost to us, not to mention all the other children who escaped Windcity, pirates, and more to be with us today. Thank you, sweet lady."

He smiled at Mrs. Francis, who immediately blushed crimson and curtseyed again. The King looked into the weathered face of Mr. Kipling.

"You, sir, are an inspiration to us all. You have proven that no one is beyond redemption and that love can be found in the darkest of places. It is an honour to have you among us and no surprise that you should win the heart of such a gentle and wonderful woman."

Mr. Kipling smiled and bowed his head.

"I am the King of this realm and so I am the law. I have never had the pleasure to perform a marriage. There is a first time for everything, I suppose. These are troubled times. Darkness waits to bring us down." His brow furrowed. "Let us make this union a symbol of hope that one day we will be able to live without fear, free and happy forever. Mimi?"

The King beckoned Mimi forward. Looking around,

suspicious of laughter at her attire, she held out her hand to the King. Resting in her palm were two simple bands of gold. The King smiled at her and picked up the smaller of the two. He gave it to Mr. Kipling.

Mr. Kipling took the ring carefully between his thumb and index finger. Holding Mrs. Francis's hand in his own and looking into her eyes, he said, "Dearest Isobel. I was lost. The world was a cold and empty place. With you at my side, I'll never be lost again."

Tears filled the little woman's eyes. She answered, "Rupert, I was waiting for you all those years to come for me. I just didn't know it."

There were sniffles from the children gathered near and Mimi's eyes looked suspiciously shiny. Hamish X reached out and took Parveen and Mimi by the hand, squeezing tight.

The King spoke. "Repeat after me. I, Rupert Milne Pendergast Kipling …"

"Milne?" Mimi murmured.

"Pendergast?" Hamish X whispered.

"Shhh." This from Parveen.

"I, Rupert Milne Pendergast Kipling …"

"Take you, Isobel Annabelle Francis …"

"Take you, Isobel Annabelle Francis …"

"To be my wife and partner …"

"To be my wife and partner …"

"In sickness and in health, through good times and bad …"

"In sickness and in health, through good times and bad …"

"As long as you both shall live …"

"As long as we both shall live … even longer if at all possible. Indeed, I do." Mr. Kipling slipped the ring onto

Mrs. Francis's finger. The fit was tight but he managed with a minimum of effort. The King smiled and turned to Mrs. Francis.

"Now it's your turn," he began.

Before he could start the vows Mrs. Francis blurted, "Yes! Yes I do! I will and yes … forever!" She placed the ring on Mr. Kipling's finger and planted a huge kiss on his lips, flinging her arms around his neck and pulling him down to her level. All the children laughed. When she finally broke free of the kiss, Mrs. Francis blushed and said, "I don't like long ceremonies."

The King raised his arms. "Excellent, then let's jump to the end. I now pronounce you husband and wife. You may kiss the bride. Again." Mr. Kipling was only too happy to oblige.

Mr. Candy and Mr. Sweet

Standing on the mountainside in the driving rain, Mr. Candy and Mr. Sweet gazed through their goggles at the seemingly solid rock of the cliff face.

"Interesting, Mr. Candy."

"Very, Mr. Sweet."

"Switch to infrared."

The goggles on their faces hummed softly and the view of the mountainside shifted. Displayed in their goggles was the rock face outlined in luminous red heat patterns. Where the cliff had seemed solid, a glowing cavity now appeared.

"Incredible," Mr. Sweet shouted over the wind. "A false rock face. It's very realistic."

"Very clever," Mr. Candy agreed. "The way into the Hollow Mountain."

"At last."

"At last."

Mr. Sweet pressed the side of his head and spoke into the air. "All units advance on these coordinates. We begin the assault in ten minutes from my mark. Mark." He lowered his hand. "A great day, Mr. Candy."

"A great day, indeed, Mr. Sweet."

Chapter 20

The reception was in full swing. A long table had been brought out for the wedding party, and there Mr. Kipling and Mrs. Francis (she had decided to remain Mrs. Francis rather than confuse the children) sat together holding hands as they watched the spectacle on the lawn before them. Mimi, Parveen, and Hamish X sat on one side. The King sat on the other.

A feast had been prepared and served. Everyone had their fill of roast beef, mashed potatoes, and steamed carrots. (Mrs. Francis had demanded that the wedding dinner be something nutritious for the children.) After the feast had been cleared away, there were plenty of rich desserts for everyone.

The kitchens, under Mrs. Francis's careful direction, had outdone themselves creating a variety of delicious treats. There were cakes, candies, tarts, and cookies, and even a chocolate fountain designed by Noor and Parveen. Children gathered around the spouting geyser of sweet liquid, dipping in pieces of fruit or marshmallows on long wooden skewers. The younger children were practically caked with chocolate up to the elbows, but no one scolded them. Everyone was having too much fun. George raccoons wandered about carrying trays of little sand-wiches, bonbons, tiny savoury pies, and glasses of fruit punch.

There were entertainments of every kind imaginable. The children had been practising, and now they displayed their incredible skills. The gymnastics class tumbled and contorted, performing acrobatic feats to the great delight of the crowd.

The highlight, however, was the Royal Swiss Guards, who put on a demonstration of tactics set to the orchestra's musical accompaniment. Marching smartly in formation out into the centre of the green, they went on to form intricate shapes through shockingly precise patterns. They created circles that collapsed into diamond shapes then exploded into stars that rotated on their axes. The crowd shouted with pleasure at each new and amazingly executed manoeuvre.

Hamish X watched the proceedings with a heavy heart. Everyone seemed so happy. He looked over at Mimi as she sat leaning forward in her chair, gazing enviously as Cara and Aidan marched by in perfect rhythm. He looked at the light in Mimi's eyes and he had to smile in spite of his sadness. *She'll be happy here*, he thought to himself.

He looked past Mimi at Parveen and saw the little boy fiddling with something in his hands. It looked like a hand-held video game console. Parveen sensed Hamish X's gaze and looked up. He pushed his glasses up onto his nose. "It's a surprise," he said with a shrug and returned his attention to the device.

Beyond Parveen sat the newlyweds. Mr. Kipling whispered something into his bride's ear and she giggled. Mrs. Francis caught Hamish X's eye and waved a chubby hand. Mr. Kipling turned and winked at him. Hamish X winked back. Mr. Kipling kissed Mrs. Francis's cheek, setting her off giggling again. Hamish X smiled to cover his heartache. He was going away. Who knew when he would see these people again?

Finally, he looked at the King. Liam nodded as if to say he understood what Hamish X was going through.

Hamish X smiled back. It was time to go. And so, as the Royal Swiss Guards' performance built to a crescendo, he silently eased out of his chair and slipped away through the crowd.

The Guards performed their finale. They formed two rings that linked as they marched towards each other, then as the music rose to an intense climax they broke apart and coalesced into a large *I* linked to an *R*, the two first initials of the wedded couple. Everyone cheered.

The crowd was beginning to disperse when a child pointed up in the air and shouted, "Look!"

The *Orphan Queen* sailed out over the throng of children. The ship was festooned with blinking lights of all the colours of the rainbow. Streamers of silver trailed behind her as she made a stately sweep around the perimeter of the cavern. The children went wild, clapping and hollering as the airship sailed above.

"How did they git the *Queen* in here, anyway," Mimi said, awestruck. In truth, the ship was too large to take up the stairs or in the elevator. Parveen and Noor, with the help of the George raccoons, had painstakingly disassembled the airship into its component parts, carried it into Frieda's Cavern, and reassembled it there.

Parveen stood at the main table, controlling the airship via the radio transmitter in his hands. He and Noor had laboured long and hard for this moment. He furrowed his brow and concentrated on the knobs and switches beneath his thumbs.

"Magnificent, Parveen!" The King clapped. "Truly amazing!"

"He really is quite clever." Mrs. Francis beamed and squeezed Mr. Kipling's hand, proud as if Parveen were her very own son.

The airship changed direction and sailed directly inward towards the centre of the Hollow Mountain. As the *Orphan Queen* reached the midpoint the cargo doors opened and multicoloured balloons tumbled out in a great slow cascade over the delighted crowd below. Fireworks erupted in glorious showers of pink and blue sparks. Everyone gasped as the fireworks went on and on.

HAMISH X NEVER HEARD the cheers and applause as the show ended. He was walking down a long stone corridor accompanied only by a George raccoon. On his back was a heavy knapsack stuffed with food and camping gear. He still wore the Highland kilt. He had grown to enjoy the swish of the pleated woollen fabric against his legs. The rest of his wedding suit he had left on his bed. He had no need of fancy clothes where he was going. He wore his rugged flannel shirt once more, and over his pack and clothes he wore a long oilskin coat.

A George raccoon had been waiting in his quarters with his gear already packed. The mechanical creature watched as Hamish X donned his clothing and lifted the knapsack. Noticing that the book *Great Plumbers* was packed on top of his clothes, Hamish X rested his hand on the green leather binding. "What do I need this for?"

"The King thought it might be useful someday. Waste not, want not."

And now he hurried along the stone corridor, keeping the George raccoon in sight. He'd been walking for some time when he saw the faint glimmer of light up ahead. A moment later he emerged from a sheltered cave mouth into a fierce rainstorm. Thunder rumbled and lightning flashed on the mountainside.

"Good luck, Hamish X," George said through the voice

of the little raccoon. Rain beaded on its thick pelt and dripped from its whiskers. "I hope you succeed in finding the doctor."

"I hope so, too. Thank the King once again for me. And tell the others not to worry."

"I will." The raccoon waved one tiny paw and waddled back into the cave.

Hamish X stood in the rain, watching the spot where the little robot had disappeared. He hadn't felt so lonely since the first time he'd come to Windcity on that snowy day. It seemed so long ago now. He suddenly felt the urge to just go back into the mountain and join the party as if nothing were amiss, as if he'd never heard of Professor Magnus Ballantyne-Stewart. He had memories now, but it seemed that all they were good for was reminding him that he was completely alone.

He shook rain out of his eyes, rain and tears. *This is no good. You have to do this alone. Stop being a baby. You're Hamish X, hero of orphans everywhere. It's time for you to get moving.*

He looked up at the peak of the Hollow Mountain. Flashes of blue and green erupted on the mountainside. "Wow," he breathed, "the lightning is something else up here. I'd better be going."

He set off at a brisk trot, his boots skipping nimbly across the stony ground. Soon he was far away from the Hollow Mountain. Dawn found him running alongside a freight train and leaping aboard.

If he'd known that the lightning he saw wasn't lightning at all, he would have come back to the aid of his friends. As it was, he ran heedlessly on into the night.

Mr. Candy and Mr. Sweet

Mr. Candy and Mr. Sweet stepped out of the helicopter onto the mountainside. Their grey coats and suits were gone. In their stead the agents wore bulky grey jumpsuits with zips up the front. From the belts around their waists dangled small black bulbs attached by metal clips. They carried large rifles with round open barrels and on their backs were heavy steel canisters with funnels poking out.

They looked up the mountain at where the entrance was hidden.

"One minute until assault commences," announced Mr. Candy, consulting an oversized watch on his wrist.

"And not a minute before time, Mr. Candy."

The two agents swung around to look at the assembled forces ranged across the side of the mountain. There were rows of the flame-throwing Firebirds that had destroyed Windcity so handily. Behind these a row of gigantic tracked vehicles idled in the rain. Grey Agents sat at the controls in high cabs, each cab topped by a winch equipped with a gripping claw; square cargo pods made up the rear. These were the infamous child containment and transport vehicles, or CCTVs, notorious among orphans the world over.

Ranked in front of the CCTVs and Firebirds were files of Grey Agents from offices all around the world, pulled in specifically for the operation at hand. The agents, men and women alike, were dressed in varying shades of grey, in a fashion similar to Mr. Candy and Mr. Sweet. Beneath the rims of their grey helmets, their faces were grim and pale; each had the same dead, heartless expression. They looked to their commanders, Candy and Sweet, holding their weapons ready.

"Agents, the time is near," Mr. Candy said, his voice broadcast to all through earpieces integrated into the black goggles they wore. "The integration is coming. We need only retrieve the asset, Hamish X, and return to Providence with our prize. Fortunately, we have been afforded a chance to destroy one of our most hated enemies in the process. The King of Switzerland's secret refuge is not so secret any more. Tonight we shall eradicate this insult to the ODA from the face of the earth. This is the first day of a glorious future. Today we begin to claim our inheritance. Take as many of the children as you can. They will be useful in the integration. Subdue those who resist. Destroy the King. Capture Hamish X."

In a normal army, after such a rousing call to arms, the soldiers would be expected to cheer, to raise a shout, or to brandish their arms in exaltation. The Grey Agents merely nodded once and stood silently in the rain awaiting their orders. Somehow the silence, devoid as it was of emotion, was more terrifying than the bloodiest war cry.

"Very inspiring, Mr. Candy."

"Thank you, Mr. Sweet."

"Five. Four. Three. Two. One!"

The metal backpacks the agents wore erupted in plumes of green flame. They rose from the ground as one, propelled by their rocket packs, for such indeed they were, and set off in a giant V formation like a flock of lethal geese towards the cliff face.

Chapter 21

The cake was wheeled in by George raccoons: three tiers of chocolate sponge cake coated with butter cream icing and decorated with pink and yellow roses. On the top of the cake were two tiny, lifelike statuettes of the bride and groom formed out of meticulously painted marzipan. Mrs. Francis clapped her hands with delight. A George raccoon handed Mrs. Francis a silver knife. Mr. Kipling laid his hand over his bride's on the handle of the knife and together they pressed it through the lowest tier of the cake.

Everyone cheered. The King stood up. "Ladies and gentlemen! Boys and girls! Artificial intelligences! Please join me in congratulating Mr. and Mrs. Kipling-Francis!"

Applause erupted.

Suddenly, all the raccoons stood stiffly erect. Their eyes were wide open. The King stopped applauding and the clapping died down to silence.

"What is it, George? What's the matter?"

The raccoons didn't respond for three or four seconds. Then, abruptly, all the raccoons shouted in unison. "SECURITY BREACH. WE HAVE A SECURITY BREACH. INTRUDERS IN THE MAIN TUNNEL. OUTER DEFENCES FAILING. THE MOUNTAIN HAS BEEN COMPROMISED."

All thoughts of the wedding and the cake were forgotten. Everyone stood frozen in shock. None could believe what they were hearing. Even the Guards were confused.

"Is this a drill, George?" Aidan said.

"NO! WE ARE UNDER ATTACK."

A buzz of panic rippled through the crowd. "Security breach?" children asked. "How is that possible? It must be a mistake."

"George," the King barked sharply. "Where is the breach?"

"The entrance tunnel has been breached. All sensors and cameras are offline in that area. We must assume Heinrich's Cavern is compromised."

The King picked up his crutches. "Aidan: arm the Guards. Tell them to muster at the head of the stairs immediately. George, seal the elevator shaft and close the stairs at the junction between Frieda's Cavern and Heinrich's. Is there anyone in Heinrich?"

"Negative. Everyone was here for the wedding."

"A blessing. We must prepare to repel an attack, but whatever happens we have to evacuate. George, prepare the escape routes. All children muster at your emergency stations. Guards only on the elevator! Everyone else uses the stairs. Older children help the young ones! Move!"

Instantly, what had been a joyous celebration dissolved into fearful pandemonium as children rushed to follow orders. Aidan and Cara set off at a dead run for the barracks to arm themselves and lead their units. Cara looked over her shoulder and saw that Mimi was right behind them. The Texan girl had kicked off her party shoes and was running in her bare feet.

"Where do you think you're going?"

"Same place as you."

"Aidan?" Cara sounded very annoyed.

"Cara, we need every hand. She's coming with us."

Mimi grinned fiercely at Cara's deflated expression.

They entered the elevator with the other Guards just as the doors closed.

"What can we do to help?" Mr. Kipling asked the King. Mrs. Francis clutched her new husband's arm, her eyes wide.

"Mrs. Francis, if you could help organize the retreat up the stairs. Mr. Kipling, I would appreciate it if you stayed with me and helped organize the defence of the stairs. You're the only one here with any real military experience."

"But he was in the Navy!" Mrs. Francis protested.

Mr. Kipling hugged his bride and laughed softly. "Isobel, what is a cavern but a boat made of rock?"

"That makes no sense at all!"[61] Mrs. Francis said angrily. "I don't want you to get hurt. We've only just found each other."

Mr. Kipling kissed her firmly on the top of her head. "Don't you worry about me, my dear. The children need you. I can take care of myself."

Mrs. Francis looked up at Mr. Kipling's face and nodded, tears in her eyes. She kissed him once, hugged him, and then bustled away to help where she was needed.

"What should we do?" the King asked when she was gone.

"The entryway is sealed?"

"George has seen to it, I am certain."

"We must assume they will try to force a breach and that they are capable of doing so. Let's prepare a welcome for them."

The King and the ex-pirate shared a wolfish grin and set about their work.

---

[61] Mrs. Francis does have a point.

BELOW, IN HEINRICH'S CAVERN, the Grey Agents waited on the platform as the larger vehicles caught up with them. The rumbling of the big treaded trucks filled the rocky space. The vehicles had traversed the tunnel by means of extendable claws on the end of long cables, swinging like spiders from webs along the entry tunnel and out into the water of the lake. From there, they had converted to amphibious vehicles, powering across the surface of the water to the central platform.

Mr. Candy and Mr. Sweet listened as one of the other agents reported.

"They have sealed the elevator shaft. The stairs are similarly blocked. We are wiring both with explosives and should be able to break down the barriers."

"Excellent," Mr. Candy nodded. "Have all the Firebirds in position."

"Yes, Mr. Candy." The agent fired his jetpack and rose directly up the cavern to relay the orders.

"Now the real battle begins, Mr. Sweet."

"At last, Mr. Candy. At long last."

The Firebirds began to climb the stairs, their heavy steel talons striking sparks from the stone. Their long necks were extended as if to sniff for their prey above.

The two agents watched with satisfaction as the machines passed by, and then rose themselves on plumes of blue-green fire.

MIMI TUGGED at the black combat tunic. It was too tight around the neck. She had grabbed an outfit that looked to be the right size, but in her haste she'd managed to find one that was just a little too small.

"Dang, but this monkey suit itches."

"Well, scratch and be quiet," Cara snapped.

They were gathered around the elevator shaft waiting for the invaders to show themselves. Guards were ranged in a loose circle, hiding behind rocks and statues or whatever cover was available. A third of the Guards had been detailed to help Mrs. Francis in the retreat up the stairs, leaving roughly one hundred to repel the attack.

The wedding decorations in their midst seemed absurd given the seriousness of what was happening. Balloons and streamers fluttered in the wind. Hakon's Fountain bubbled on around the foot of the stairs and the elevator, its laughing gurgle in stark contrast to the tension in the air. Children were still making their way up to the higher levels on the stairs. They were crying and shouting, urging each other along. Mrs. Francis was still at the bottom of the stairs and vowing she would not start up until the last child had begun to climb. Hundreds of raccoons helped her in her labours.

King Stephen's Stair was blocked off at the floor of Frieda's Cavern by a sheet of steel that completely covered the opening around the elevator shaft. The Guards listened tensely to the clangs and scratching sounds that echoed off the metal plate as the intruders prepared to break through.

Mimi and Cara hunkered down behind a carving of Queen Helga, taking cover behind the stone folds of her elaborate gown. The King, Aidan, and Mr. Kipling crouched behind the wall of the fountain on the opposite side of the stairs. The King was sweating from the strain of holding such a cramped position.

"You should go, Sire," Aidan said gently. "This is our job. The others will need your leadership."

King Liam wiped his brow with a shaking hand and shook his head. "No, I must stay. This is my proper place. George will take care of the children."

"I just wish they'd get on with it," Aidan said impatiently. "The waiting is the hardest part."

Mr. Kipling laid a restraining hand on the boy's arm. "Don't ask for trouble. It will find us soon enough."

As if in response to his words, a sudden, massive explosion sent chunks of shattered steel rocketing all over the cavern. The Guards ducked to avoid flying shards. Black smoke billowed up from the twisted metal plate that had blocked the opening. Screams of panic and fear erupted on the stairs as children tried to push the climbers ahead faster. Several George raccoons took up stations in a line at the bottom of the stairs, forming a furry line of defence.

"Children! Children! Remain calm!" Mrs. Francis called.

The Guards clutched their weapons tighter and waited for the invaders to surge through the hole and attack. A minute passed, then another. Just as they slightly relaxed their grip there came a soft roaring sound and two figures dressed all in grey rose through the blasted opening on plumes of blue-green flame, hovering in the air above the hole.

"Grey Agents!" Mimi spat, peeking out around the carving.

The two figures were indeed Mr. Candy and Mr. Sweet. They swivelled their birdlike heads back and forth, their goggled eyes surveying the cavern around them. All the Guards trained their pistols steadily on the two intruders. Finally, one of the agents spoke.

"We come to offer terms. I am Mr. Sweet. This is my colleague, Mr. Candy."

"How do you do?" The other agent ducked his head once in greeting. "Which one of you is the so-called King of Switzerland?"

Aidan made to stand up but King Liam pushed him back and rose to his feet. He threw aside his crutches and hobbled forward a few steps until he was a few metres away from the Grey Agents.

"I am Liam, seventy-seventh King of Switzerland. This is my realm. These are my people. You are trespassing here."

Mr. Candy took over. "Forgive my rudeness, King Liam, but you do not seem well. Surely, a battle is the last thing you want right now. How can you hope to stand against the might of the ODA? It is folly. You will all be destroyed. Let me offer you a deal. If you surrender now, we'll be gentle. The children will be distributed to our clients worldwide, you will survive, and no one will be hurt."

King Liam laughed. "Your concerns for my health are laughable, Mr. Candy. Don't you remember me? It was you and your experiments that made me this way."

Mr. Candy and Mr. Sweet tilted their heads to one side in unison and stared at the King. "You don't seem familiar," Mr. Candy said after a moment.

"But we have had so many children through our laboratories over the years," Mr. Sweet added.

King Liam smiled grimly. "I assure you, I am well enough to defy you and repel your invasion of our home. There will be no terms. There will be no surrender. You must leave immediately or face the consequences."

The Guards roared their approval. Mimi roared along with them. Mr. Kipling merely drew his saber and held it loosely at his side.

Mr. Candy held up a hand for silence. When the jeering stopped he spoke. "All this ugliness may be avoided. We will pack up and leave, never to return. You can live in peace. All we ask is that you give us Hamish X."

There was silence. Mimi suddenly realized that Hamish X was nowhere in sight. She looked all around at the Guards gathered on the field and she didn't see him anywhere. In fact, she hadn't seen him since the reception started. She was about to say something but held her tongue, not wanting to give anything away to the Grey Agents.

"I'm sorry to disappoint you, but he isn't here. I'm afraid you are out of luck." The King smiled sweetly.

"You're lying."

"No, Mr. Candy, I am not. I know that for someone such as you, for whom lying is a matter of habit and necessity, you imagine that others are equally deceitful. No, I am not lying. But know that, if he *were* here, I wouldn't hand him over to you. You will never let us live in peace. As long as the ODA exists the world is not safe for children anywhere. If you seek to come any further we will resist with all our strength to the last boy and girl … and raccoon."

"Raccoon?" Mr. Candy cocked his head and frowned. "How ridiculous."

As one, each of the George raccoons on the stairs made a rude noise. The Grey Agents blinked in surprise.

"Very well," Mr. Sweet said, regaining his composure. "We will destroy you utterly."

As he finished speaking, a stone ricocheted off his jetpack with a loud clang.

"Go stick that in yer *utterly*, ya creep!" Mimi held a bigger rock and cocked back her arm for another throw. Her second rock sailed through empty space as the agents dropped quickly down through the hole.

"Prepare yourselves," the King shouted. He tried to hurry back to the cover of the fountain but stumbled and fell. Aidan and another Guard ran to his aid, pulling him to safety as the first Firebird's menacing snout poked through the hole. The Guards opened up with their pistols, firing blue stun bolts at the flat head of the mechanical beast, but they had little effect. The creature sprayed a tongue of liquid fire in a deadly arc around the hole. The Guards were forced to drop behind their meagre cover. A few unlucky ones had their hair singed or set alight. Fortunately, their fellows patted out the flames before any real injury occurred.

The wedding tent and all the flowers withered and caught fire. The wedding cake slumped in the sudden heat, dissolving into a pool of marzipan and molten sugar. The mechanical bird rose up out of the hole, to be followed by another and another.

The Battle for the Hollow Mountain had begun.

Chapter 22

When the alert had sounded Parveen and Noor set off at breakneck speed, forcing their way up the stairs to get to the workshop. They burst into their workroom and looked around at all the projects they had been tinkering with.

"If only we had more time," Parveen panted. "So many things have not been tested satisfactorily."

"Just grab everything we can," Noor cried, twisting the end of her ponytail in her fingers. "It'll have to do."

They gathered up all the gadgets they could carry, hanging them on belts and stuffing them into backpacks. Thus equipped, they took off as fast as their legs could carry them back against the flow of panicked children being herded by raccoons.

When they returned to the stairs, they looked down to the floor of Frieda's Cavern two hundred metres below and were dismayed.

Fires raged everywhere. At least a dozen Firebirds were marauding through the Royal Park. The Guards were trying to contain the mechanical beasts, but their stun guns had no effect at all. They were forced back, reduced to serving as distractions as they tried to draw the things away from the children retreating up the stairs.

The children were on the verge of hysteria. A solid wall of terrified faces looked up at the brother and sister. As desperate children reached the top they flooded past, tumbling out into the safety of the open courtyard that was the Workshop level. Going against the flood of orphans seemed impossible.

"There's no way for us to get past them," Noor shouted over the chaos. "The elevator's tied up. What do we do?"

"Watch," Parveen shouted.

He reached into his pack and pulled out a remote control. He raised the aerial and pointed it out into the cavern. Out of the corner of the ceiling the *Orphan Queen* emerged into the light. Under Parveen's guidance it cruised towards the top of the stairs. In such dire circumstances its decorations seemed totally inappropriate, but Parveen had no time to worry about appearances. The children began to shout and point, afraid that this was some new element of the assault.

"George!" Parveen shouted. One of the raccoons nearby turned to him, eyes glittering. "We need room to board the airship." The raccoon nodded, and soon a dozen of the little creatures were forming a cordon by linking arms and pushing gently but firmly against the flow of children.

Parveen and Noor stepped into the space the raccoons had created and waited for agonizing seconds for the airship to approach. Parveen cast a worried eye below, but the bird things hadn't noticed its passage. The two children held their breath and waited.

MIMI PULLED CARA behind the statue of Queen Gerta just in time to rescue her from a gout of flaming liquid. The Texan girl covered the Guard with her own body as the searing heat scorched her back. Cara rolled Mimi away from her.

"Just get off, will you?" Cara snarled. Then she saw Mimi's smoking uniform and felt ashamed of her anger. "Are you all right?"

"Ain't nuthin'," Mimi said curtly. "Them fire things are gonna bake us all like chimichangas, make no mistake."[62]

Cara nodded. "What can we do? The pistols are useless."

Mimi scowled. She looked around. Everywhere, the birds were pushing them back. There had been some injuries but nothing serious yet. Mrs. Francis was still hurrying kids up the stairs. She wasn't at the bottom any more but she was a long way from the top. Just one of those mechanical creatures could wreak havoc. Mimi had to do something.

She looked at her belt and saw the loop of climbing rope that was standard equipment for the Guards. The rope was terrifically strong, reinforced with synthetic fibres to make it less prone to fraying and breakage. She smiled. Taking the rope from her belt, she tossed one end to Cara. The other, she began tying into a noose.

"Tie that around the base o' that statue but good, got me?"

Cara nodded and did as she was told, doubling the knot and tugging to make sure it was secure. Satisfied, she asked, "What's the plan?"

"Watch!" Mimi ran out into the open, into the path of the nearest Firebird.

"Hey! Over here, ya big stupid thing." The creature's head swung around, following the sound of Mimi's voice. The deadly funnels dripped liquid fire. "Yeah, you. I'm right here, you big ugly turkey."

---

[62] A chimichanga is a Mexican food consisting of yummy spicy fillings sandwiched between two tortillas and then deep-fried to a delicious crispiness. I truly love them, but this really isn't the time to be discussing Mexican food. Return to the story immediately.

"You're insane!" Cara shouted. Mimi ignored her.

The creature started towards her, its long neck straining in her direction. Mimi raised the rope and spun it around her head. As the creature prepared to spout flame, Mimi hurled her makeshift lasso around its neck and pulled. The head of the metal monster was yanked sideways and the flames sprayed wide of Mimi to fall harmlessly across the lawn.

Mimi let go of the rope and ran. The beast took off after her, its metal talons sending clods of earth flying. When the creature reached the end of the rope, secured to the statue, its head was jerked violently back. The cord was so strong and the force of the creature's movement so great that the head of the mechanical bird was severed neatly by the tightening noose. The head went spinning through

the air to land with a sizzling splash in the fountain pool. The rest of the machine fell flat on the grass, carving a furrow in the soil, liquid fire dribbling out into a pool at the top of its neck.

Mimi leapt onto the mechanical carcass and crowed, "Don't mess with Mimi Catastrophe Jones!"

A ragged cheer went up from the beleaguered Guards. Everywhere, the defenders reached for their ropes and hoped to imitate her achievement. Mimi looked up and pointed.

"Look!"

The *Orphan Queen* approached from above. The cargo doors hung open and Noor stood in the hold.

Inside the bridge, Parveen manned the wheel. A raccoon stood at the trimsman's post, manipulating the levers with its tiny paws. "We have to go lower," Parveen shouted.

"Yes, sir."

"Aye. You're supposed to say 'aye.'"

"What's wrong with your eye?"

"Nothing … On a ship you don't yes you say—" Parveen realized he was explaining ship's etiquette[63] to a mechanical raccoon and shook his head. "Never mind. Just

---

[63] *Etiquette* is another word for "manners." It is shortened from the French words *être une racquette*. Literally translated, this means "to be a racquet." Tennis was so important to the Kings of Renaissance France that King Louis the Thirteenth dressed his entire court as tennis racquets. Appearing this way in public was deemed to be the height of fashion and grace. The hopeful dressed as tennis racquets and hung around, hoping the King would notice them. For some reason, the term came to be synonymous with politeness. Words are weird. The word *synonymous* is worth a whole footnote on its own but I don't have time right now. Get a dictionary.

take us lower." He clicked on the speaking tube attached to the wheel and shouted into it. "Noor! Get ready to drop the payload."

"Understood," came the tinny reply.

Below, the Firebirds were all gathering to greet the airship. They raised their snouts in unison and sprayed gouts of fire up at it, but the vessel stayed just out of reach.

"That's as low as we get, Noor!" Parveen shouted down the tube.

"Okay!" Noor shouted back. "Bombs away."

Noor tipped a sack of orange and white spheres out of the cargo door. The objects dropped down among the gathered bird machines, clattering like hail against their metal skins. Some of the spheres shattered, but most landed on the soft earth in the midst of the Firebirds.

In seconds they turned into a swarming mass of hamsters, pink ears flickering, pink noses quivering. The furry creatures skittered up the towering legs of the Firebirds and along their squat bodies, traversing the long necks and finally reaching the blunt heads. Several simulated rodents latched onto the skulls of each creature. Once they were all in position, they detonated.

The scene was awe-inspiring. The birds, invincible only moments before, were reduced to flailing helplessness. They spun and danced, jittered and strained, smashing into one another as they collapsed into bizarre convulsions. Fire spewed from their snouts in uncontrolled bursts, showering everything in their path with flame. Fortunately, the Guards had pulled back out of reach.

In less than a minute the Firebirds lay on the scorched lawn in a heap of wreckage. Here and there a metal limb jerked involuntarily, but there was no doubt that the birds were out of the fight.

The Guards cheered loudly, waving to Noor in the airship. Mr. Kipling raised his hand and gave the thumbs-up. Parveen, in the bridge, saw the gesture and returned it.

The King called, "Everyone! To the foot of the stairs!"

The Guards took advantage of the momentary lull to regroup around their King. When they had gathered at the bottom step, King Liam, coughing from the smoke from the many fires raging around them, addressed his troops.

"Everyone accounted for?" The Guards nodded. "Well done, Mimi. You're an inspiration." Mimi blushed as Guards slapped her on the back. Even Cara nodded. The King continued. "Parveen and Noor have given us a moment's reprieve. We must take advantage of it. I want half of you to go up the stairs and help Mrs. Francis now. The rest stay here. We hold the stairs as long as we can. I am going up. I have to prepare for the departure. The rest of you, good luck. Aidan is in charge. Be brave. I'm proud of all of you. Don't take any unnecessary risks. Stay only until the children are free. We'll be sealing the next cavern as soon as you are through. Let's go."

He turned and hobbled up the stairs. Aidan took control. "Platoons one through eight go with the King. The rest stay here."

Cara stepped forward. "I'm staying."

"No you aren't. You're in charge of those platoons. You go."

"I can't leave you behind now." Cara looked close to tears, her usual haughty scowl dissolving under some softer sentiment. "I can't be alone."

Aidan hugged her. "You won't be. I'll be up in a moment. You'll see. I need you to lead. Understand?"

Cara looked into his brown eyes and nodded at last.

Blinking away tears, she turned and led the Guards up the stairs.

Mimi watched her go and called, "I'll keep an eye on 'im!"

Smoke was still curling from the twisted hole in the plating that led below to Heinrich's Cavern, but so far the bird creatures were the only things that had come through. Aidan and the rest of his Guards checked their equipment and prepared to hold the line. "Okay, people," he said grimly. "They're gonna send their worst. We have to do our best." They ranged themselves around the hole and braced for the onslaught.

What came out of the hole was the last thing they could have expected.

THE GREY AGENTS stood on the stairs below, in neat rows, their jetpacks idling, waiting for the next phase in the attack. Mr. Candy and Mr. Sweet huddled over a small television monitor at the head of the line. They watched in growing disbelief as the Firebirds were defeated, first by the girl from Windcity and then by the strange little hamsters dropping from the airship. Mr. Candy tossed the monitor aside to fall hundreds of metres and crash on the rock platform below.

"Mr. Sweet, it would seem that the first wave has been repulsed."

"Indeed, Mr. Candy. What's next?"

Mr. Candy looked over the edge of the stairs and saw the CCTVs labouring up the stone steps to join the assault.

"Shall we release the next wave?"

"Yes, Mr. Candy. Let's."

Mr. Candy pressed a long finger to his temple and said in a clear voice, "Open CCTV cargo doors."

Immediately, all the cargo bins on the back of the lumbering vehicles opened. Out of the bins came a swarm of colour that massed into a gigantic cloud in the middle of the cavern. Once all the tiny objects were congregated they moved in concert towards the opening, flocking past the watching agents with a sound like a hundred electric fans and sweeping up through the hole into the cavern above.

THE GUARDS HEARD the swarm coming, a hum that grew steadily louder. Out of the hole came a throng of fluttering ... butterflies. The tiny creatures were of myriad hues, delicate and beautiful. The Guards watched as the butterflies wafted up into the air and formed a sort of cloud of hovering colour.

"I don't get it," Mimi breathed. "Butterflies? What's the idea?"

The swarm emerging from the hole petered out, and finally all the butterflies were massing together in the air metres over their heads. As the Guards watched, one of them delicately fluttered down. The creature flitted above them as if deciding where to alight. The little butterfly was so beautiful, tinted in the most delicate shades of blue and green, that one Guard, a girl with straw-coloured hair, held out her bare hand.

"No," Aidan said sharply. Too late. The little butterfly landed on her palm. Instantly there was a flash of blue light and the girl went rigid. She slumped to the ground, unconscious.

"Hoods on! Gloves on!" It was all Aidan had time to say before the swarm descended.

Chapter 23

Noor joined Parveen in the bridge. They hovered close to the stairs, watching the progress of the refugees. Children scrambled up the stone steps with the help of the George raccoons and the Guards.

"We seem to have bought them some time," Noor said. She pinched Parveen's cheek. "Well done, little brother."

Parveen squirmed away from her hand. "Please. No pinching."

"We make a good team, Parv. I'm so glad we found each other."

Parveen nodded. "Indeed. But the name is Parveen. You've been listening to Mimi too much." He turned his gaze to the stairs below. Mrs. Francis hustled children along. "We can't win this fight."

"I agree," Noor said, her quick nod sending her ponytail bouncing. "The escape pods are on the upper levels. We have to get everyone up there and away before the Grey Agents overwhelm them."

"Escape pods?"

"They're capsules that can be launched down tubes hollowed out of the mountainside. They lead to an underground river. We can all float to safety, but we have to stall the ODA long enough to get all the kids away." Noor's attention was drawn to the swarm of colour down at the base of the stairs. "What is that?"

A couple of hundred children were still on the stairs as the butterflies entered the cavern. Some of them stopped to look at the new arrivals in wonder.

"Am I seeing things?" Parveen said. "Are those butterflies?"

"It would seem so," Noor answered. She picked up Mr. Kipling's binoculars from the map table and took a closer look. She saw the butterfly light in the Guard girl's hand and the girl fall stricken. "Oh, no. Those aren't real butterflies. They're a trick."

Parveen took the binoculars from her and looked. He watched in horror as the butterflies descended en masse on the Guards around the breach. Some Guards were able to cover their exposed skin, but he saw many fall motionless to the ground.

"We've got to help them," Parveen cried. "But how?"

MIMI WAS ONE of the lucky ones, pulling her hood down over her face and adjusting her goggles. She already had her gloves on and so was immune to the butterfly effect. The light before her eyes was suddenly blotted out by a flurry of tiny flapping wings. She flapped her hands around her face, but it was no use. She staggered blindly, heading in one direction and hoping it wasn't taking her straight into the hole. Several panicked steps took her out of the attacking swarm at last. She burst into the light and ran straight into a statue, knocking the wind out of her lungs. She gasped through her breathing mask and looked around.

The swarm was thickest around the hole. Dark figures staggered in the heart of the cloud. One by one, individual Guards fought their way free. Coated with butterflies, they looked like delicately winged moving carpets.

Mimi was about to go to the aid of the Guards when a figure dressed in red and white dashed into the fray waving a burning branch. Mr. Kipling, who'd been looking for his peaked cap in the wreckage of the wedding tent, had been separated from the Guards when the swarm attacked. Fortunately, he still wore his white gloves from the wedding. Around his face he had wrapped a white scarf that covered everything but his grey eyes. Swiping his makeshift torch back and forth he waded into the swarm, looking for Guards who were still upright. The butterflies shrank back from the heat; any that came too close ignited and shrivelled to crispy black husks.

Several more Guards struggled free, guided by the flaming torch. Many, too many more lay on the ground, immobilized by butterfly stings.

Mimi shouted, "Over here! Over here!" The Guards followed the sound of her voice, staggering blindly towards her. She grabbed the closest by the hand and pulled him over to a spot where a bonfire of broken chairs, shattered and set alight in the Firebird attack, burned brightly. The heat was enough to keep the butterflies at bay. She dragged another Guard over, and another. Soon a dozen Guards were swiping the clinging butterflies from their goggles.

"How many did we lose?" Aidan's voice was so welcome that Mimi felt tears start in her eyes. He grabbed her arm and shook her. "Mimi? How many?"

"Loads. I couldn't count 'em all."

Mr. Kipling dashed out of the cloud waving his torch. Mimi thought it was a miracle he hadn't been stung. The man joined them by the fire. "You know, I never liked butterflies. Too fluttery for me by half! But these really take the biscuit."

Aidan pulled a burning stick from the flames. "Grab a torch, everyone. We're going to get our people out of there."

"Oh no," one of the other Guards gasped and pointed. "The stairs."

In the heat of the attack they had forgotten the refugees climbing above. Butterflies were separating from the main group and heading for the vulnerable children, who were looking behind them and pointing. Mrs. Francis urged them to climb, but the butterflies were already alighting. Here and there a child slumped motionless on the stone steps. The other children, filled with terror, began to push the ones in front. Panic was spreading.

"We gotta help," Mimi shouted.

"What about our comrades?" Aidan pointed at the Guards lying unconscious around the breach. "We can't just leave them."

"We have to fer now," Mimi said. "Our job's to protect the children. We cain't do nuthin' fer these fellars if we lose the whole mountain."

Aidan was torn, his eyes wide behind the goggles. Finally, he decided. "Grab a torch and follow me."

The Guards did as they were told and soon they were racing up the stairs to the aid of the escaping children.

MRS. FRANCIS WATCHED the approaching swarm with mounting terror.

"Stay calm! Stay calm! Don't push!" she cried but no one was listening. Children were climbing over each other to get to safety. The raccoons were doing their best, but they were small and not as strong as the panicked children.

"Oh dear," Mrs. Francis gasped. Her wedding dress was torn and smeared with soot. She looked up and saw that the gate to the Workshop level was less than a hundred metres away, but it seemed like miles.

"Help me!"

The little woman turned to the sound of the terrified voice. A tiny girl, the last of the long line of children, sat a few steps above Mrs. Francis. "I hurt my foot." Mrs. Francis looked behind her and saw that the closest butterfly was scant metres away. She dashed up, crushed the little child to her ample bosom, and began to grimly climb the steps.

Mrs. Francis had never had a child of her own. The tiny girl in her arms was a stranger. She didn't even know her name. There are some people, however, to whom all children are important and special and worthy of any sacrifice. Mrs. Francis knew that she would not be able to outrun the butterflies. She had never been fit, had always been chubby, and right now she was close to exhaustion. So she did the only thing she could do: she stopped and covered the girl with her voluminous wedding dress and braced herself for the sting of the first butterfly.

"What's your name, child?"

"Olive," the girl sniffed.

"Olive. What a lovely name. Don't cry, Olive. I'm Mrs. Francis and I'm here to take care of you."

They huddled closer and waited for the end.

Instead, they felt a strong wind rush over them from above. The wind was accompanied by a loud roar. Mrs. Francis raised her head to see the rear of the *Orphan Queen*, its great propellers blasting a strong current of air over the huddled woman and child. The back cargo door was open and Parveen stood there. He saw Mrs. Francis and waved.

Mrs. Francis hazarded a look over her shoulder and saw no butterflies. Their tiny wings weren't strong enough to counter the propellers' blast. They were being held at bay. Around the corner of the stairs rushed the remaining members of Aidan's group. Mr. Kipling saw Mrs. Francis and ran forward. He threw aside his torch and crushed her in a bear hug.

"Darling! Are you all right?"

"I am now!"

"Enough mushy stuff," they heard Mimi say. "Let's hightail it!" Mimi pushed the adults along. Mrs. Francis held tight to Olive and together they mounted the stairs. Above them, the last of the refugees passed through the gate. Guards and raccoons stood beckoning. Mimi waved to Parveen as they passed and he gave her the thumbs-up.

MR. SWEET and Mr. Candy flexed their fingers and checked their jetpacks. All the other agents followed suit. Satisfied, Mr. Sweet turned to Mr. Candy. "It would seem that the time has come to get our hands dirty, Mr. Candy."

"Indeed it has, Mr. Sweet. Indeed it has."

They thumbed their ignition buttons and rose through the breached gate into the cavern beyond.

CARA WAITED with the Guards at the metal plate that served as the gate to the Workshop Cavern. The final refugees hurried in, with Aidan and Mimi bringing up the rear. Cara hugged Aidan fiercely. He hugged her back briefly and then pushed her away.

"Where are the others?" Cara asked.

"The butterflies," he said bitterly. "They didn't make it." Cara's face was a picture of shock. "We don't have time to worry about that now. Is everybody up in the Nurtury?"

Cara nodded. "George has been shuttling them up in the elevator. Just these ones here to go."

"Good," Aidan said. "Quick. Let's get the gates closed."

"Wait!" Mrs. Francis pushed forward. "Parveen and Noor are still in the airship."

"That's right!" Mimi dashed back through the gate to the top of the stairs. What she saw filled her with dread.

The airship was making a wide turn pursued by a flock of Grey Agents. The *Orphan Queen* was nowhere as fast as the agents' jetpacks. As she watched, the first of them approached the open cargo hold and attempted to enter the airship. Suddenly, the agent clutched at his head and then dropped like a stone to the floor of the cavern far below.

INSIDE THE CARGO HOLD, Parveen picked up another hamster bomb from the box at his feet. He looked out at the open air and tried desperately to keep his balance. He had tied himself off with a piece of rope, but standing was next to impossible with Noor at the controls. He regretted allowing her to take the wheel. There was no helping it now, though. She wasn't doing badly, but the middle of a battle was not exactly the ideal time to learn how to navigate smoothly.

Parveen saw another Grey Agent approaching. It was a female. Parveen found her pallid skin and blank expression somehow more disturbing than the male version. He wondered briefly and incongruously if the Grey Agents married or had children like normal people. He didn't have more than a second to ponder the question before the agent swooped into the cargo hold, directly at him.

Parveen cocked back his arm and threw a hamster bomb, but he missed. Silently wishing Mimi were here, he braced himself as the agent bowled him over. She wrapped her hands around his throat and began to squeeze. Parveen battered the strong hands with his smaller fists, but to no avail. They rolled around the cargo hold, the plume of blue fire from the jetpack scorching the planks of the deck.

Parveen knew he couldn't continue in a wrestling match with the agent: she was far larger and much stronger. He turned his head and saw the gaping cargo door. Just then Noor made another of her hard turns, and he pushed off with all his strength. Parveen and the agent rolled up and out of the cargo door and into space.

Parveen fell until he reached the end of the rope. The agent's grip was jerked loose as they bounced from the impact. Parveen looked down past her blank, goggled face and saw the fire-dotted lawns hundreds of metres below.

The jetpack on the agent's back was still firing. It spun the dangling combatants in a great swinging arc. Parveen knew the rope would hold both of them forever. In desperation he leaned closer to the pack and saw a cluster of hoses running down the side of the metal device. He reached down, grasped the largest of the hoses, and pulled with all his might.

The hose ripped free and sprayed some form of liquid into the air. The flame on the jetpack fizzled and died. The agent looked over her shoulder, the same blank expression on her grey face. Parveen took the opportunity to wrench his whole body in one titanic wriggle. The agent's grip slipped and she fell, looking up at Parveen with a strange expression on her face, neither fear nor anger, merely puzzlement: a look Parveen would never forget. Turning away before the creature struck the ground, he began hauling himself back up towards the ship.

"Parveen!" He heard Mimi's voice and stopped climbing. He looked and saw her standing at the top of the stairs, waving her arms. She cupped her hands to her mouth and shouted. "We have to close the gates. Come on! Now."

Two agents spotted Mimi and swooped towards her.

She turned to meet their attack, pulling her combat stick from her back and swinging hard at the closest one. Parveen watched long enough to see the agent reel back from the impact of the blow before he turned his attention to the hole and saw more agents pouring through the breach. He redoubled his efforts and finally heaved himself into the cargo bay.

As soon as he got his breath back, he pushed himself to his feet and raced up the corridor that ran the length of the ship, then through the galley and into the bridge. He stopped, horrified at what he saw.

The wide glass windscreen in the front of the bridge was shattered. Two agents held Noor in their grip. As he leapt forward to stop them they launched themselves out of the shattered windscreen, carrying his sister away.

"NO!" Parveen screamed. The agents roared off, his sister thrashing between them. He ran to the shattered window and watched them carry his sister down to the hole and through. Several other agents rose in their place, heading in a V formation straight for the airship.

Parveen was an intelligent boy. The whole of his being cried out to go and help his sister immediately. His practical side, however, told him that without a plan he had no chance of getting her back. He looked to the top of the stairs and saw that Mimi was still battling the two agents, swinging her stick wildly and fending off their attacks. The gate was open above her. Parveen went to the wheel and spun it. The airship turned sharply, drawing the agents after it. Parveen aimed the vessel straight for the open gate. He pushed the throttle forward to full power.

Mimi drove her stick into the belly of one attacker then spun and batted the rifle barrel of the other just in time to make a shot fly safely over her head.

"Is that all you got?" She danced from foot to foot, holding the stick at the ready. The two agents floated in front of her, calculating their next move. Mimi glanced past them and saw the *Orphan Queen* approaching, its long nose heading straight at her. Through the shattered windscreen she saw Parveen, his face grim and determined, holding the wheel steady.

"Holy monkeys!" Mimi gasped. "He's lost it." She turned on her heel and ran for the open gate. "Out o' the way! Ever'body back!"

The two agents watched her retreat with surprise. They looked at each other, shrugged, and turned to investigate the loud humming noise building behind them. They had an instant to register the bulk of the ship approaching before it smashed into the stairs and scraped them like a grey smear on the stone steps.

The pursuing Grey Agents had managed to catch up with the *Queen* just seconds before the impact. Three of them had already been in the cargo hold when the ship crashed, two were underneath, and one, a female agent called Miss Gumdrop, had managed to fly down the corridor to the bridge, arriving just in time to see Parveen tie himself to the wheel.

"Stop!" Miss Gumdrop levelled her rifle at Parveen.

"If you say so," Parveen said and pointed forward.

Miss Gumdrop saw the grey stone stairs looming before them. "Goodness," she said, before the crash sent her hurtling forward, smashing her head on the window's frame as it suddenly stopped when she didn't. Her hat was dashed from her head and a mess of brightly coloured cables flew in every direction.

The ship slid into the open gate and smashed, its wreckage filling the opening like a very messy plug. Mimi and the other Guards had managed to get clear just in time. Effectively, the door was closed.

Mimi scrambled over shattered stone and airship wreckage. "Parveen!" She clawed away broken scrapes of hull and tattered shreds of gas envelope. "Parveen!!!" Her efforts became more frantic. Aidan and Cara joined her in pulling debris aside. In a minute, they had managed to clear a path to the shattered bridge.

"Parveen! Can you hear me?" Mimi shouted, on the verge of hysteria.

A square of hull planking jerked and then fell to the floor with a clatter. Parveen's head and shoulders appeared in the gap. "Yes. I can hear you. I think anything with ears can hear you, and even some things that sense only vibrations."

Mimi laughed and tears of relief leaked from the corners of her eyes as she reached down, grabbed his tunic by the shoulders, and pulled him out of the wreckage. She shook him angrily. "Are you nuts? What's the deal? Crashin' like that ... you coulda bin killed!"

Parveen dangled in her grasp and shrugged. "It was a calculated risk. The gate is blocked now. The agents will have some difficulty getting through. Now," he said patiently, "please put me down."

Mimi laughed and hugged him once. She dropped him onto his feet.

Parveen reached back into the debris and hauled out a metal cylinder with grey nylon straps.

"Is that a jetpack?" Mimi asked.

"One of the agents was wearing it. She has no further need of it."

Mimi smiled fiercely and looked past Parveen into the wreckage. "Is thur another one o' them things handy?"

Aidan broke in. "All right. We don't have time for souvenir hunting. This level is secure. We're retreating. We'll use the time to make sure everyone gets out. Everybody up to the stairs, now!"

"But we've stopped 'em. It's time ta regroup," Mimi disagreed. "They'll take forever ta git through this mess."

As if to prove her wrong, a dull explosion rippled through the rock beneath their feet. The wreckage of the *Orphan Queen* shifted slightly.

"Then agin, I could be wrong."

Mimi and the rest of the Guards ran for the stairs on the heels of Aidan and Cara. Parveen ran a few steps after them and stopped, ducking behind a statue of some King or other. He watched until he was sure the others were up the stairs and out of sight. When they were gone he slung the jetpack over one shoulder and jogged to the doors of the tech department and the lab that he and Noor had been using that very afternoon.

"Don't worry, Noor," he said to himself as another explosion shook his makeshift barricade. "I am coming for you."

Chapter 24

Mr. Candy and Mr. Sweet watched from aloft as the CCTVs roamed about Frieda's Cavern. The lumbering vehicles had made their way up the stairs and through the shattered gate. Now the cranes on the back of each vehicle were rising and falling, plucking unconscious children from the ground and placing them in the cargo containers in neat rows.

"The butterflies were most effective, Mr. Sweet."

"Indeed, Mr. Candy. Now we will have plenty of energy for the final integration. They are not very ripe but they should provide a sufficient boost to open the gate."

"But we have not found Hamish X. I thought the boy would have challenged us by now."

"Indeed, Mr. Candy. And I have not detected his electronic signature anywhere in the mountain. I had assumed the stone was shielding it from us but I am beginning to think the King wasn't lying."

Mr. Candy shook his head. "Of course the King was lying. The boy must be here. We must scour the higher levels."

A loud crash echoed off the stone walls. "Ah," Mr. Sweet said, looking up. "The blockage has been cleared. Send in the troops."

IN THE NURTURY, the gathered refugees heard the shattering crash below and knew they didn't have much time. Great arched doorways had already been unsealed. These portals led to the escape pods designed to ferry the residents of the Hollow Mountain should their safety be threatened.

The children were lining up, carrying whatever meagre possessions could be crammed into a single backpack. The younger ones were crying and the older ones were on the verge of tears. Guards urged the children forward. George raccoons were everywhere, doing what they could to keep the exodus orderly. Still, progress was agonizingly slow.

"Come on! Come on! Keep moving! We don't have much time," Aidan shouted.

"No pushing and shoving," Mrs. Francis called, waddling here and there, helping where she could.

Aidan motioned for Mimi, Cara, and Mr. Kipling to step aside. They formed a small circle and spoke in hushed tones.

"We have to hold the Grey Agents off long enough to get the pods loaded," Aidan said. "We have to make a stand here."

"I'm in," Mimi said grimly. She checked her stun pistol. "They ain't gittin' past me, if I can help it."

"I have a question," Mr. Kipling interjected. "Where is the King?"

"Here." The King's voice came from above. As one, they looked up the stairs. They saw a strange and wonderful sight.

The King was taking the steps three at a time. His incredible progress was made possible by the fact that his entire body was encased in a suit of shining chrome armour. King Liam bounded down the stairs with easy grace, coming to a stop before them. He was smiling, his head encased in the silver helmet.

"I'm sorry I've taken so long, but George tells me you have all done wonderfully well. This thing," he waved the metal arms, "is difficult to get into unassisted."

"Sire, what are your orders? We're all ready to fight to the end."

"I know you are." The King smiled sadly. "I don't think you'll like my orders very much. I want you to get out. I want all of you to get into the escape pods and go. I will stay behind and hold them off for as long as I can."

"But we can't leave you here alone," Cara cried.

"Oh, I won't be alone, will I, George?"

All the raccoons stopped what they were doing and looked to the King. "No," they answered in unison, hundreds of tiny voices speaking all at once. "We are with you, King Liam." The raccoons began to congregate near the King. They came from everywhere, hundreds of furry bodies massing in the open space of the cavern floor. They sat up in rows, their bright black eyes blinking in their masked faces.

"You see?" the King said lightly. "George will be with me."

Aidan and Cara saw the King's determined expression and knew there was no dissuading him. They dropped to one knee and bowed their heads.

"Oh, I wish you wouldn't do that. It makes me embarrassed," the King laughed, laying a large metal finger delicately on each of their heads. "Now go. Make sure my children are safe."

Aidan and Cara rose and turned to their duties. "Let's get a move on," Aidan bawled, but his voice cracked and Mimi swore he was about to cry. Mr. Kipling followed the brother and sister after doffing his peaked cap and sketching a quick bow.

Mimi shook her head. "You ain't gonna make it outta here alive."

"Dear Mimi," Liam said softly. "How proud I am to have earned your friendship. I was never meant for a life outside the Mountain. I've known that for a long time. You have a full life ahead of you. I am going to stay and make sure you have it, you and all the others." He smiled and patted her shoulder with a shining metal hand. "Who knows? I may even win. Miracles happen." A huge boom echoed through the chamber. "Hurry, they'll be through any minute."

Mimi gritted her teeth and forced herself not to cry. "You've made miracles happen. For me and Parveen and ..." Suddenly, something occurred to her. She narrowed her green eyes. "You know where Hamish X is, don't ya?"

The King's face clouded. "He is gone. He went to find his destiny."

Mimi was crushed. "How could he leave us at a time like this? We need him here!" She felt her face flush with anger. How could he leave her without saying goodbye?

"Don't be angry at him. He had no idea this would happen. He was long gone when the attack began." An explosion rocked the Workshop Cavern below. The King's head snapped around and the silver helm snapped with it. "I must be going now. Hamish X wanted me to say goodbye." The King turned to go.

"Where did he go?" Mimi demanded.

"Central Africa," King Liam called over his shoulder as he bounded towards the stairs. "To find Professor Ballantyne-Stewart." And then he was gone.

Mimi watched as the raccoons headed after their master, and then she turned to join the others.

ONE LEVEL BELOW, agents were piling through the newly cleared wreckage of the airship and gathering in the centre of the cavern. About fifty of them had made it through when the King appeared at the head of the stairs.

Chapter 25

"Grey Agents, you are not welcome here." The King descended the stairs, step by step, his silver suit shimmering in the light of the Daniel's Panels overhead. "This is my home. Leave now and none of you will be harmed."

The agents looked at each other and then back at the apparition walking down towards them. Mr. Sweet and Mr. Candy were not yet among them. Rows of grey faces, goggles trained on the King, stared without expression. As one, the agents raised their rifles.

"It's going to be that way, is it?" The King chuckled. "Very well."

Down the stairs behind him came a deluge of tiny furry bodies, hundreds of George raccoons tumbling headlong and hurling themselves into the massed ranks of the agents. The agents staggered back in shock before remembering they were holding rifles. They began firing at the oncoming beasts, the bolts of energy issuing from their weapons striking individual raccoons. The effect was horrifying, with raccoons flailing about in bizarre contortions and falling in a smouldering lump on the stone floor. The smell of burning filled the air.

The attack of the raccoons gave the King the time he needed to leap down from the stairs directly into the midst of the beleaguered agents. He swung his metal fists with augmented speed and strength. Each blow sent an agent reeling, many too damaged to rise again. The raccoons were taking their toll as well. Alone, a raccoon isn't much of a threat, but twenty of the creatures leaping on one agent were enough to pull the wretched being from its feet.

Any agent trying to rise up into the air using a jetpack was not immune to attacks. King Liam picked up raccoons and tossed them aloft at the agents. The raccoons latched onto their victims. The agents frantically clawed at the raccoons, trying to fling them off, but the raccoons crawled for the heads of their victims and wrenched their hats off, plunging clever little fingers into the mass of wires in the agents' skulls. Agents plummeted to the cavern floor, writhing and convulsing.

The agents were soon fighting a rearguard action, backing into a defensive square and shuffling back in the direction of the exit. One of their number, a Mr. Floss, thumbed his radio. "Mr. Candy! Mr. Sweet! We are under attack! Please advise!"

Mr. Candy and Mr. Sweet stopped supervising the loading of the children and stood stock-still. They consulted video projections on the inside of their goggles and saw the fury of the King's attack and the overwhelming number of raccoons.

"Raccoons, Mr. Candy?"

"Raccoons indeed, Mr. Sweet."

"It would seem that it is time to unleash the full measure of our disapproval upon the King of Switzerland and his furry automatons."

"Agreed, Mr. Candy. Activate the Teddy."

Mr. Candy pressed a long finger to his temple. "Activate the Teddy."

One of the CCTVs stood alone in the middle of Frieda's Cavern. While the others roamed hither and yon, gathering up prone children with their cranes, this lone vehicle remained completely still, idling gently. Now, the top of the cargo pod folded open. When the two flaps were completely extended a huge metallic claw, loosely covered in tattered brown fur, reached out and grasped the side of the cargo pod on one side. Then an equally vast claw reached out and grasped the opposite side. With an ear-splitting roar, amplified by the surrounding stone walls, a terrible creature hauled itself erect, towering five metres into the air.

The ODA, being experts in the art of terrifying children, had brought all the powers of their twisted minds to bear on the creation that hoisted itself up from the cargo pod that was its home. The Teddy was indeed a giant teddy bear, but this version of the common stuffed toy loved by children the world over was a twisted and terrifying parody of the original. Its body was covered in filthy brown fur, matted with mud and oil that leaked from its mechanical workings. The vast head the creature sported was horrific.

Instead of the customary benevolent smile there were clashing steel fangs. One of its round ears dangled from a shred of fabric. Its button eyes were glossy, dead camera lenses that whirred, extended, and retracted as the Teddy continually focused and refocused, trying to assess its new surroundings.

The Teddy was designed to seek and destroy an individual target keyed into its electronic brain. Mr. Candy pulled a video image from his own feed and sent it to the computer processor that was the Teddy's brain. The Teddy stood eerily still as it processed the image, lubricating oil dripping from its vast claws and fangs. After a few seconds it sent a signal confirming that it had received and understood the communication.

The metal monster heaved itself out of the cargo pod, setting the CCTV's tortured suspension rocking wildly. The steel bear feet of the Teddy gouged holes in the turf as it loped across the ruined gardens and mounted the stairs.

IN THE WORKSHOP COURTYARD the raccoons and the King had pushed the Grey Agents back to the gate. There the retreat halted, though, as the agents held off wave after wave of the raccoon assault. Smoking, mangled raccoons with electronic innards were splayed out on the flagstones all around.

The King stopped. He struggled to breathe. Though the suit translated his tiniest movement into action, amplifying his strength enormously, the sustained action was taking its toll on his sickly body. On top of that, the basketball game with Hamish X had sapped his energy dangerously. His chest heaved and his eyes watered. He was almost at the end of his endurance. Fortunately, against all hope, it looked as though the agents were stymied. If he could hold them off for a few more precious minutes, the escape pods would be off. He was just beginning to think everything was going to be all right when he heard the heavy tread on the stairs below.

Clang! ... *Clang!* ... *Clang!* Something was coming ... something big. Closer and closer the echoing clank approached. The impact of each step shivered through the stone and into the King's suit.

"This doesn't sound good," the King said to the raccoons ranged around.

"No, Sire, it doesn't," they answered.

The King lifted one of the raccoons in a metal hand. "Go. Find Hamish X. Tell him what has happened and help him if you can," he whispered into the ear of the George raccoon. "Hurry."

He put the creature down and it scuttled away, up the stairs, heading for the Royal level. The King watched it go, then turned to face his fate.

The agents at the gate scattered. Out of the gate emerged the giant furry nightmare that was Teddy. The thing ducked under the frame of the entranceway. The huge bulk of the beast's body was barely able to fit through the debris-choked gate. Once inside, the great shaggy head swivelled back and forth, lenses whirring in and out until its gaze settled on King Liam in his chrome armoured suit.

"Oh, my," the King said softly, drawing himself up to his full height. He raised his hands in a defensive posture.

"*Roooooowwwwwwr!*" With an inhuman howl the Teddy raised its metal claws, lowered its head, and charged.

Chapter 26

Mimi and Cara raised their heads from loading their escape pod. Mrs. Francis was safely inside the pod, sitting in the cushioned bench that ringed the inside of the sphere. Mr. Kipling stopped with one leg in the entry hatch.

The Escape Pod System was devised and constructed in the reign of Queen Josephina, fifty-third Queen of Switzerland. She was renowned for her fear of enclosed spaces and wanted to be sure escape was possible in the event of a cave-in. She'd had a crew widen existing tunnels to accommodate spherical capsules designed to carry inhabitants down through the mountain into an underground river that flowed out through the roots of the Nutterhorn.

The pods were hidden in a compartment cunningly carved behind a stone slab in the wall of the Nurtury Cavern. The compartment was a long tunnel with round hatches every ten metres. The hatches opened into individual pods. Once a pod was loaded and the hatch sealed, it would launch automatically down long stone tubes.

Guards stood at the hatches to the pods, supervising the loading. They were almost done when the fierce roar echoed from the Workshop tier below, cannoning off the stone walls and up the stairs.

"What in all heck was that?"

"It sounded like some kind of animal. Aidan, shouldn't we go and help the King?" Cara asked.

Aidan was pacing back and forth by the slab. "No," he snapped, "the King told us to go. We're going." He stopped pacing when the terrifying roar repeated itself. He stared out through the opening, his hand gripping the hilt of his pistol.

"Aidan," Mimi said, "we gotta go help."

"No!" Aidan shouted, spinning and glaring at her. "No! He gave us an order. Load the pods. NOW!"

Cara and Mimi were cowed by the ferocity of his tone. Cara spoke. "Yes, Captain. I believe everyone is secured. Shall we give the order to close the pods?"

"Yes," Aidan said, calmer now. "Close the pods."

"Close pods!" Cara shouted the order. Each Guard echoed the order in turn as they stepped into the pods and pulled the hatches closed. As each one thudded shut there was a hiss and the pod slid out of its socket. The pods fell away, down stone tubes into darkness, carrying their precious cargo to safety.

At last, the only pod remaining was the one containing Mr. Kipling, Mrs. Francis, and ten frightened children.

Aidan came over to the open hatch where Mimi and Cara waited. "In you go, girls."

"You first," Mimi said, scowling.

Aidan looked into her eyes. "It's bad enough that my King has sent me away. Let me be the last to leave, at least."

Cara looked at her brother for a long moment and then nodded. "You did everything you could." Impulsively, she kissed his cheek before stepping into the pod.

"We'll git 'em back fer this," Mimi swore. She stepped into the pod after Cara. The girls settled onto the bench beside Mrs. Francis. They fastened their belts. Cara held out a hand to Aidan.

"Come on, little brother," she said softly.

Aidan stood in the hatchway and smiled sadly. "I love you, big sister. Goodbye." He slammed the hatch shut.

266

"Aidan!" Cara screamed but it was too late. The pod dropped away and fell into darkness.

THE TEDDY shambled in a headlong rush at the King, razor-sharp claws extended. Raccoons leapt at the beast, clinging to its metal limbs and attempting to slow its progress, but without any real effect. The King waited until the Teddy was only a few steps away before leaping up, directing both feet at its furry face.

The creature reached out mid-stride and swatted the King like a fly, sending him tumbling through the air to crash into the stone wall of the cavern. The Teddy skidded to a stop. Swarming with raccoons, it shook itself like a dog, sending furry tormentors scattering like drops of water. Then it swung its massive head until it locked onto the King's prone body. Liam stirred painfully.

The King was having trouble rising. His left arm was useless, crushed in the impact with the wall. He pushed himself into a sitting position with his right arm. His legs were sluggish but he managed to force himself upright. He looked at the floor beside him and saw a raccoon twitching, its mechanical back broken but its eyes still aware.

"Oh George, it pains me to see you like this."

"Don't worry about me, my King. One of us is even now making its way out. I will live on."

The King smiled and reached out, scratching the twitching creature on the top of its flat skull. "Old friend," Liam rasped. "I will miss you. Even if you are only a machine."

"My ... King," the raccoon croaked, its vocal projection systems badly damaged. "I will hold you in my hard drive, forever."

"That will have to do. Goodbye, George."

The raccoon, and all the raccoons in the chamber, went still. The King turned to the Teddy and waited.

The Teddy seemed to sense that its prey was wounded. It made a leisurely approach, traversing the flagstones with slow, heavy steps. The paving shattered under its ponderous clawed feet. The King waited until it was less than five metres away—and then leapt with all his strength, his one good arm extended.

The King's leap carried him between the monster's mighty paws. King Liam latched his legs around the creature's neck. He immediately began punching the glossy surface of an eye lens with his right arm. Glass shattered. Half-blinded, the Teddy roared in fury, grabbed hold of the King's legs, and ripped the annoying pest from its head. It threw the King with all its strength.

The King sailed through the air again. Slamming into the doors of the elevator, the armour shattered. The King tried to rise but couldn't. He lay with his back to the doors. He watched the Teddy approach.

The creature took its time to close the distance. Cautiously, it nudged the King with its massive toe. The King tried to move away but now the armour was a dead weight, shattered and broken, holding him in place.

"My you are an ugly thing," King Liam coughed. A trickle of blood leaked from the corner of his mouth, dribbling down his pale cheek. "They've escaped. They're beyond your reach." He smiled grimly into the eye that remained intact, knowing that his image was being conveyed back to Mr. Candy and Mr. Sweet. "Hamish X is gone."

The Teddy reached down and lifted the King in its mighty paw. Liam was helpless in his ruined armour, his limbs dangling uselessly. With one claw, the Teddy flicked off the King's helmet, letting it fall to the stone floor where it clattered like an empty can. King Liam closed his eyes and waited for the end.

"*Noooo!*" The cry was filled with rage. Liam opened his eyes in time to see Aidan leap from the stairs above the Teddy. The Guard Captain landed on the monster's shaggy shoulder, a stun pistol in his hand.

"How's this for a pain in the neck?" Aidan growled. He jammed the pistol into a joint between the shoulder and the humongous head. He fired and kept firing until the pistol's energy was drained.

Sometimes luck is fickle. Sometimes it is kind. Sometimes every particle of the world aligns to give you the best of all possible results. This was one of those rare times. Though the monstrous teddy bear was overwhelmingly huge and powerful, the pistol managed to strike it in the most vulnerable spot, the central power conduit that ran from its brain to its spine. The creature went completely rigid and then fell with all the grace of a small building, crashing headlong to the cobbles and sending pieces of shattered stone flying in the air.

Aidan leapt to the ground as the Teddy fell, rolling and ending up at the side of his King. He looked down at King Liam and his heart was wrenched by what he saw. Liam was still trapped in the massive paw of the lifeless beast, his face pale, his eyes closed. The unruly red hair was plastered to his forehead with sweat and soot. A trickle of red threaded its way from the corner of his mouth and across his white skin.

"Majesty," he said with a choked sob, desperately pulling on the massive claws, trying to loosen the Teddy's death grip.

The King opened his pale eyes. He blinked, coughed, and winced at the pain. Looking up into Aidan's tearful face, he smiled. "Captain," Liam said, his voice a raspy whisper. "I gave you an order."

"I'm sorry, Sire. The rest are safely away. I couldn't leave you alone."

The King smiled and coughed again, blood dribbling down his chin. When he was finally able to speak again he said, "I must admit, I'm glad you are here."

"I'm where I belong, Sire."

"I hate you seeing me like this ... So helpless."

"My King, you are many things, but you have never been helpless." Aidan took the King's hand in his own. "Rest now."

"Yes," Liam whispered, his breath uneven. "I could do with a little sleep. So tired." The blue eyes fluttered closed. The King took a ragged breath and then another ... then was still. And so, King Liam, seventy-seventh King of Switzerland, Master of the Hollow Mountain, was no more.

"So sad," said a voice. A shadow fell across the Guard Captain and his King. Aidan looked up to see Mr. Candy and Mr. Sweet standing over him. "Still, it's what he deserved."

Aidan raised his pistol, aimed at Mr. Sweet, and thumbed the trigger. Nothing happened. The charge was gone, expended on the Teddy. Mr. Candy tilted his head to one side. Holding out a closed fist, he opened his gloved fingers to reveal a butterfly. The colourful insect darted across the empty space between the agent and the boy and stung Aidan's exposed neck. The Lieutenant of the Royal Guards fell across the body of his King.

Chapter 27

The door to the laboratory swung open. Two Grey Agents stormed into the room, rifles poised to deal with any stray children. They were part of a detail that was sweeping the entire mountain, gathering up any children who might be hiding and taking them into custody. They were surprised to discover that one of their number was already there.

A Grey Agent stood in the middle of the room holding a small, dark-skinned boy in his arms. The agent wore a jetpack on his back. The boy was unconscious, hanging loosely in the agent's grasp.

"How did you get in here ahead of us?" one of the agents, a Mr. Toffee, demanded. "We were the first ones in this quadrant."

The strange agent shrugged. He took a couple of steps towards the newcomers but still didn't speak.

"What's your name and unit number?" the second newcomer, who was called Miss Nougat, demanded. "Why don't you speak? Are you damaged?"

The strange agent walked straight up to them. When he was less than a metre away the little boy he was holding came to life, tossing two orange objects at Mr. Toffee and Miss Nougat. The agents had no time to react: the hamsters latched onto them, skittered up to their skulls, and delivered their lethal charge. Toffee and Nougat fell in a heap on the laboratory floor.

Parveen eased back into the robot's arms and thumbed the small black remote control box. The jetpack flared to life. The robot hovered out of the laboratory door and floated down the corridor into the courtyard.

Parveen peered through slitted lids as he guided the robot agent through the maze of wreckage from the battle between the Teddy and the King. His heart ached when he saw the fallen body of King Liam looking tiny and frail in the metal frame of his armour. He saw Aidan tossed onto a cart. The Guard Captain still breathed, so Parveen knew he was alive. An agent rolled the cart towards the elevator that was now functioning.

I can't do anything for him yet, Parveen thought. *I must find Noor*. Everywhere, the bodies of raccoons lay smouldering and inert on the stone paving. He felt some satisfaction seeing the fallen agents sprawled out like tumbled scarecrows here and there.

No time to mourn now, Parveen said to himself. *Must find Noor.*

He floated on past agents who were searching the wreckage. Above, in the Nurtury and residences, he heard explosions. He hoped the other children had gotten safely away.

Gliding to the stairs, he floated down the stone steps through the wreckage of the doughty *Orphan Queen*, feeling a pang of sorrow for the craft that had brought them through so much. He stopped short when he saw what had become of the green wonderland of Frieda's Cavern.

Everywhere fires burned. What had once been beautiful gardens were now torn and charred wastelands, ravaged by the attack of the Firebirds and the treads of the CCTVs. The ungainly tracked vehicles were moving around the cavern, loading the bodies of stunned children into their large, gaping cargo holds.

"You there!"

An agent stood on the stairs below. Parveen touched a knob on the hidden remote and the robot tilted its head.

"Get moving!"

The robot, guided by Parveen, nodded and started down the stairs. Parveen sent the robot floating in a straight line out into the open air, heading as fast as he could for the ruined gateway to Heinrich's Cavern. He did his best to avoid crossing paths with any more agents. The risk of finally having someone figure out that the robot wasn't actually an agent became greater with each encounter. He reached the gate without further incident and headed down into the lowest cavern.

He sailed towards the loading platform. On the stone apron a long row of CCTVs idled, the noise like a herd of huge beasts grumbling. Agents were supervising the loading of more unconscious children into the cargo pods. Parveen floated down for a closer look.

The back walls of the pods were lowered to form ramps. Agents carried children up the ramps and laid them in little compartments like letters in little cubbyholes at the post office. Mr. Candy and Mr. Sweet stood together deep in conversation. Parveen steered well clear of them.

She must be in one of these, Parveen thought. He floated along the line of vehicles, getting as close as he dared, scanning the interior of each vehicle for a sign of his sister, Noor. He had gone down the entire line without success and was just starting back up when the farthest of the CCTVs raised the ramp of its cargo pod and slammed it shut. The CCTV started forward, heading for the exit tunnel.

Parveen knew he didn't have much time. He had to find his sister soon. He continued back up the line, scanning the pods as quickly as he dared. At last, his heart leaped. He saw a head of glossy black hair done up in a ponytail that dangled almost to the floor of the pod. Parveen turned the robot and headed up the ramp of the vehicle.

Floating into the cargo pod, he came to the cubby holding Noor. She looked to be sleeping deeply, breathing slow and even. Her face was peaceful. Was there any lasting damage? He didn't know. He could only hope the effect would wear off if he got her away.

He made the robot lower him into the cubby alongside her. He crawled in, unhooking his bag from the belt of the robot. He had food and some essential tools in the bag, packed in haste while the battle raged in the Workshop courtyard.

When he was safely stowed he guided the robot out of the cargo pod and down the ramp. Using the remote, he directed the robot in a straight line, far away from the cargo vehicles, and then pressed a button. The robot reached into its coat pocket, pulled out a hamster, and slapped it against the side of its head. The effect was instantaneous: the robot agent convulsed and then collapsed on the platform. Agents gathered around, looking down at the heap of grey clothing.

Mr. Candy and Mr. Sweet jerked their heads towards the fallen robot. "Leave him. There's no time," Mr. Sweet instructed. The agents dispersed, returning to their individual tasks.

"We've lost another agent, Mr. Sweet."

"Indeed, Mr. Candy. Those hamsters are disturbingly effective. We must develop a countermeasure."

"Not a pressing need. Once the integration is achieved and the portal opened, it will all be moot."

"Moot indeed. Still no sign of Hamish X."

"Sadly no. I believe the King was indeed telling the truth when he said the asset was not here. What shall we do?"

Mr. Candy thought for a moment. "I think we can make Hamish X come to us."

"How, Mr. Candy?"

"I think the destruction of the Hollow Mountain will be a clear message to Hamish X. He'll know we have these pathetic children, his *friends*"—Mr. Candy spat the word out as if it burned his tongue—"and he will come to take them back, Mr. Sweet. Is the charge in place? Shall we get out of this miserable mountain?"

"Indeed, Mr. Candy. Indeed on both counts."

Mr. Sweet and Mr. Candy fired their packs and set off in the direction of the tunnel.

PARVEEN KNEW he had no chance of getting out of the cargo pod with his sister without being caught. He resigned himself to travelling in the cargo pod to its final destination, hoping there would be some opportunity for escape along the way. He huddled up close to his sister, throwing his arms around her inert body and hugging her tightly.

"Don't worry, Noor. We won't be parted again." The cargo pod door squealed as it rose. With a clang, it slammed shut, plunging Parveen and Noor into darkness.

AN HOUR LATER, Mr. Candy and Mr. Sweet stood on the mountainside, a helicopter idling nearby. Cold rain pelted down in the grey dawn.

"Many have escaped, Mr. Candy," Mr. Sweet said. "There are far too few children in the cargo pods."

"There are enough. They will serve us well during the integration. When the portal opens, it won't matter any more."

"Yes, Mr. Candy," Mr. Sweet nodded. "Shall we send Hamish X a message?"

Mr. Candy turned to Mr. Sweet and did something very odd for an agent: he smiled, showing yellow, discoloured teeth. Mr. Sweet smiled back, his teeth also ghastly and yellow-grey. Mr. Sweet held out a black box with a single red button in the centre. Mr. Candy plunged a long gloved finger down onto the button.

A deep rumble shook the mountainside. Beneath the earth, a detonation occurred that smashed through sheets of bedrock, bursting the crust of the earth like a pimple and releasing molten rock from deep within the root of the Hollow Mountain. Boiling red lava percolated up through the strata and began to fill Heinrich's Cavern in a rising red tide.

By the time the flow erupted out of the tunnel, sweeping down the mountainside like a river, the helicopter was long gone, winging its way across the lightening Swiss countryside. The Swiss people woke to the news that there'd been a volcanic eruption in the Alps for the first time in modern history.

"I do love an eruption, Mr. Sweet."

"It's very bracing, Mr. Candy."

Earlier, when they had climbed into their helicopter and lifted off, neither of them noticed the raccoon watching them from behind a rock. The creature blinked its black eyes. With a flick of its tail, it turned and headed south.

EPILOGUE

Hamish X did not, unfortunately, hear the news about the bizarre eruption. He had managed to run through the night, feeding on the amazing stamina his boots provided. He kept to the back roads and smaller highways, resting in the daytime on a moving freight train and running at night. He headed south.

After three days of travel he arrived in the Greek city of Athens in the early evening. The ruins of the Acropolis were framed in the orange glow of the setting sun as he jogged through the narrow streets through the busy traffic. A trip to the train station and he had the contents of the locker in his backpack: money, and several passports from different countries with several different identities.

It was dark when he arrived at the shores of the Mediterranean at the port of Piraeus, the shipping centre for Athens. In the blackest part of the night he trotted along the wharves, looking for a vessel that would suit his purposes. He wanted to get to Africa, and these fishing vessels plied the waters off the North African coast. At last, he saw a rusted, leaky tub of a ship and decided it would do.

Climbing the anchor chain, he slipped over the rail and onto the deck. No one was about. He padded along the deck until he came to a broad hatch. Hamish X lowered himself down into the hold.

The stench of fish was overwhelming, but he breathed deeply to inure himself to the horrible smell. "It may be bad," he whispered to himself, "but it can't beat Caribou Blue." The thought of the horrible cheese filled him once more with a sense of loneliness that he hadn't known since before he came to Windcity and met Parveen and Mimi. "I hope they're all right," he murmured to himself as he curled behind a pile of rope, hidden from sight. "I'll find the Professor and come right back. I'll see them again in no time." On that happy thought, he closed his eyes and let the gentle rocking of the ship send him off to sleep.

He was having a dream about Mimi and Parveen, smiling and murmuring in his sleep when, hours later, he woke with a knife pressed to his throat.

He opened his eyes and looked up to see a girl with dark, filthy hair and bright blue eyes leaning over him.

"One move and you die," she hissed.

"Fine. I won't move. Who are you and what's the big idea?"

"My name is Maggie," the girl grinned fiercely. "And we're taking over this ship."